FIGHT OR FLIRT ON THE SCENIC ROUTE

MARGARET AMATT

LEANNAN
PRESS
INDEPENDENT PUBLISHER

LEANNAN PRESS

First Published by Leannan Press 2025

Book Cover designed by Margaret Amatt

eBook ISBN: 978-1-914575-29-7

Paperback ISBN: 978-1-914575-28-0

CHAPTER ONE

Elise

'Elise, a moment, please.'

Elise Reid looked up from her screen in the busy office. Gill Campbell's voice was unmistakable. Some called it shrill, and it had a pitch that could probably attract any stray dog passing the modern office block in central Glasgow. But it carried authority, and when she came looking for you, it was rarely a good sign.

Inwardly wincing, Elise arranged her face in a smile. 'Sure... Do you want me to come to your office?'

'Yes, now, please.'

At least she added the "please". Elise got up and followed Gill through the main room that was filled with desk pods. Everyone suddenly looked very busy now that Gill was on the floor. She swung her arms as she walked, almost bouncing in her wedge heels, her lanyard swinging around her neck. An outsider might think it looked quite a cheery walk, but Elise knew better. Gill had spent her life working in hospitality; she knew how to put on a face. Elise could spot it a mile off.

She did it so often herself.

And that face wasn't confined to work. Elise had spent most of her life perfecting it – the polished exterior that told the world she was fine, thriving even, while everything underneath felt like a barely functioning shitshow. In her twenties, she'd mapped out a future, determined to be in control of something, anything. But those plans had unravelled spectacularly. Now, freshly thirty – a milestone she'd pretty much ghosted – there was no getting away from the fact that she was at an age in her life that didn't match the stage she felt she should have reached – either personally or professionally. She looked the part, played the part, but inside, she wasn't sure she'd ever figured out who she was when no one was watching.

Working as a project manager for a tour company was a good job. It paid bills, and she was getting used to life in the city, even if it would never appeal to her as much as life in her hometown surrounded by friends and everything familiar. But she couldn't go back. Ever. Her name was mud in Glenbriar, and she didn't have the strength to face anyone back there.

Once enclosed within the translucent walls of Gill's office, Elise followed Gill's aloof gesture and sat on a comfy seat in the corner of the room. Gill lifted a coffee cup from her desk, then came over and sat on the other side of the low table from Elise.

This little nook she'd created in her office seemed more informal than sitting at the desk, but, like the cheerful façade, it was nothing but window dressing. Elise knew not to think that Gill would have anything nice to say, no matter how much sugar she coated it in.

What the hell have I done?

Elise racked her brains, trying to think if she'd made a stupid mistake. Which she had – many, though all of them were in her private life and didn't apply here.

'I have to thank you.' Gill sipped on her coffee. 'We wouldn't have been able to get the new Glenbriar branch up and running without your intel on the town.'

The name alone sent a pang through Elise. She missed it. Until last year, it had been her home. She'd grown up there, had family there. All her once friends were there, though she'd pretty much given up on them – not because she didn't care, but because she understood their reasons for not wanting to see her. She couldn't afford to let her mind wander there just now. Gill's words made no sense. Elise frowned. Yes, she'd played a crucial role in the setup of the Glenbriar branch, as she would have with any new project. The fact that the new branch was in her hometown was largely coincidental. She hadn't brought any intel – how could she? It was a lovely place, but not that much different from other small towns in Scotland. So what was Gill leading to?

'Um... Thank you.' Elise gave her a little smile, crossing her legs so her knees jutted out from beneath her skirt. Being slightly taller than average was a bonus sometimes, but on these low chairs, it was awkward to look professional when her instinct was to rest her legs out in front.

'There's a problem however.' Gill clasped her hands together and cocked her head to the side, still with a very sweet smile on her face.

'I see.' Elise raised her chin. Now they were getting to it. 'What's happened?'

Gill sighed. 'We're having staffing issues.'

'Oh? I thought everything had been sorted.'

'So did I, but we've had two people pull out only today. One of them is the manager, which has really thrown things into disarray. I might have to step in myself for a while. We've got the inaugural tour coming up and there's no way I'll be able to recruit someone in such a short time.'

Elise's heart leapt. Was Gill expecting her to volunteer? In all honesty, it was more like the kind of job she wanted, but not in Glenbriar. No way could she go back to living and working there. Not even for a little while. There were too many people she really didn't want to see again. Aidan – the ex she'd cruelly left for his cousin, Finlay. Finlay himself, who Elise had dumped too, only for him to marry one of her best friends. The awkwardness was off the charts. She hadn't even dared to go to their wedding, which only made her feel worse. Facing any of them – let alone her other friends, who now saw her as the villain – was something she needed to avoid for the sake of her own sanity.

'That doesn't sound good.' Elise clasped her hands together, putting on her best sympathetic face, but giving nothing away.

Gill nodded, her eyes searching Elise's. 'You've been very dedicated since you started here last year. That's why I'm bringing this to you.'

Elise's heart hammered in her chest. Bringing what to her exactly?

'I can't be there for the long term, so I'd like you to consider running the Glenbriar branch. It would be a promotion and, as you know the town well, it seems ideal.'

Didn't it just. Only an idiot would turn it down. Elise steadied her breathing. She was going to have to be that idiot, because she couldn't do it.

Her nails dug into her palm as she clenched her fists.

'I'm flattered, truly.' She swallowed, her mouth suddenly very dry. 'But I feel my strengths lie here. I've moved my life to Glasgow. I don't live in Glenbriar anymore.'

Gill's lips pressed into a thin line. 'But you know the place, the people. You could commute from here. I believe it only takes about ninety minutes, maybe even less. Or I'm sure finding somewhere to stay wouldn't be a problem.'

If only Gill knew how popular a place Glenbriar was and how that bumped up the house prices, making it a very difficult place to find good accommodation.

'I'm not asking you to make an immediate decision, though I would like you to think very carefully about it.' Gill blinked, almost batting her eyelashes. She picked up her mug and took another sip of her coffee, then placed it back on the table with a resonating smack. 'There's a more pressing issue unfortunately.'

Elise's insides tensed. There was more?

'The other member of staff we've lost was the guide for the inaugural tour. I'm struggling to find anyone who can step in. You, however, used to guide tours according to your resume.'

'I did but—'

'Then I need you to do it. We need someone experienced, someone who can handle a last-minute change without a hitch. And that person is you.'

Elise's breath caught in her throat. The walls of the office seemed to close in around her. She hated guiding tours. Giving up that job had been one of her favourite moments in life so far.

She closed her eyes briefly and drew in a breath.

'Postponing is not an option.' Gill clapped her hands on her knees. 'Our clients have booked their holidays, and it's our responsibility to deliver. It's a critical moment for the business, and, as this tour is the first one to leave from the new branch, we can't afford for it to go wrong.'

'I understand the importance, but I'm not a guide anymore. I've worked hard to get where I am. Stepping back into that role... Well, it feels like a demotion.' And the whole idea of putting herself on display like that made her insides squirm.

'I know it's not ideal.' Gill pulled a wide smile that couldn't have been more fake. 'But let's be clear, this is not a demotion. This is a one-off. To reflect that, I'm offering to pay you both your normal wage and the tour guide's wage. Plus, you can have the whole week off following the tour to make up for it. I think you'll find that a very generous offer.'

Elise ran a hand through her long dark hair, gathering the strands together and drawing it over her shoulder. It sounded like a very good offer, but could she bear it? Running a tour from Glenbriar wouldn't be the same as living there. It wasn't likely anyone she knew would be on it. These tours usually attracted foreign visitors.

'It's only five days.' Gill lifted an iPad. 'To the Isle of Skye. It won't be a difficult one.'

Elise squared her shoulders. 'Ok, fine,' she said, though her heart thudded an erratic beat. 'I'll do it.'

'Splendid.' Gill clapped her hands together. 'I knew we could count on you.'

Elise nodded, offering a tight-lipped smile.

Duty... or fate... or something called her back to Glenbriar. Hopefully, she could sneak onto the coach, do the tour and be back in Glasgow before anyone even noticed she was gone.

Chapter Two

Gabe

Gabe Wilder leaned against the weathered brick wall of the small bus station in Glenbriar, ran a hand through his thick, dark hair, and smiled. He was back in his old stomping ground – for now, anyway. Not that he ever stayed in one place for long. His podcasts, *Wilder at Heart*, meant he travelled here, there, and everywhere, raising awareness of environmental issues and making a name for himself in the process.

His best friend, Aidan, and Lilah, Aidan's lovely young wife, huddled close over a phone, reading something. Gabe's smile grew. They were so adorable. But seeing them thick as thieves made him question his sanity for about the hundredth time that morning. While travelling was part of his life, what he was about to embark on definitely wasn't the kind of travel he was used to. He had possibly signed up for one of the wackiest things in his entire life – which was saying something.

A coach tour!

On paper, it didn't sound wild at all – but for a man who'd made his name in the wilderness, it shoved him completely out of his comfort zone. He still couldn't quite believe he was doing it. Aidan wasn't exactly a coach tour type either, but he and Lilah had won tickets and decided to use them. Gabe had bought one at their insistence that they could all have a laugh together, though he wasn't convinced he wouldn't end up being anything more than a gooseberry.

Sanity questioned for the hundred and first time that day.

'Are you looking up the evening entertainment?' Gabe eyed the phone. 'Or will I end up being in bed by seven?'

'Probably.' Aidan smirked. 'With one of the local bar staff.'

'Oh, ha-ha.'

Lilah stifled a laugh, though she probably didn't realise that Aidan wasn't joking. Gabe didn't say no to hookups, and if it passed the time this week, he'd welcome one with open arms.

Aidan shook his head. 'You never know, you might end up meeting a nice single girl on the tour.'

Gabe raised an eyebrow. 'I doubt it. It's not exactly the kind of trip that attracts single women... Not in an age bracket that I'd be looking for anyway.'

'Not fancy being someone's boy toy, no?' Aidan winked at him, and Gabe refrained from telling him to eff off only because Lilah was there.

'I wonder where Scarlett is.' Lilah looked around.

'She's always late.' Aidan checked the time on his phone. 'But she better get here soon. We need her for the tickets.'

Gabe frowned. Why the hell were they talking about Scarlett? She was Aidan's red haired little sister – red by name, red by nature. 'Is she coming too?'

'She's the one who won the tickets,' Aidan said. 'She invited us.'

'Wait... What?' Gabe straightened up and folded his arms. 'I didn't know that.'

Aidan shrugged. 'I thought I'd said. Sorry. But it doesn't matter, does it? She'll probably keep out of our way.'

'You think?' Gabe muttered, rubbing the stubble along his jawline. 'This better not be some crazy attempt at a setup. You know I'm not going to date her, right?'

People were always trying to set him up, convinced the man they viewed as a local celeb needed to settle down. But Scarlett? No way. Dating his best friend's sister was not on his bingo card.

'No, no.' Aidan held up his hands and pulled a face. 'God no. It's nothing like that.'

'Yeah?' Gabe wasn't entirely convinced. His eyes roamed around, observing some more passengers who had just arrived. Most of them looked to be at least in their sixties, possibly seventies.

'Definitely not. She's got a boyfriend. He's coming too.' Aidan glanced at Lilah, and they shared a look.

'Ah, ok.' That was a relief, though it meant he'd be playing gooseberry to two couples.

Sanity questioned for the hundred and second time that morning.

'We're a bit worried about her actually,' Lilah said.

Gabe's brows knitted together. 'How so?'

'She's always falling in with dodgy blokes.' Aidan's jaw clenched. 'And this current one, Leon... well, let's just say he's not exactly Prince Charming.'

'This is starting to sound like a setup again.' Gabe raised an eyebrow. 'I'm not going to flirt with her or something and try to split them up. No offence, but I don't want to date your sister... or anyone like that – friends, exes, whatever. It makes everything too messy.'

Aidan cocked his head. 'You're telling me.'

Yeah, there was no need to remind Aidan about messy relationships. He'd had a roaster of a breakup, and his ex had gone off with his cousin – only to do the dirty on him too.

'Leon doesn't strike me as the coach tour type.' Lilah glanced around. 'I think that's why Scarlett wanted us to come too. To keep him in order.'

'He sounds like a dick.' Gabe winced, glancing around. He'd have to modify his language in this group.

'Won't be the first time I've had to step in with her boyfriends,' Aidan said. 'She's always drawn to guys who end up being no good for her. But we should give this one the benefit of the doubt. He might be ok really.'

'He might not even come.' Lilah checked her phone again.

Gabe's gaze swept over the small crowd gathered. He didn't wish Scarlett – or anyone – a toxic relationship, and he sincerely hoped both she and this man were happy together... and that they showed up. Otherwise, he'd be stuck with her, and he wasn't sure he could handle it.

His eye landed on a shock of bright red hair, unmistakable even from a distance. Scarlett strode towards them, and trailing behind her was a young man with a buzz cut and an expression of abject disgust on his face. He made no attempt to hide his distaste as he looked people up and down, screwing up his nose at everyone.

'Hi.' Scarlett headed straight up to them. Her boyfriend followed, narrowing his eyes at Gabe, who smiled at him.

Little shit. Aidan might be prepared to give him the benefit of the doubt, but to Gabe, he looked like trouble.

'Hey.' Lilah gave Scarlett a brief hug. 'And hi, Leon.'

He grunted, not looking at any of them.

'This is Leon,' Aidan said. 'Scarlett's boyfriend. Leon, meet Gabe, my friend, who's also on the tour.'

Another grunt.

'Delighted to meet you.' Gabe put on his most enthusiastic tone and exchanged a grin with Aidan, the two of them almost bursting into a laugh.

A large white coach drew up and its arrival prevented Gabe from saying something he regretted – even in jest. They lifted their luggage and started moving closer, along with the rest of the group.

Gabe frowned at Leon, who had his arm around Scarlett's neck in a way that looked more threatening than romantic. Aidan was looking too and didn't seem best pleased either.

The coach doors swung open, and the tour guide stepped out in a purple uniform. Gabe's jaw dropped, and he turned to Aidan. Aidan's eyes went wide. So did Lilah's.

'What the fuck?' Scarlett gaped at the guide too, and several people turned around and tutted at her.

The air seemed to grow thick with tension; all his group locked in a silent exchange of horror.

Elise Reid – Aidan's ex, the woman who had caused such a stir and broken so many hearts – stood on the bottom step of the coach.

'She's the tour guide?' Gabe's voice was hoarse.

They were doomed, and they hadn't even got on the bus.

But despite the animosity that curdled in his gut, Gabe's traitorous eyes lingered on her elegant form and her long dark hair. She was undeniably gorgeous, but she was also a horrible person he'd never forgive for the way she'd hurt Aidan.

Aidan cleared his throat. 'Well, this is going to be some trip.'

That was one way to put it.

Chapter Three

Elise straightened her purple blazer and fixed a professional smile in place as she stepped off the coach to greet the awaiting passengers. She didn't make eye contact with anyone. The chances of someone recognising her were slim – but still. She was in Glenbriar now, and the risk was real. As soon as everyone was aboard, she could relax a little. Hopefully, after that, it would be plain sailing for the rest of the week.

She tucked a strand of hair behind her ear and checked her iPad one last time. If she'd had more time, she'd have liked to have read the manifest more thoroughly, but she'd simply skimmed the medical information section to check nobody had a condition she needed to know. Once the coach was on its way, she'd have a proper look. Sometimes it was easier once everyone was onboard and she could match the names to the faces. The morning was bright and promising, sunlight glinting off the sleek white coach that would carry them northwest through the Highlands to Skye. Perfect weather for the promotional photos Marketing would want. Perfect conditions for the inaugural tour from Glenbriar.

'Good morning!' She stepped down to greet an elderly couple, who beamed back at her. 'Welcome to Highland Horizons' Spectacular Skye Adventure. I'm Elise, your tour guide for the week.'

The words flowed easily. She hadn't done a coach tour for a few years, but it all came back. She'd practised her script and learnt what she could about the places they were visiting on Skye, so that when she spoke about it, it would feel natural.

'We'll be departing in approximately twenty minutes. Plenty of time to get settled. May I see your booking confirmation?'

She checked their paperwork, ticked them off on her passenger list, and directed them to the driver who was loading luggage into the hold.

A small crowd had gathered now, and Elise moved up onto the first step of the coach, giving her just enough height to address them properly. She clasped her hands together, smile firmly in place.

'Ladies and gentlemen, welcome to what promises to be a week of unforgettable Scottish magic. I'm Elise Reid, your tour guide as we journey from Glenbriar through the northwest Highlands to the Isle of Skye.' She beamed around the assembled group, fixing her perfect smile in place. 'We'll be making our first stop at the charming town of Fort—'

Her words faltered as her gaze swept across the back of the assembled group. A face caught her attention, and her heart stopped.

Aidan.

'Um… the town of Fort William.' She did a double take. *Jesus Christ.* It was definitely him. With his thick, dark curls and deep brown eyes, he was unmistakable. But what the hell was he doing here? She should have checked the bloody list.

Aidan McBride was here. Her ex-boyfriend. The man who'd started the slow downfall of her life. She'd dated him for nearly three years before he 'disappeared' to Canada. His leaving had hurt so hard. She'd later got engaged to his cousin in what she now recognised as an ill-conceived attempt at revenge… possibly self-destruction. Or maybe just a desperate grab at happiness.

Her hand tightened on her iPad. Her lungs seemed to have forgotten how they were supposed to work, but her mouth kept moving – somehow. Her brain was short-circuiting. Next to Aidan was Lilah – his wife now – twirling a lock of her curly ginger hair around her finger. And also Scarlett, with her distinctive red hair, Aidan's half-sister. She didn't seem the type to be on a coach tour, and definitely not with Aidan. Elise had never thought they were that close.

Her eyes travelled to the man beside them and her stomach plummeted. Gabriel Wilder. Tall, broad-shouldered, with that perpetual lop-sided grin of his that made middle-aged women and teenagers alike wet their knickers over him and his *Wilder at Heart* podcasts.

She stepped onto the ground to start checking people in, wishing she'd at least glanced at the names on the passenger list.

Not that it would have changed much. It wasn't like she could get out of it.

'Your booking reference, please.' Her voice sounded distant even to her own ears as she took the number from the next couple.

Why the hell was Gabriel on a coach tour? Surely he was all rugged adventure holidays? He was Aidan's best friend and someone Elise had never got on with, even before the split. And definitely not after it, when he sent her that scathing message. He'd made it abundantly clear what he thought of her character, her decisions, her very existence.

What were any of them doing here?

Her professional smile was starting to ache at the corners, but she held it in place through sheer force of will.

The queue was moving, and they were coming closer. They must have seen her. What did they make of her being here? Maybe they all thought she was a liar, someone who claimed to be a project manager for the company in Glasgow, but was actually just a tour guide.

She cringed inwardly because she didn't want to have to go into the details of why she was here – that would mean having conversations with them, which she really wanted to avoid. Her hands were trembling, and she pressed the iPad against her chest as if it might shield her from what was happening.

An elderly gentleman asked something about bathroom breaks, and Elise answered automatically, years of customer service experience coming to her rescue when her conscious mind had all but shut down. 'And there is a toilet on board too.'

'Thank you ever so much.'

'You're in seat 7D, just about halfway down on your right,' she told a middle-aged woman. 'Lovely view from that side as we head north.'

The woman beamed at her. 'First time to Scotland. So excited!'

'You're in for a treat,' Elise replied.

She sneaked a glance over the woman's shoulder. Four people to go before... *them*. Four blessed strangers to process before she'd have to face Aidan, Lilah, Scarlett, and Gabriel. Four more moments of pretending everything was fine.

'Booking reference?' she asked a tall woman with a camera hanging around her neck.

'QT549.' She showed Elise a phone screen.

Elise found her name on her list. 'Anna Thompson. Seat 3A. You'll have an excellent view for photographs from there.'

'I'm hoping to catch some wildlife. Eagles, maybe even an otter if I'm lucky.'

'There's a wildlife spotter's guide in your welcome pack,' she said.

Three more passengers to go. Watching eyes burned into her.

'Seats 14A and B, towards the back on your left,' she said to an older woman by the name of Rita Miller – who looked vaguely familiar – and a younger man, Lloyd Miller.

'He's my son,' Rita told Elise.

She smiled. 'That's lovely. Make yourself comfortable.'

Two more to go. Then it would be them.

Sweat prickled at Elise's hairline. Her purple blazer suddenly seemed stifling.

'Seats 5C and D, just there.'

Aidan, Lilah, Scarlett, and Gabriel were next, along with another young man with a buzz cut and a very sour expression. Presumably he was Scarlett's boyfriend, but that didn't explain Gabe's presence.

The iPad felt slippery in Elise's damp palms. She forced her professional smile to remain fixed in place as they approached. Who would hand over their booking reference first? Would any of them speak to her? Would they all pretend they'd never met?

She braced herself as Aidan stepped forward, but at the last moment, Gabriel moved in front of him. He towered over her, all six-foot-something of him. His dark hair was longer than she remembered, curling slightly at the collar of his jacket – a brown leather thing that looked like it had weathered the wilds for a decade and come out unscathed. Unlike her composure, which was rapidly disintegrating under his direct gaze.

'Hi,' he said, and nothing more. Not that she'd expected it.

But even that one word in his low, rumbling voice hit her like a physical blow. She met his eyes for the first time in what? Three years? And felt that old familiar crackle of mutual dislike. Except there was something else there, too. Something that made her insides tighten and her skin prickle.

Gabriel Wilder was infuriatingly handsome. More so than she remembered. The passing years had only refined his features, adding character lines around his startling blue eyes and confidence to his broad shoulders. He'd always been attractive in that rugged, outdoorsy way, but now there was a maturity to him that she found—

No. She was not going to notice that. She was not going to notice him at all beyond what her job required. After all the messy relationships, she'd researched a lot about what attracted people to each other. This was just a chemical reaction to his physical attributes.

'Booking reference?' Her voice came out more clipped than she meant, though still professional. A minor victory.

He held out his phone, displaying the confirmation email. Their fingers didn't touch during the exchange, but Elise felt the warmth of his hand's proximity like a brand.

She looked down the list and saw his name screaming loud and clear. Maybe it was better this way. If she'd seen this earlier, who knew what she might have done.

'Right. You're in seat 15D, the second last row on the right.'

Gabriel's eyes hadn't left her face. The weight of his stare was like a physical pressure, forcing her to meet his gaze again despite her best intentions. The moment their eyes locked, something electric passed between them – not attraction. Definitely not. Antagonism. History. The shared knowledge of everything that had happened.

His mouth quirked up briefly at one corner. 'Thanks.'

'Enjoy the trip.'

He raised an eyebrow slightly, a gesture she'd always found infuriatingly smug. 'I'm sure I will.' As he stepped past her onto the coach, his thick forearm brushed against hers. Even through the fabric of her blazer, the brief contact sent an unwelcome jolt through her system – anger, irritation, annoyance. Definitely one of them.

She took a steadying breath, acutely aware that her cheeks were flushed. The morning wasn't particularly warm yet, but she felt overheated, off balance. Gabriel had always had that effect on her, from the very first time Aidan had introduced them. That immediate, instinctive clash of personalities. That irrational, visceral response to his presence.

And now she'd be trapped on a coach with him for a week. With all of them.

She turned to face the next in line, struggling to maintain her professional demeanour when her insides felt like they'd been put through a blender.

Gabriel bloody Wilder and his intense eyes and his stupidly handsome face weren't going to derail the tour... or anything else. Not today. Not ever.

Aidan stepped up, Lilah tucked against his side like she'd been designed to fit there. His arm was draped around her shoulders, her ginger curls spilling over his hand where it rested. They were laughing at something private, their faces tilted towards each other like he was deliberately not wanting to notice Elise. Could she blame him?

Her throat tightened. They radiated contentment, that settled happiness of two people who had found their place in the universe, which happened to be right beside each other.

'Booking reference?' she asked, her smile firmly back in place despite the tremor in her hands.

Aidan caught her eye only briefly as he said, 'We're with Scarlett. She has the reference.'

Scarlett nudged forward and held out her phone. Elise checked the number.

Lilah gave her a faint smile, then nuzzled against Aidan's cheek, and he chuckled, a low, intimate sound that Elise remembered all too well.

'You're in 15A and B.' Elise checked the list with her stylus.

Aidan nodded, adjusting his backpack strap with his free hand. His dark curls were shorter than when she'd last seen him, but his profile was achingly familiar. He and Lilah moved past her, still wrapped up in each other, still not properly acknowledging her existence.

'This is bizarre.'

Elise turned to find Scarlett still standing before her, hands on her hips, red hair burning like embers in the morning sun.

'A little.' Elise gave her a smile, as she was trained to do. 'I didn't expect to see you on this tour.'

'Likewise.' Scarlett pulled a face. She must be about twenty-five now, though Elise would always think of her as a teenager. Still, she looked more grown up than when Elise last saw her. She'd grown out her pixie cut into a neatly styled long bob that looked very vibrant with the red dye. 'I won the tickets and thought the two of them might like to come. Then Gabe decided to tag along for some reason.' She dropped her phone back into her bag. 'Is this going to be weird? I feel like it might be.'

'We'll keep it professional,' Elise said, which wasn't exactly an answer to Scarlett's question.

Scarlett's mouth quirked up at one corner. 'Sure.'

'You're in seats 14C and D.' Elise's gaze drifted to the sullen young man trailing behind Scarlett, engaged in what appeared to be an intense text conversation.

'Come on, Leon.' Scarlett turned to him. 'You'll get left behind.'

Leon looked up from his phone, his expression thunderous. 'Good.' He slouched onto the coach with narrowed eyes. 'This is going to be shit. Four hours on a coach... There'd better be decent Wi-Fi.'

'There is Wi-Fi,' Elise confirmed. 'Though it can be patchy in the more remote areas.'

Leon made a disgusted sound. 'I told you this was a stupid idea,' he muttered to Scarlett as they headed up the aisle. 'We could've flown to Ibiza for what this cost. Beaches, clubs, actual sunshine instead of whatever depressing weather we'll get in the middle of nowhere.'

'Leon! I got it for free. I won it, remember? You're not paying anything for it.' Scarlett rolled her eyes. 'You'll like it once we get there.'

'No, I won't,' Leon muttered.

Elise clutched the iPad to her chest, breathing very deliberately and trying to process what had just happened. She checked in the remaining passengers, her mind wandering all over the place. Scarlett had won the trip... That explained some of it. But why bring Gabriel? *Wilder at Heart* had made him quite the celebrity during the lockdown, and people in Glenbriar raved about him – including Elise's sister-in-law, Amanda, who thought the sun shone out of his arse. Only a couple of weeks ago Amanda had arranged for him to sing at some charity do she was organising. You'd have thought she'd secured Bruno Mars the way she went on and on about it.

Elise's brief eye contact with Gabe had been enough to res-urrect years of mutual animosity in an instant. Some people just didn't fit together, like puzzle pieces from different boxes, and she and Gabe had been mismatched from the first moment Aidan had introduced them. Gabe had been all easy smiles for Aidan, but when he'd turned those startling blue eyes on her, something had shifted. A subtle cooling, and they'd never warmed up since.

After Elise got together with Finlay and Aidan returned from Canada, she'd received a message from Gabe. It still struck her how odd it was – he never messaged her.

You broke Aidan's heart, and now you're using his cousin to patch up your own. Finlay deserves better than to be your consolation prize.

She'd never responded to it, but it still stung – partly because, in her darkest moments, she'd feared it might be true. Gabe – like most people – had resolutely sided with Aidan and Finlay. Elise was seen as someone who'd played them both.

Maybe she had. But no one ever really took the time to consider what it had been like for her when Aidan went to Canada. Least of all Gabe.

Elise took a deep, steadying breath. After her breakups, she'd gone to counselling. She'd needed to understand why her relationships always went pear-shaped… and why it always seemed to be her fault.

It had been uncomfortable, at first. She wasn't used to speaking aloud the thoughts she kept under lock and key. Thoughts like *maybe I'll never find true love*, or *maybe I push people away before I get the chance to.*

Her counsellor had spoken about early conditioning – how the way people look at you when you're young, before you're even sure who you are, can shape the way you see yourself forever. Elise hadn't wanted to talk about that part.

About being fourteen, tall and glossy-haired, already looking like an adult. Fielding comments from her dad's friends that made her skin crawl.

About learning to smile through it, to pretend it didn't matter.

To dress the way people expected.

To use her looks like armour – all part of a façade.

But the truth was, it had messed with her. She'd never known how to separate attraction from approval, or control from connection. And when someone tried to get close – *really* close – she either braced for rejection or smothered them with sharp edges until they backed off.

Perhaps that was why Aidan had run in the first place. They were both young when they started dating. Everyone said what a great-looking pair they were, but they'd never really communicated. Not properly.

Even with Finlay, she'd kept so much of herself tucked away.

Sometimes it even happened with her friends. She knew she'd been called aloof before because there were only certain parts she allowed people to see: the polished, poised, impossible-to-hurt version of Elise. Not the one who sometimes cried in the shower for no reason. Or flinched when someone reached for her unexpectedly.

She was trying to be better now. To catch herself when she wanted to run or lash out. But it was a lonely kind of work, the sort no one applauded. No one saw. And she didn't dare mention it, in case it looked like she was throwing a pity party.

Now was the time to remind herself that she was a professional – a woman with a career she cared about, a life she'd rebuilt from the ashes of her past trauma and her disastrous relationships.

Gabe's opinion of her shouldn't matter.

But it did. Somehow, it still did.

And she felt like she needed to explain herself – like there were loose ends waiting to be tied up.

For now, though, she just had to stay professional.

As she climbed aboard, her gaze landed on Gabe immediately. He was watching her with those too-perceptive eyes. Probably waiting for her to do something that would confirm whatever negative opinion he still held of her.

She wouldn't give him the satisfaction. This week would be a masterclass in professionalism. She would be the perfect tour guide – knowledgeable, friendly, unflappable. Gabriel Wilder and his judgmental stares could go to hell.

She could do this. She would do this.

She made her way to the jump seat near the front of the coach, designed for the tour guide. From here, she'd use the microphone to address the passengers, point out sights of interest as they travelled through the Highlands.

She could also, thankfully, keep her back to the passengers. Including the five seated at the rear of the coach.

Her palms were damp with sweat as she settled into her seat and reached for the microphone. This was it. No turning back.

She took a deep breath, steadying herself before addressing the coach.

'Ladies and gentlemen, welcome aboard. My name is Elise Reid, and I'll be your guide for the Highland Horizons Spectacular Skye Adventure. We're about to embark on a journey through some of Scotland's most breathtaking landscapes. As we travel, I'll be pointing out places of interest and sharing some of the rich history and folklore of the Highlands.'

Through the large front windows of the coach, she watched Glenbriar recede as they merged onto the main road heading north. Soon, the town would give way to the gentler landscapes of Perthshire, then the more dramatic scenery of the northwest Highlands. On another day, with another group, she might have been thrilled by the route ahead – eager to share in the passengers' excitement.

Today, she was simply focused on survival. One mile at a time. One hour at a time. One day at a time.

'Please make yourselves comfortable. There's complimentary Wi-Fi on board – the password is in your welcome packs – and feel free to use the USB charging points at your seats.'

As she spoke, a prickling sensation developed between her shoulder blades. Someone was watching her – really, it could be anyone. She was on a coach with sixty-odd people. But Gabriel always had this effect on her – his eyes were like lasers, and they were boring a hole right through her, right now.

She wasn't going to look back to check. She didn't have to. And no way was he getting the satisfaction of knowing he'd rattled her.

Her hand tightened around the microphone, her knuckles whitening with the pressure. A headache was building at her temples, a dull throb that no doubt would intensify as the day progressed. The coach's air conditioning seemed suddenly inadequate, the recycled air too thin to fill her lungs properly.

What she'd hoped would be a quick few days was suddenly looking like an unscalable peak and a complete nightmare.

Chapter Four

Gabe

Gabe twisted in his seat, the faux leather squeaking as he leaned across the narrow aisle to speak to Aidan. The coach rumbled beneath them, winding north, and he still couldn't believe it – Elise Reid, of all the bloody tour guides in Scotland, was the one narrating their trip. 'This is going to be a long five days,' he whispered.

Aidan's jaw tightened, the muscles working beneath his stubbled cheek. 'You're not wrong.' His eyes fixed on the headrest in front of him.

'I had no idea she was still a tour guide.' Gabe frowned. 'Didn't she get a new job in Glasgow?'

'This company is based in Glasgow.' Aidan shrugged. 'They just opened a branch in Glenbriar. That was why they did the prize draw that Scarlett won. Part of a larger publicity stunt, I guess, but I certainly didn't know she was working for them, or I wouldn't have come. We made our peace last year, but that doesn't mean I want to spend time in her company.'

Lilah nestled into Aidan's shoulder and placed a gentle hand on his arm. 'It doesn't matter if she's here or not.' Her sweet smile and wild ginger hair always made her look like a flower fairy or a Celtic princess. 'We're here to enjoy ourselves. She's doing her job. We'll just keep out of her way as much as we can.'

Gabe raised an eyebrow. Lilah was either a saint or delusional. Possibly both. How could they keep out of her way when they were stuck on the coach with her?

'All I'm saying is, awkward.' Gabe held up his hands.

'Yup,' Aidan agreed.

A familiar protective anger rose in Gabe's chest. The way Elise had jumped from Aidan to Finlay when Aidan had already been suffering would never not be something that pissed him off. Watching Aidan fall apart after his dad died had been awful. Aidan's dad had been one of the good ones. He'd been there for Gabe growing up in a way his own father never had.

Thank god Lilah had come along and helped Aidan find his feet again and get over both his father and Elise.

Gabe clapped Aidan on the arm. 'I suppose, on the bright side, she'll have to watch you and Lilah being disgustingly happy together for five solid days.'

Lilah laughed, leaning closer to Aidan, who automatically dropped a kiss on the top of her head.

'Revolting. I might actually be sick.' Gabe glanced away with a laugh. He was joking – mostly. But a small part of him, a mean part, found their constant affection hard to watch. Not because he begrudged them their happiness – hell no. Aidan deserved it after everything. But it highlighted the empty space beside Gabe. The space he filled with work, casual hookups, and loud opinions about climate change.

Not that he'd ever admit out loud that he was lonely. Not even to himself. Being lonely felt like a weakness.

Gabe fished in his backpack for a snack as the coach continued on. Nibbling on his carrot sticks like Bugs Bunny, he scrolled his phone for a bit, trying – and failing – to ignore Elise's voice as she spoke over the microphone. He knew this part of the country well enough not to need a commentary.

A sharp whisper from the row in front caught his attention.

'Do you ever stop talking?' Leon snapped under his breath. 'Honestly, it's constant jabbering with you. You never know when to shut up.'

Gabe lowered his phone slightly, ears pricking up. The tone in Leon's voice set off warning bells in his head.

Scarlett's bright red hair was just visible through the narrow gap between the seats. Next to her, Leon slumped with his black hoodie pulled up despite the warmth of the coach.

'I was just excited,' Scarlett whispered back, her voice small in a way that didn't suit her at all. She was normally so loud. Sometimes to the point of being annoying, but that didn't justify someone speaking to her like that.

'You're always bloody hyper,' Leon muttered. 'About everything. It's fucking exhausting.'

'Sorry,' Scarlett said, and Gabe's frown deepened. She shouldn't be apologising for being enthusiastic. That was like apologising for having freckles or red hair – it was just part of who she was.

He leaned forward slightly, trying to hear better without making it obvious he was eavesdropping. There was something off about Leon. Gabe had sensed it from the start. And this was doing nothing to change his mind.

'I told you I didn't even want to come on this stupid trip,' Leon continued, his voice low but sharp. 'Wasting a week looking at boring scenery with your brother and his mates.'

'I won the tickets. I couldn't just not use them.'

'You could have sold them. Or given them to someone else.'

'But I wanted to go with you.'

Leon made a sound that might have been a laugh but had no humour in it. 'Yeah, well, maybe you should start thinking about what I want for a change.'

Gabe's jaw tightened. He glanced across the aisle, wondering if Aidan could hear the conversation too. But he was still wrapped up in his little bubble with Lilah, the two of them looking at something out of the window and smiling. Gabe hesitated, torn between not wanting to overreact and a growing certainty that something wasn't right.

'Don't touch me,' Leon snapped, when Scarlett apparently tried to take his hand. 'I'm still pissed off with you.'

'For what?' Scarlett asked.

'What do you fucking think? I just told you. For forcing me to come here. And for being so loud and embarrassing all the time.'

'Pipe down, mate,' Gabe said, through the tiny gap in the seats. 'You're being very loud and not very pleasant.'

'For fuck's sake.' Leon pulled up his hood and slouched back with a thump.

Aidan frowned over at Gabe silently asking what was going on.

Gabe jerked his head towards the seats in front of him. 'Your sister's boyfriend is being a grade-A prick,' he leaned over and whispered. 'Is he always like this?'

Aidan's expression darkened. 'What's he saying?'

'I don't want to repeat it,' Gabe said. 'But it's out of line.'

'I knew he was trouble,' Lilah murmured, looking genuinely upset. 'Poor Scarlett.'

Aidan ran a hand over his face. 'Let's keep an eye on him.'

'I don't understand why she goes for these losers,' Aidan whispered.

'Low self-esteem,' Lilah said. 'She puts on a brave face, but I think deep down she doesn't believe she deserves better. I used to be the same.'

Aidan squeezed her hand.

Gabe had never thought of Scarlett as having low self-esteem. She always seemed so confident, with her bold fashion choices and outspoken opinions. But then, he knew better than most how easy it was to project one image while feeling something entirely different beneath the surface. His whole persona was built around *Wilder at Heart*, but the outgoing, ever-cheerful, laid-back man people saw on their screens wasn't truly him – not always. Sometimes he could be like that, but other times, he preferred his own company and lived a bit too much in his own head.

Five days stuck on a coach with this guy was going to be horrific. Worse even than being stuck with Elise. Gabe slumped back in his seat, stretching his long legs as far as the limited coach space would allow. Through the window, the familiar rolling hills of Perthshire were giving way to higher hills, stretching into the distance. At the front of the coach, Elise's voice flowed through the speakers again, clear and confident. Gabe wanted to hate it on principle.

'We're now approaching Roy Bridge,' she said. 'As we travel onward, you'll see the Nevis Range more clearly and eventually Ben Nevis, the highest mountain in Scotland, which is just outside Fort William. That's where we'll be making our first stop.'

Gabe glanced to his right, across Lilah and Aidan, where the mountains loomed dark and imposing despite the summer sunshine. He knew those peaks well – had climbed most of them over the years, sometimes for work, filming segments about conservation efforts or climate impact, sometimes just for the pure joy of standing at the top and feeling small against the vastness of the world.

He hadn't planned to spend his summer holiday on a coach tour. In fact, he hadn't planned to take a holiday at all. His podcasts were still doing well – better than he'd expected when he'd started recording them from his bedroom during lockdown. The documentary series that had followed had opened doors he'd never imagined possible. There were meetings scheduled with production companies, talks of a bigger platform, more exposure for the environmental issues he cared about.

Taking time off felt like losing momentum. But his producer had pointedly mentioned the word 'burnout' after Gabe had snapped at a sound engineer for breathing too loudly, and here he was, on a Highland Horizons coach to Skye with his best mate, his best mate's wife, his best mate's sister, and her prick of a boyfriend.

Oh, and Elise bloody Reid.

This was him supposedly relaxing. He needed a reset, probably a change. But stepping away from *Wilder at Heart* would be crazy when it was still so popular. Admitting that it had lost its spark, and that filming had become a chore rather than a joy, felt almost like a failure. Maybe after a break, everything would be fine again. And this week would be a pause on his hectic life if nothing else... That was the theory anyway.

'The Nevis Range,' Elise continued, 'also boasts Aonach Mòr, which has a gondola system to take visitors to the top. In the Nevis Range, you might see golden eagles, red deer, pine marten and water voles, as well as snow bunting, ptarmigan, and rare butterflies like the mountain ringlet and chequered skipper.

There are also seventy-five different species of lichen, thirty-three of which are considered rare in the UK.'

Gabe raised an eyebrow, mildly impressed despite himself. That was actually correct – a lot of people he met spouted a lot of nonsense when they were pretending to be knowledgeable, but Elise seemed to know her stuff... or she was good at remembering facts and presenting it like she knew what she was talking about. Not that he'd tell her that.

Being a passenger like this was strange. Normally when he travelled, it was with a specific purpose – filming locations, inter-view subjects, sometimes speaking engagements. He even wrote songs and performed them either as part of his podcasts or at open-mic nights and occasionally concerts. They were usually soft-rock ballads with messages about the planet – sometimes obvious, sometimes hidden. He planned his own itineraries, made his own decisions, controlled his own schedule. Handing control over to someone else was both unsettling and oddly lib-erating.

He didn't have to think about where they were going or how to get there. Didn't have to worry about finding accommodation or deciding what sights to see. It was all mapped out, planned to the minute by Highland Horizons.

Gabe glanced out as they passed a loch, sunlight glinting off its surface like scattered coins. He'd swum there once, on a rare hot day several years ago. The water had been breathtakingly cold despite the heat, and he'd emerged gasping and laughing, his skin prickling with goosebumps.

He couldn't remember who he'd been with that day. Maybe Aidan. Maybe one of his short-lived relationships? The kind that burned bright for a few weeks and then fizzled out when his work took priority.

'There are lots of lovely cafés with spectacular views that are extremely good for lunch and cakes, for those who might be feeling peckish after our journey so far,' Elise said. 'We'll be there in about thirty minutes.'

Objectively, Elise had a nice way of talking. That wasn't a betrayal of Aidan to acknowledge, just a statement of fact. She had a good speaking voice, appropriate for her role as a tour guide. That was all.

Gabe's stomach rumbled. No matter how much he ate, he was always hungry but rarely put on weight – just muscle.

'I told you to leave me alone!' Leon snapped from the seat in front. 'Are you deaf as well as annoying?'

The coach fell oddly quiet, the sounds of conversation dropping away as heads turned towards the source of the disturbance.

'I just asked if you wanted some water,' Scarlett said, her voice small but carrying in the sudden silence. 'You don't have to bite my head off.'

'You've been poking and prodding at me for the last twenty minutes,' Leon said, loud enough that everyone in the vicinity could hear.

'No, I haven't.'

An elderly woman a few rows ahead, who was in Gabe's sight-line, turned around, her face pinched with disapproval.

Gabe caught Aidan's eye across the aisle, a silent question passing between them. Aidan looked as alarmed as Gabe felt.

'I was just being nice,' Scarlett went on, a tremor in her voice now. 'What's wrong with that?'

'What's wrong' – Leon's voice dropped to a dangerous growl that raised the hairs on the back of Gabe's neck – 'is that you never listen. You never fucking listen when people tell you to back off.'

Gabe saw Scarlett's hand move, perhaps to touch Leon's arm in a placating gesture, and then everything happened very quickly.

Leon knocked her arm away with enough force that she hit the window with a dull thud. 'Don't,' he spat, looming over her in the confined space of their shared seat. 'Touch. Me.'

'Hey!' Aidan was on his feet instantly, his face thunderous. 'Keep your hands off my sister!'

Gabe had moved too before he'd consciously made the decision, following Aidan into the narrow aisle. The coach swayed beneath them as it rounded a bend, forcing them to grab the backs of seats to keep their balance.

'Mind your own business.' Leon turned in his seat to face them. But when he made eye contact with Aidan, a flicker of doubt registered on his face.

Scarlett looked up at Aidan and Gabe, her eyes wide with a mixture of shock and something that might have been relief. 'It's fine,' she said.

'It's not fine.' Aidan looked at Leon. 'You don't get to talk to her like that. Move away from her. Now.'

For a moment, Leon seemed to consider defiance. His jaw worked, his fingers curling into fists at his sides. But then the coach jolted over a pothole, momentarily throwing everyone off balance, and in that split second, Aidan and Gabe seized their chance.

Aidan reached down and grasped Leon's hoodie by the shoulder, hauling him upward. 'I said, move away from my sister.'

Gabe stepped in from the side, inserting himself into the space between the seats, using his considerable height and broad chest as a barrier between Leon and Scarlett. 'Come on, mate.' His voice was quiet despite the anger coursing through him. 'Let's all calm down before someone does something they'll regret.'

'Get your hands off me!' Leon twisted in Aidan's grip, his face contorted with anger. 'This is between me and Scarlett. It's none of your business!'

'You made it our business when you put your hands on her in front of the entire coach,' Gabe said.

'This is ridiculous,' Leon protested, still struggling against Aidan's hold. 'She was the one who wouldn't leave me alone! I asked her nicely and she kept pushing and pushing—'

'That's enough,' Aidan cut him off. 'I don't care what she did or didn't do. You do not touch my sister like that. Ever.'

Scarlett hesitated, looking between the three men with wide panicked eyes. 'Please let's all just sit down—'

'I don't think him sitting anywhere near you is a good idea.' Aidan narrowed his eyes at Leon again. 'Not if you're going to push her about.'

But they didn't have a lot of options. Leon would have to sit somewhere. Gabe didn't fancy being beside him the rest of the way either, but it seemed like the safest solution – and the only other empty seat – except Leon wasn't likely to agree.

'I didn't push her,' Leon insisted, his voice rising again. 'I just moved her hand. She fell against the window because the coach turned!'

Gabe's insides burned. Classic abuser tactics – minimise, justify, blame the victim. Exactly the way Gabe's father treated his mother. The way he used to treat Gabe himself, until Gabe had learned he didn't need to put up with that kind of shit anymore, and left.

He glanced at Scarlett, searching her face for signs that this wasn't the first time.

What he saw made his stomach clench. Beneath the embarrassment and the immediate distress was a weariness that suggested this was familiar territory. Not necessarily the physical aspect, but the public humiliation, the anger directed at her for simply existing too loudly in Leon's space.

'You're blowing this completely out of proportion,' Leon said to Aidan, his voice taking on a wheedling quality now. 'Ask Scarlett – she'll tell you it was nothing. Just a misunderstanding.'

'I know what I saw,' Aidan replied coldly. 'And I know what I heard. You threatening my sister, insulting her, and then physically intimidating her.'

'I didn't threaten her!'

'Shouting at someone to back off sounds pretty threatening to me,' Gabe interjected. 'Especially when it's followed by shoving them into a window.'

'And who asked you?' Leon glowered at Gabe. 'This has nothing to do with you!'

Gabe pulled himself to his full height and looked down at Leon. 'I'm not going to sit back and let anyone treat another human like that.'

Leon's face darkened. 'You think you're really something, don't you? With your fancy podcasts and your celebrity friends. Well, guess what? You're just a jumped-up YouTuber who got lucky. In five years, no one will even remember your name.'

The attempted insult was so pathetic that Gabe laughed. 'You might be right, but that's irrelevant.'

A woman with short grey hair, wearing a floral scarf, stood up from her seat, her expression outraged. 'What is going on?' she demanded in a plummy accent. 'This is disgraceful behaviour!'

'Sorry,' Gabe said. 'Bit of a misunderstanding—'

'He attacked me!' Leon spun around to appeal to the woman, though he couldn't get past Gabe and Aidan without pushing them out of the way. 'They both did! They're trying to keep me away from my girlfriend!'

'Because you pushed her into a window, you lying little—' Aidan's retort was cut short as Leon suddenly went limp, like he'd fainted. Then he raised his arm and went to throw a punch at Aidan. Gabe grabbed his arm from behind, preventing him from moving it.

'Get the fuck off me. This is assault.'

Gabe's grip on Leon's arm tightened. 'That was not a smart move.'

'I didn't do anything,' Leon insisted.

'Yes, you did,' Gabe said. 'And now you're going to sit down next to me, shut up, and stay away from Scarlett for the rest of this journey.'

'Or what?' Leon challenged, though his bravado was clearly slipping. 'You're going to break my arm? Because if you do, you'll be arrested.'

Gabe leaned in slightly. 'Or we'll see just how quickly this coach can make an unscheduled stop to drop you off in the middle of nowhere.' He let go of his arm.

The coach hit a bump, sending all three men lurching sideways into the seats where a middle-aged couple was sitting. The woman squealed in alarm as Gabe's shoulder collided with her husband.

'Sorry!' Gabe gasped, trying to right himself. 'Really sorry about that.'

'This is completely unacceptable,' the husband spluttered.

'Utter hooligans!' The woman glared at them.

'You were being very rude to the young woman,' a man with glasses said from across the aisle from Scarlett, looking up at Leon. 'I heard you quite clearly.'

Several other passengers in the vicinity murmured in agreement.

Leon's face darkened further. 'Mind your own business!' he snarled. He kicked out, and his foot connected with the back of a seat, causing a woman to cry out.

Aidan and Gabe exchanged a look. They couldn't let this go on for another five days.

CHAPTER FIVE

Elise

Not long until Fort William, bathroom stop, food break, then back on the road. The trip was running smoothly enough – if you didn't count the fact that Elise had spent the last hour and a half working out how best to avoid certain people for the next few days. At least she was far enough away not to have to look at them and also had a good reason to keep her back to them.

'Coming up on Fort William soon,' Kev, the driver, murmured beside her. His eyes remained fixed on the road, his somewhat wrinkled hands steady on the wheel. 'About twenty minutes. Weather's holding up.'

'Yeah, it's looking pretty good.' She smiled, appreciating his steady presence. Thirty years of driving coaches meant he was experienced and an aura of calm radiated from him. 'I'll make the announcement in a few minutes.'

A sharp noise, kind of like a bark, sounded from the back of the coach, followed by other loud voices. Elise frowned.

'What on earth?'

'Trouble brewing?' Kev raised an eyebrow as he checked his rear-view mirror. 'Want me to pull over?'

'Not yet.' She set her iPad down. 'Let me see what's happening first.'

The mere thought of confrontation made her palms sweat. Conflict resolution was definitely not in the job description when she'd agreed to cover this tour. But then, neither was 're-unite with your ex-boyfriend and his best friend who despises you.'

Several passengers had turned in their seats, craning necks to see the source of the disturbance. A prickle of irritation ran up her spine as she rose from her seat, steadying herself against the gentle sway of the coach. It was quite clear who the voices were coming from, and it made her heart hammer. What the hell were they playing at? For all she didn't much like Gabe, she'd never taken him for violent, and Aidan definitely wasn't, so why did it look like they were threatening Scarlett's boyfriend?

'Stop attacking me,' Scarlett's boyfriend yelled.

'You really need to sit down,' Gabe said.

Elise smoothed down her company blouse and squared her shoulders. Months of avoiding confrontations in Glenbriar, months of carefully building a new life in Glasgow, and here she was walking straight into the middle of a fight with two men she really wanted to avoid.

'Just stop it, Leon,' hissed Scarlett's voice. 'Please.'

'Excuse me.' Elise injected every ounce of professional authority she could muster into her voice. 'What seems to be the problem here?'

Three heads turned towards her simultaneously. Leon's face was flushed with anger. Aidan's expression shifted from determination to surprise. And Gabe – Gabe's piercing blue eyes narrowed when they landed on her, his mouth tightening into a hard line.

The air between them crackled. For a split second, Elise wasn't a professional tour guide handling a disturbance – she was just Elise Reid, a woman, open and vulnerable. Why did it seem like Gabe could see right inside her with those eyes? She gave an involuntary shudder, not sure she wanted to know what he might find there if he could.

The entire coach seemed to be holding its collective breath, all eyes on these three men.

Leon's face was flushed, a vein pulsing in his neck. 'Tell these two to back off!' he spat. 'It's none of their business.'

'It became our business when you started threatening my sister,' Aidan said.

Standing side by side, Aidan and Gabe formed an imposing barrier, broad-shouldered and solid. They weren't touching Leon, but they didn't need to – they had him effectively trapped between them, using nothing but their physical presence as a cage.

'You might want to arrange for this boy to find alternative transportation when we reach Fort William.' Gabe gestured towards Leon.

'I need to know what happened before making any decisions.' She kept her voice level. 'Company policy requires—'

'Company policy?' Gabe raised an eyebrow. 'Does company policy cover what to do when a passenger threatens someone with physical violence?'

Elise's gaze darted to Scarlett, who was hunched against the window, her makeup was smudged beneath one eye.

'I understand everyone's upset,' Elise went on, 'but we need to calm this situation for the sake of all our passengers. Maybe you could all just sit back down.'

Gabe shook his head. 'Yes, that's what we're aiming for.'

Leon wasn't small, but next to them, he looked diminished. Sweat beaded on his forehead.

'You can't keep me here,' he said, but his voice had lost some of its conviction.

'No one's keeping you anywhere.' Elise steadied herself. 'But realistically, there's nowhere else for you to go. So you'd be better sitting back down and trying to keep calm.'

The coach slowed abruptly, and everyone swayed. Elise caught herself on the back of a seat, her hand brushing against Gabe's arm. Even that brief contact felt charged, electric. She pulled away quickly, meeting his gaze for a fraction of a second.

His eyes had darkened, something unreadable passing across his features before his attention snapped back to Leon.

Elise held up her hands. 'Can you all just go back to your seats, please?'

Aidan shook his head. 'He's not sitting next to Scarlett.' He eyed Leon. 'Take the seat beside Gabe like we suggested, will you?'

'Fuck off.'

A collective gasp followed Leon's utterance and Elise ground her teeth. This wasn't getting any better.

'Please, sir.' Elise eyeballed Leon.

'I haven't done anything. They're making it up because they want to look like hard men.'

Before Elise could respond, a voice spoke up from a seat near-by.

'If I may...'

Elise turned to see Lloyd, the man who'd got on with his mother, adjusting his glasses.

'These guys' – he nodded towards Aidan and Gabe – 'are doing the young woman a favour.' He spoke with an educated, pleasant accent. 'This man' – he gestured at Leon – 'was being verbally abusive to her. Quite aggressively so. I don't think it's a good idea to let him sit next to her.'

'Lloyd, don't interfere.' His mother smacked his arm lightly. 'It'll make things worse. Don't get involved with these... weirdos.'

She said the last word quietly, but Elise heard it and judging from the expression on Gabe's face, he had too.

Leon's face darkened. 'Everyone should just mind their own fucking business. I knew this would be a nightmare.'

'Please, sir. If you would just lower your voice and sit down. We'll be in Fort William in about fifteen minutes. We can talk about it when we're off the coach.' And hopefully they'd all have calmed down a bit.

Elise glanced towards Scarlett, who seemed to be trying to disappear into the upholstery. Her usual vibrancy seemed dulled. Her punky clothes – torn jeans and a band t-shirt – suddenly looked less like a fashion statement and more like protective armour on a very vulnerable person.

Lilah leaned over the aisle to talk to her, and she barely looked up.

Elise was caught in an impossible position. Company policy was clear about threats and violence – zero tolerance. But ejecting a passenger in the middle of nowhere wasn't something she could do lightly. If they could just get to Fort William.

'Everyone needs to take their seats,' she said again. 'Leon can sit at the front, near me. There's a spare seat there.'

'This is bullshit,' Leon muttered.

'Watch your language,' Gabe said.

'I've had enough of this. Scarlett!' Leon shouted. 'Are you really going to let them do this?'

Scarlett flinched, shrinking further into her seat.

'She doesn't want to talk to you,' Lilah said.

'Let her speak for herself!' Leon took a step back towards them.

Aidan moved to intercept him. 'That's enough.'

'Get out of my way!' Leon's hand shot out, shoving Aidan's shoulder.

It was like pushing against a brick wall. Aidan barely moved, but his expression darkened dangerously.

'Bad idea,' Gabe said quietly.

Elise stepped forward, her pulse ringing in her ears. 'Stop this right now. We don't need a fight.'

Leon's eyes fixed on her, wild with frustration. 'You're all against me!' he snarled. Then he shoved past Aidan and barrelled forward.

Elise had no time to react. Leon's shoulder rammed into her chest, the impact knocking the breath from her lungs. She stumbled backwards and landed heavily in Lloyd's lap. He looked wide eyed and taken aback.

'I'm so sorry,' she gasped, heat flooding her cheeks.

'It's ok,' he replied.

Before she could answer, another pair of hands closed around her upper arms. Larger hands, stronger, with a grip that was firm but surprisingly gentle. She was lifted effortlessly, set back on her feet in the aisle.

Gabe.

He steadied her for a moment, his hands lingering just long enough to ensure she wouldn't fall again. His palms were warm through the fabric of her blouse, the heat of them seeping into her skin. Elise found herself noticing irrelevant details – the faint callouses on his fingers, probably from rock climbing; the clean, woodsy scent of him; the way his dark hair fell across his forehead as he looked down at her.

But he didn't meet her eyes. His gaze was fixed on the front of the coach, his jaw tight. He released her quickly, as if the contact burned him, and stepped back, his attention still on Leon, who was storming towards the driver.

Gabe and Aidan followed, their expressions thunderous.

'I'm so sorry about that,' Elise said to the man, who was adjusting his glasses.

'No harm done.'

Her chest smarted where Leon had rammed into her, and she knew she'd have a bruise tomorrow. The tour company's insurance forms flashed through her mind – 'Describe the incident in detail' – and she suppressed a groan. The paperwork alone would be a nightmare.

Ahead of her, Leon reached the front. 'Stop the coach!' he shouted. 'I want off!'

Kev's startled eyes appeared in the rearview mirror. He glanced at Elise as she caught up, making her way past Aidan and Gabe.

Gabe and Aidan had stopped a few paces behind Leon, boxing him in against the front of the coach. Their postures were alert, ready, as if expecting him to try something else.

Elise pushed her way past them. Her shoulder brushed against Gabe's arm as she squeezed through the narrow space, and she felt him tense at the contact. Neither of them acknowledged it.

'Leon.' She kept her voice level despite her racing heart. 'Kev will pull over at the next safe spot. I need you to calm down until then.'

Leon's laugh was bitter. 'Calm down? With these two breathing down my neck? They should be the ones kicked off, not me!'

'No one said anything about kicking you off,' Elise replied, though that was exactly what she was considering. 'But your behaviour is disrupting the tour for everyone.'

'My behaviour?' Leon's voice rose incredulously. 'What about them?' He jabbed a finger towards Aidan and Gabe.

'We weren't the ones threatening a young woman,' Gabe said coldly.

'Or pushing her about,' Aidan added.

Elise shot them both a warning look. 'You're not helping.'

Gabe's eyebrows rose slightly, but he fell silent.

The coach began to slow, the indicator ticking as Kev prepared to pull into a large layby. Through the windscreen, Elise saw the scenic stretch of road ahead, the mountains rising darkly against the sky.

Leon's gaze fixed on her. 'You're taking their side. You don't even know what really happened.'

'I'm not taking anyone's side,' Elise said, though she knew it wasn't entirely true. The evidence against Leon was damning. 'I'm trying to resolve this situation in a way that's fair to everyone.'

'Fair?' Leon scoffed. 'There's nothing fair about this!'

The coach eased into the layby, the air brakes hissing as it came to a stop.

Elise met Kev's questioning gaze and nodded slightly. As Kev reached for the door controls, she turned to face the three men, acutely aware that she was standing much closer to Gabe than she wanted to be. The heat radiating from him was intense.

The coach door hissed open, letting in a rush of fresh air.

Leon hesitated before jumping off, as if only now realising the consequences of his demand. The layby was nothing more than a small gravel strip beside the main road with a scrubby woodland behind it. The next town was Fort William, still over fifteen minutes away by car.

Elise took a deep breath and followed him. She needed to handle this professionally, regardless of the personal complications. 'Leon, if you choose to leave the coach here, I'll need to document that you left of your own accord.'

'Own accord?' Leon scoffed. 'I'm being forced off!'

'No one's forcing you,' Aidan said quietly. 'You demanded to be let off. The driver complied.'

Leon's gaze darted between them.

'You have two choices,' Elise said. 'Either return to a seat – not next to Scarlett – and comply with the rules of conduct for the remainder of the journey or disembark now. But I can't allow you to continue disrupting this tour. Any further attempts to assault people and I'll have to call the police.'

He seemed to deflate slightly, the bravado leaking out of him. 'Get my luggage,' he demanded.

'Mind your manners.' Gabe glowered at him.

'Kev will open the luggage compartment.' Elise signalled to Kev, who pressed the control to release the side storage panels. Then she stepped back onto the coach and lifted the microphone. 'Ladies and gentlemen, I apologise for this disruption. We'll be underway again in just a few minutes. Please remain seated.'

An older man raised his hand. 'Is everything alright? Should we be concerned?'

'Everything's under control,' Elise assured him, though that was a blatant lie. She had no idea what was going to happen next or what the hell to do about it. Never in her career had anything like this happened.

Aidan and Gabe were standing like guardians to ensure Leon didn't try to re-board or cause further trouble.

'You think you're so much better than everyone else! Both of you!'

Elise hurried back outside, hearing Leon shouting again. The last thing they needed was for the confrontation to turn physical.

Leon hoisted his backpack onto his shoulder. 'Scarlett's coming with me.'

'No, she's not,' Aidan replied.

Leon sneered. 'You can't stop her if that's what she wants.'

'No chance are you getting to take her with you wherever you're going,' Gabe said. 'You're an unsafe person.'

Leon gave him the finger.

Elise stepped forward. 'Scarlett has made no indication that she wants to leave, and you can't force her.' She checked her watch. They really needed to get moving, but could she just leave Leon here? A twinge of guilt twisted in her stomach. The professional part of her brain listed all the company regulations that justified leaving him here – the threatening behaviour, the physical aggression, the disruption to other passengers. The human part wondered if she was doing the right thing. Despite everything, abandoning someone on a remote stretch of road felt wrong.

Kev had come to the door and was watching them.

'I need to call the manager,' she told him, pulling the work mobile from her pocket. 'Company policy requires documentation for incidents like this.'

Kev nodded. 'Take your time. Better to get it sorted properly. I'll keep an eye on this lot.'

Elise moved to a spot in the layby where she could speak without being overheard by the passengers. The last thing she needed was for them to hear her uncertainty. A tour guide was supposed to inspire confidence, to make everything seem under control even when it wasn't.

She scrolled through her contacts, finding Gill Campbell's number. Her finger hovered over the call button. This would be an admission of failure, wouldn't it? The inaugural Glenbriar tour, and she already had a battle on her hands before even reaching their lunch stop. Not exactly the launch Gill was looking for. This was the kind of thing that would spread over social media and review sites like wildfire.

Elise pressed call. The phone rang once, twice, three times. Each ring seemed to echo her racing thoughts. What if Gill didn't answer? *What if I made the wrong decision?* What if this incident damaged the company's reputation... or hers?

How the hell could it play out without utter carnage?

Chapter Six

Gabe

Gabe watched Leon from the corner of his eye, tracking his movements like he might a wounded animal. Something unpredictable was simmering in there and this wasn't really a safe location. Gabe's eyes travelled up and down the busy road. Traffic rushed past with sharp blasts of air. A lorry rumbled by, momentarily blotting out Elise's voice as she talked with someone on the other end of her phone.

'Do you think he'll do a runner?' Aidan murmured, not taking his eyes off Leon, who'd slumped onto a large rock at the edge of the layby, his expression murderous.

'I hope not. That would be crazy…' Though everything he'd done already was unhinged so Gabe wouldn't put it past him. 'But where would he go?' Gabe nodded towards the busy stretch of Highland road.

'I can't believe all this.' Aidan sighed and ran his hand through his hair.

'This is exactly why I don't do relationships,' Gabe muttered.

Aidan folded his arms and gave him a look. 'Because you're afraid you'll shove your girlfriend in front of a bus full of pensioners?'

'No, you eejit. Because of the drama.' He rubbed at his cheek.

Aidan snorted, but Gabe wasn't kidding. Aidan had gone through the drama with Elise before finding Lilah. And so many friends had gone through similar. His own mother suffered day in, day out at the hands of a dickhead Gabe wouldn't even consider calling 'Dad'. He'd lost that right long ago. Relationships caused pain and heartache.

They watched as Leon kicked at the gravel, sending stones skittering across the tarmac. The situation was a powder keg.

'She's been on that call for ages,' Gabe muttered, eyeing Elise. She stood some metres away, her back turned to them, one hand pressed against her ear to block out the sound of another lorry roaring past. Her dark hair whipped around her face in the breeze.

'Not an easy one to explain to the boss, I guess,' Aidan said. 'Sorry, we've got a violent passenger. What's company policy on abandoning people in the middle of nowhere?'

'Let's see what's going on.' This waiting was driving Gabe mad. He made his way across the layby towards Elise.

'... I get that, but what am I authorised to do here?' Her voice was professional, though taut with frustration. 'The other passengers are waiting, and – no, I haven't – yes, I realise that...'

She glanced up, noticing Gabe, and gave him a quick, harried look that seemed to say both 'help me' and 'go away' simultaneously.

'Is there any progress?' he asked when she paused for breath.

Elise held the phone down. 'I'm on hold again,' she whispered. 'My manager's checking with legal.'

'Legal?' Gabe frowned. 'Christ, is it that complicated? The guy assaulted someone. He should be off the tour.'

'I'm trying,' she said, 'but I can't just abandon a customer in the middle of nowhere.'

'He wants to leave anyway.'

'Yes, but if something happens to him after I dump him at the side of the road, guess who's liable? The company. And guess who gets the blame? Me.' Before Gabe could respond, she straightened. 'Yes, I'm still here.'

Gabe folded his arms, studying her. He'd never understood how Aidan had fallen for someone so... He ground his teeth, not sure exactly what he was thinking. She annoyed him though because... Well, he didn't really know why. Or if he did, he couldn't admit it. Not even to himself. The simmering dislike was visceral and raw, not rational.

His frown deepened as his brain nudged him with some uncomfortable truths, but he didn't even entertain them. He didn't like Elise. And that was that.

'No, I understand that completely,' she continued, 'but the situation is escalating, and the other passengers—'

She was cut off again, and Gabe watched as she closed her eyes briefly, perhaps counting to ten in her head.

'Look, we need to sort this. Leon's on edge, and I don't fancy spending my entire holiday playing bouncer,' he said.

'I'm doing everything I can.' She smiled, but it was the fakest thing he'd ever seen.

'How much longer is it going to take?'

'They're giving me my options.' She narrowed her eyes. 'And it would go faster without interruptions.'

He raised his hands in mock surrender. 'Ok, I get the message.' He backed off, still watching her. What was it about her that got under his skin and pissed him off? Returning to Aidan, he pulled a face to indicate that he'd learned nothing from their interaction.

A few moments later, Elise marched towards them and Gabe caught a slight tremble in her fingers as she tucked a lock of hair behind her ear.

'Well?' Aidan asked when she reached them. He stood with his arms folded, his gaze periodically flicking towards Leon, who had taken to throwing pebbles at a nearby sign.

Elise let out a sigh. 'My manager says I have to let him off the tour, if that's what he wants.'

'Thank Christ for that,' Gabe muttered.

'But...' She shot him a sharp look, 'I also have to offer to call a taxi to take him to the nearest town. I can't just leave him here.'

Aidan nodded. 'Makes sense.'

'Ok,' Gabe said. 'So, let's call him a taxi and send him on his way.'

Elise winced slightly. 'If he agrees to it.'

'And if he doesn't?'

'Then I need to document that he refused assistance, and he's on his own.' She squared her shoulders. 'But I have to make the offer.'

'Do you want us to stick with you when you talk to him?' Gabe raised an eyebrow.

Elise flattened her lips together. 'He already feels ganged up on, so don't crowd him and let me do the talking.' She stepped forward, getting closer to Leon, and Gabe moved too, almost shadowing her but still keeping his distance.

'Leon,' she began, 'I've spoken with my manager, and we've come to a decision about the situation.'

Leon looked up. 'Yeah? And what's that, then?'

'Since you've expressed a desire to leave the tour, we're prepared to accommodate that request.'

'Like you have a choice. I'm not your prisoner.'

'That's true, but we can't in good conscience leave you here at the side of the road. My company is willing to arrange and pay for a taxi to take you to Fort William if you don't want to get back on the coach. Once you're in Fort William, you'll have access to train and bus services back to Glenbriar or wherever else you might want to go.'

Leon's eyes narrowed. 'And that's it? I don't get a refund?'

Gabe glowered at him, and Aidan scoffed, saying, 'You didn't pay anything in the first place. Scarlett won the tickets.'

'The taxi fare is on us,' Elise said. 'As a goodwill gesture.'

'Which is more than fair,' Gabe added. 'All things considered.'

Leon's gaze shifted to Aidan, then to Gabe, and his scowl deepened.

'Fine,' he muttered. 'Whatever. Call the taxi.'

'Please,' Gabe added, giving him a pointed look. 'Manners cost nothing.'

'I'll do it right now,' Elise said.

As she stepped away to make the call, Leon resumed his sullen examination of the ground. Gabe and Aidan exchanged glances. The time it took for the taxi to get here would be longer than Leon getting back on the coach and going with them, though it was probably better if he didn't get back on.

Elise made the call, her back straight, her free hand gesturing occasionally as she spoke. Despite everything, Gabe found himself watching her. How did she keep so calm? He'd have kicked Leon off straight away and left him to his own devices.

Elise pocketed her phone and got back on the coach. Gabe frowned. 'What's she doing now?'

Aidan gave a little shrug. 'Maybe checking Scarlett's ok. This is not going to be a nice trip for her now, is it?'

'Nope.'

'Sad, because she's the one who won the tickets. It wouldn't surprise me if she wants to get off in Fort William and go home too.' Aidan took in a deep breath. 'I think this trip is doomed.'

Elise came off the coach carrying an iPad and went straight to Leon. She started explaining something to him and a frown grew on his face.

'You want me to sign that I'm leaving willingly?' Leon's incredulous tone carried across the layby. 'Are you taking the piss? They chucked me off. I had no choice.' He pointed at Gabe and Aidan.

'It's procedure,' Elise replied. 'It simply states that you're choosing to leave the tour and that we've offered alternative transportation, which you've accepted.'

'So it's to cover your arse, basically.'

'It's to cover everyone and to document the agreement we've reached.'

Leon stood abruptly, causing Elise to take a small step backward. Gabe and Aidan both tensed, ready to move.

'I'm not signing anything,' Leon said. 'Just call the bloody taxi like you said you would.'

'I've already called for the taxi,' Elise explained patiently. 'This is merely to—'

'I don't give a fuck what it's for,' Leon cut her off, his voice rising to a shout. 'Screw your company policies, your forms, and your bullshit. I just want to get the hell away from this tour and all of you!'

'I think you should lower your voice—'

'Or what?' Leon stepped closer to her. 'You'll kick me off the tour? Oh wait, that's already happening, isn't it?'

'I understand you're upset—'

'You don't understand shit,' Leon spat. 'Just fuck off and leave me alone until the taxi gets here!'

'Watch your mouth,' Gabe said. 'You don't talk to her like that. She's just doing her job.'

Leon turned his glare on Gabe. 'Whatever.'

'Sign the form like she says.' Gabe eyeballed him. 'It's not a request.'

'Bully,' Leon muttered, but he grabbed the iPad and the stylus from Elise and scrawled on the form.

'Thank you.' She took it back from him with shaky fingers.

Gabe turned away and paced the layby, looking for any sign of the taxi. As he walked back, he caught Aidan's eye. Aidan raised an eyebrow.

'What?' Gabe asked.

'Awkward this, isn't it? Given the history.'

'I don't have a history with her. She has a history with you.'

'And you've made it very clear over the years how you feel about her.'

Gabe shrugged. 'No one deserves to be spoken to like that, regardless of who they are. She's here to work.'

'True.'

The minutes stretched into what felt like hours as they waited for the taxi to arrive. Gabe leaned against a post, arms folded across his chest. Every time Leon moved, Gabe tensed, ready to intervene if necessary. It was exhausting, but he couldn't bring himself to relax. Not with Leon's mood swinging like a weathervane in a gale.

Finally, a white taxi appeared, pulling into the layby. Its arrival meant an end to this particular standoff, though the ripple effects would no doubt continue long after Leon was gone.

'About time,' Gabe muttered, checking his watch. 'Think he'll make this difficult?' He eyed Leon.

'Probably.' Aidan rolled his eyes.

Elise approached the driver's window, leaning down to speak with him.

Leon remained where he was, as if debating whether to comply or create a final scene. The seconds stretched uncomfortably until, with a visible slump of his shoulders, he began walking towards them, not looking at any of them directly.

The taxi driver, seemingly sensing the tension, got out to open the boot with a slight frown. Leon got in and pulled the door shut with unnecessary force.

They stood in silence as the taxi made its way back onto the road. None of them spoke until it had disappeared around the bend, carrying Leon away from their tour and, Gabe hoped, out of Scarlett's life for good.

'Well,' Aidan said finally, 'that's that, then.'

Elise exhaled slowly, a long breath. 'Thank you both for your help. Now, let's get this tour moving again. We're running so late.'

Gabe followed Aidan back onto the coach, many curious stares and whispered speculation following them as they made their way down the narrow aisle.

Lilah sat beside Scarlett, one arm draped protectively around her shoulders, her head bent close as she spoke.

A pang of sympathy tugged at Gabe's chest, mixed with a fresh surge of anger towards Leon. Whatever had transpired between them before his outburst, Scarlett didn't deserve to be left feeling like this – embarrassed, abandoned, and turned into an unwilling spectacle for a coach full of strangers.

'Has he gone?' she asked quietly as they reached the seats.

Aidan nodded. 'A taxi took him to Fort William. He didn't want to get back on the coach.'

Scarlett looked up. Her eyes were rimmed with red, though she'd clearly made an effort to fix her makeup.

Gabe settled into a seat next to Aidan as the coach finally rolled off again.

'Ladies and gentlemen,' Elise's voice came over the microphone. 'Thank you for your patience during our unscheduled stop. Unfortunately, due to our delay, we will need to adjust our schedule slightly. We'll still be stopping in Fort William for lunch as planned, though our time there will be shortened by a few minutes to keep us on track for the afternoon.'

A murmur rippled through the coach – disappointment from some, understanding from others.

'I apologise for any inconvenience this may cause. If anyone had specific issues that might be affected by this change, please speak with me privately.'

'She probably hates me,' Scarlett said. 'I've ruined the tour.'

'You haven't ruined anything.' Aidan leaned over to speak to her. 'If anyone's to blame, it's Leon, not you.'

Scarlett didn't look convinced, but she nodded slightly, her gaze fixed on her hands in her lap.

The woman in the seat in front turned and looked through the gap. 'Is the girl alright? Such a dreadful business earlier.'

'She'll be fine, thank you,' Aidan replied.

About ten minutes later, they turned off the main road and Elise's voice came through the microphone.

'Ladies and gentlemen, we're just arriving in Fort William,' she announced. 'Due to our earlier delay, we'll have one hour and thirty minutes here instead of the originally planned two hours.'

A murmur of disappointment rippled through the coach, which Elise acknowledged with a sympathetic nod before continuing.

'I know it's less time than we'd hoped for, but we need to keep to our schedule to ensure we reach our hotel by check-in time. There are several lovely cafés and restaurants within easy walking distance for lunch. Let me know if you need help to choose one.'

'Lunch plan?' Aidan asked as passengers began to get ready to leave.

'Somewhere quiet,' Gabe suggested. 'Away from the rest of the group might be sensible. Otherwise, we'll have people yapping about Leon nonstop.'

Aidan nodded in agreement. 'Good idea.'

They waited until most of the other passengers had disembarked before making their move.

Fort William was a hive of energy. Visitors moved between shops selling everything from authentic Scottish woollens to mass-produced tartan tat. A group of hikers in serious-looking gear consulted a map outside an outdoor equipment store, while nearby, a family debated the merits of various ice cream flavours displayed in a café window.

'I think there's a place down here.' Aidan led them away from the main street and onto a quieter lane lined with a mix of residential buildings and small businesses. A café appeared after a short walk – a cosy-looking place with hanging baskets of summer flowers framing its entrance.

'The Nevis Kitchen,' Lilah read from the sign. 'Looks perfect.'

Inside, the café was warm and inviting, with wooden tables, mismatched chairs, and local art adorning the walls. They found a table towards the back. Scarlett slid into a seat with her back to the door.

Gabe sat last, scanning over the blackboard behind the counter at the list of lunch foods.

'I'm not really hungry,' Scarlett said.

'You should probably eat something.' Lilah sucked her lower lip before glancing at Aidan.

'Yeah,' Aidan agreed. 'It's a long way otherwise.'

The door opened, and Gabe looked around to see a pair of people from the tour. The man with glasses whose lap Elise had fallen into and an older woman – possibly his mother. Scarlett had also glanced around and seen them. She groaned.

'I feel like a circus freak.'

'It's ok.' Lilah reached over and patted her hand. 'They're not looking and even if they see you, I don't think they'll say anything.'

A waitress came and took their orders, then a heavy silence fell over the table. No one wanted to mention Leon's departure and what it meant for Scarlett and the rest of their trip.

Tension gripped Gabe's shoulders, and he had a mad impulse to walk out and get a train back to Glenbriar – or anywhere. Why was he here anyway? Obviously, Scarlett felt a lot worse than him, but this whole trip felt like a disaster, and they'd barely got going.

After lunch, they didn't have much time left before the coach was due to depart. They went into a couple of shops, Gabe and Aidan enjoying all the outdoor equipment stores. Aidan and Lilah were missing their beautiful husky dog and bought her some treats.

'I'm going to step out for a minute,' Gabe told Aidan. 'Need to find the gents.'

He made his way out of the shop, relieved to be alone with his thoughts for the first time since the chaos had begun. While he genuinely needed to find a bathroom, space to breathe was just as essential. Near the car park, he spotted a set of public toilets and ducked inside, splashing cold water on his face after washing his hands. The mirror reflected a more tired version of himself than he'd expected. So much for a relaxing Highland break.

He'd joined the tour looking for a few days of easy companionship, beautiful scenery, and perhaps the chance to scout some locations for future environmental podcast episodes. Drama and confrontation hadn't figured into his plan. Why would they? Or was this just normal life? For other people? He was used to doing things on his own terms. Sometimes these days he worked with bigger companies and producers, but even then, he had freedom and people usually bending over backwards to accommodate him. Not that he craved that here, but everything felt so alien.

He pushed open the restroom door with more force than necessary, still distracted by his tangled thoughts, and nearly collided with a woman emerging from the ladies' room opposite. Elise. His heart plummeted. They both pulled up short, that peculiar social dance of avoiding a collision made awkward by their mutual surprise at finding themselves suddenly face to face, alone in a narrow corridor.

'Sorry,' they said in unison.

'I... um...' Her lip twitched like she was attempting to smile but not managing. 'I should thank you,' she said. 'For your assistance with the... er, situation this morning.'

'It's fine.' He shoved his hands into his pockets. 'Though I'm not sure how helpful we actually were. I just know we couldn't sit by and let him behave like that.'

'Agreed.' She met his eyes directly, and his insides shifted so weirdly he almost registered a physical pain. What the hell? 'It's probably better that he's not on the coach, but his exit wasn't the prettiest.'

'No.' He raised an eyebrow. 'That's true.'

'Anyway.' Elise glanced away. 'The tour is almost back on track now, and hopefully nothing else happens.'

Gabe nodded. 'Let's hope.'

With the smallest of smiles she headed out, holding the door for him but scuttling off very quickly once he was through. Well, they'd managed a micro moment without fighting or glaring at each other, which was something, but an oddly unsettled sensation trickled through Gabe's veins. It wasn't the same as not wanting to be here, more like he'd forgotten to do something, or something was going to happen that he hadn't prepared for. Only he had no idea what.

Letting out a slow breath, he raked his fingers through his hair and looked about for the others. He could try to figure out the nonsense in his head another time, because right now, he needed to get back on the coach.

Chapter Seven

Elise

Elise ticked off items on her checklist, her stylus stabbing at each bullet point as if the iPad had personally offended her. Outside the coach windows, the main street of Fort William bustled with tourists, including her own passengers who were making their way back after their cut-short time here.

She glanced at her watch and swallowed a sigh. Five minutes until they were due back and she had to plaster on her tour guide smile and pretend everything was absolutely fine, that they weren't running behind schedule on their inaugural trip and the whole thing was already a shitshow.

'Bloody Leon Fletcher,' she muttered under her breath. 'There's a name I won't forget in a hurry.'

Kev chuckled and shook his head. 'In all my years of driving, I've never had a passenger demand to be let off in the middle of nowhere. That's a first.'

'Same.' Elise watched a retired couple peer into a gift shop window across the street. 'I'm just hoping the rest decide to stay aboard.'

'You handled it well.' Kev took a sip of coffee from a paper cup. 'That young man was a right radge. Nothing to be done with his sort. What was he even doing on a tour like this in the first place? No offence to his girlfriend, but they don't look the type.'

'She won the tickets in the promotional draw.'

'Ahh.' Kev raised his bushy eyebrows. 'That makes more sense. Oh well, at least she's not losing any money.'

'I wonder if she'll choose to leave herself. It'll be a bit weird for her carrying on.'

'Maybe, though she might realise she's better off without him.'

'Who knows? I just want today to be over.' She checked out the window. In fact, the whole tour couldn't end quick enough. 'We should probably open up and start letting people back. The quicker we get away, the better.'

Elise got off the bus to welcome people, only to hear the work phone vibrating against the plastic tray table. She turned around to see Kev leaning over, looking at the screen.

'It's Gill,' he said. 'You probably want to take it.'

Elise's stomach performed an Olympic-worthy dive. With a sigh, she stepped back onto the coach and lifted the phone.

'Gill, hello.' She walked a little away from the coach as she spoke.

'Elise.' Gill's crisp tone came through sharp as a dagger. 'I've got an update on your little situation.'

Your little situation. As if Leon's explosive departure was her doing.

'Ok,' Elise said.

'I've contacted the police who are going to make a record of what happened. And I've checked with the taxi company. They've confirmed the passenger was dropped at the station without incident.'

'That's good to hear.'

'Yes.' Gill's voice had that particular quality that Elise knew so well – pleasant on the surface, but with undercurrents of something less friendly beneath. 'Let's just hope that's all the drama we have for the rest of the week. What's happening with the other passengers who were with this man? Are they staying on?'

'As far as I know.'

'Well, for goodness sake, keep a close eye on them. It's almost a pity they haven't all chosen to end their trip. I think I'd prefer to refund or compensate them than have them onboard.' She let out an audible sigh. 'I don't suppose it's something you could persuade them to do?'

Elise swallowed and shook her head, though she was aware Gill couldn't see her. 'No. I'd rather not.' She wouldn't with anyone, but especially not that group.

'I can imagine. But if they make any signs of wanting to leave, then let them.'

'Ok. I will. I should go. That's most people back, I think. And we should crack on.'

'Yes. Well, keep me up to date.'

Elise pressed her fingertips to her temples, where a headache was beginning to throb.

'Did you enjoy your time in Fort William?' She hitched on a smile as she returned to the door of the coach where passengers were still boarding.

'Lovely little shops.' A woman handed Elise a paper bag. 'Got you a wee sweetie. For all your trouble earlier.'

'That's very thoughtful. Thank you.'

'Not your fault that young man was behaving like a hooligan,' the woman's husband added. 'You handled it well.'

Elise murmured her thanks again. How kind. She tucked the bag into her pocket before glancing up and finding herself staring at Gabe. Their gazes locked, and something electric passed between them, a raw and primal sensation that made Elise's mouth go dry and her heart stutter in her chest.

For an insane moment, she forgot she was standing in a car park in Fort William. Forgot she was on the clock. Forgot everything except the intensity in his laser blue eyes as they bored into hers with an almost predatory focus.

He didn't smile. Didn't nod. Just kept his eyes on hers. Heat bloomed low in her belly. That look told her he was thinking things that had absolutely no place on this tour – or anywhere in her life.

But god help her, she was thinking the same. If they cleared the coach, she'd jump him. All that pent-up hatred would spill out – but not in a fight. No, it would be something much hotter. Something far more cathartic.

'If you'll take your seat, we'll be departing shortly.' She kept her voice steady despite the chaos in her head.

One corner of his mouth quirked up. Not exactly a smile; something far more dangerous. 'That was a nice gift that lady gave you,' he muttered. 'Is that because you're not sweet enough already?' Such teasing should have annoyed her, but instead, it sent another inappropriate thrill through her body.

'I couldn't possibly comment.' She stepped aside to let him pass, and as he did, his arm brushed against hers. The brief contact was like touching a live wire.

Holding her breath, she turned her focus to the next passenger.

Once everyone was accounted for, she took her position at the front of the coach, microphone in hand.

'Right, everyone. I hope you enjoyed your lunch in Fort William. We're now heading west towards the Kyle of Lochalsh. We have some spectacular scenery ahead of us...' She settled into a familiar spiel.

Kev started the engine and pulled onto the main road, weaving through the town. As they travelled onward, the road narrowed further, hugging the contours of the land. Kev slowed the coach, handling each bend carefully. Still, Elise found herself leaning slightly in her seat, as if her body could help guide the large vehicle through the tight spots.

'These roads were not built with modern coaches in mind,' she commented. 'But Kev here has plenty of experience, so we're in safe hands.'

Kev gave a modest grunt in response, his eyes never leaving the road.

'The Highlands were much more isolated before these roads were improved,' Elise continued. 'Communities were often cut off for months during winter. Today, we complain when the Wi-Fi drops for five minutes.'

A ripple of appreciative laughter spread through the coach.

They crested a rise, and suddenly the landscape opened up before them. Hills rolled away to the horizon, their slopes patched with heather and gorse. In the distance, the glint of water signalled their approach to the western seaboard.

'Ladies and gentlemen,' Elise said, 'here we have one of the most beautiful views in Scotland.'

Several passengers murmured in appreciation.

'We're now beginning our descent towards the coast,' she continued. 'From here, it's about an hour and twenty minutes to the Skye Bridge, depending on traffic.'

Elise continued her commentary when needed, every now and then glancing back to check everyone was seated and that no further drama was unfolding behind her. They made good speed and right on time, the Skye Bridge loomed ahead, a graceful arc of concrete spanning the narrow strait between the mainland and Skye. Elise leaned forward in her seat, microphone in hand. 'We're now approaching the Skye Bridge,' she said. 'Until 1995, the only way to reach Skye was by boat. The bridge was originally a toll bridge, but those tolls were abolished in 2004, and now travellers can go across freely.'

The late afternoon sun glinted off the water of Loch Alsh like little gems on the surface.

'And now,' she said as the coach reached the highest point of the bridge, 'we are officially crossing onto the Isle of Skye – or Eilean a' Cheò in Gaelic, which means "Island of Mist".'

The road curved along the coastline, offering tantalising glimpses of beaches and cliffs. Elise pointed out landmarks as they passed.

'We're staying in Portree,' she continued, 'the main town on the island. The name comes from the Gaelic "Port Rìgh," meaning "King's Port," after a visit by King James V in 1540. Today, it's known for its pretty harbour with colourful houses and excellent seafood.'

The coach rounded a final bend, and Portree came into view, nestled around a natural harbour. The iconic row of painted houses along the waterfront glowed in the late afternoon light – pink, blue, yellow, and white facades, creating a picture-postcard scene.

Kev pulled the coach into the car park of the hotel, which was a large country house on a hill above the village. Elise descended the coach steps, straightening her jacket as she approached the hotel entrance. The manager was already waiting.

'Ms Reid? I'm Fiona MacLeod, hotel manager. You made it.'

'Sorry about the delay.' Elise shook her hand.

'No problem. Thank you for calling ahead and letting us know, and you're here now.'

Elise stood by the door, counting passengers as they disembarked. The next twenty minutes passed in a whirl of organised chaos as Fiona distributed keys and answered questions about mealtimes, and local shops, while Elise dealt with the ones about tomorrow's itinerary.

Gabe, Aidan, Lilah, and Scarlett had taken their keys and gone. Elise rolled her shoulders discreetly, trying to ease the tension that had accumulated, as she watched the last passenger head up the stairs. Technically, she was off duty now until dinner – a brief respite. She was still on call, of course. Tour guides were never truly off the clock, not until the final passenger was safely delivered home at the end of the trip. But for now, at least, she could breathe.

She found Kev at the bottom of the stairs looking nearly as exhausted as she felt.

'Survived, then?' he asked.

'Barely.'

'Well, get some relaxing done before later. I'm looking forward to a cup of tea and a sit down.'

The staircase creaked slightly as Elise climbed to the second floor. The hotel was old, with character, but nicely done up with modern furnishings.

She was so focused on the search for her room that she almost didn't notice the two men standing further down the hallway until she was nearly upon them. When she looked up, her heart leapt.

Aidan and Gabe were deep in conversation outside what she presumed was one of their rooms. Aidan gestured with one hand, his back partially turned, while Gabe leaned against the wall, arms crossed over his chest. His eyes flicked up over Aidan's shoulder – and locked with hers.

Their conversation continued, Aidan seemingly unaware of her presence, but Gabe's focus shifted. To her. That same electric pull that had haunted her all day crackled to life, more potent than ever. Their eyes began their own conversation, following an agenda she had no control over. He was undressing her with that look. She returned the favour, heat blooming low and hot as invisible flames licked at her core.

Christ's sake.

She fumbled to unlock her door, forcing herself to look away, but sensing Gabe's laser eyes still on her back. She slipped inside quickly and let out a long slow breath. What was that? What the hell was going on with Gabe? Why did he keep looking at her like that... And why couldn't she look away?

An almost carnal urge to have him fired up inside her. Which made no sense. She didn't even like the man. But she wanted him...

Ugh. This was so infuriating.

She dropped her bag on the bed, trying to shake off the feeling. But she knew from the online research she'd done on attraction after her breakups how indiscriminate it could be. What she had to decide was whether to act on it or not. And she wouldn't. Well, she wouldn't initiate anything.

But what if he knocked on her door?

The idea sent a shock of something – panic? anticipation? – through her system. She glanced around as if expecting it to happen. Was he out there right now, fist curled ready?

She held her breath. Minutes ticked by, and the corridor outside remained silent. No footsteps approaching. No knock.

Relief warred with an emotion she refused to identify as disappointment. Whatever bizarre tension existed between them, she shouldn't acknowledge it and definitely shouldn't encourage it.

She stripped off her jacket and headed for the shower. She needed to wash away the day's stresses and these bizarre feelings.

Elise surveyed her reflection in the mirror. The black dress was a careful choice – professional, presentable, nothing that would invite comment. Her makeup was minimal, her dark hair swept into a tidy updo. Polished, but forgettable. That was the goal. She'd spent years perfecting the art of looking good without seeming like she was asking for attention. It started with the leers from her parents' friends when she was barely a teenager, and continued with at least one sleazy man on almost every tour she'd guided since. She'd long lost count of how many times she'd had her bum slapped or endured a lewd comment.

She arrived at the hotel dining room just before seven. The room was half-filled already, her tour group scattered among the tables, mixed with other hotel guests. White tablecloths and flickering candles gave the space a warmth and looked very welcoming.

Kev was already at their designated table, looking slightly uncomfortable in a button-up shirt that strained across his shoulders.

'Evening,' he said. 'Scrub up well, don't you?'

'Thanks, Kev. You're not so bad yourself.' She sat, smoothing her dress over her knees. 'Did you manage to get some rest?'

'Aye, a wee nap. You?'

'I tried.' She pulled a face. 'I had a shower, but I ended up scrolling social media.'

A waiter appeared with menus and a jug of water. Elise ordered a glass of white wine – just one, to take the edge off while remaining professional – while Kev opted for a local ale. She surveyed the room discreetly, noting which passengers were already seated.

'Are you quite new to this job?' Kev asked once their drinks arrived. 'I've not seen you on a tour before.'

'I've only been with the company for just over a year.' Elise took a sip of her wine. 'Though as a project manager. I'm just standing in as someone is sick. I've done guiding before with other companies though.'

'Ah, I see. And are you from up this way originally?'

Elise tensed slightly. Personal questions were always a minefield. 'I grew up in Glenbriar, actually.'

'Did you?'

'Yes, and what about you? Have you always been a coach driver?'

The diversion worked. Kev launched into his career history – lorries first, then long-distance coaches, then tour work when he decided he wanted more regular hours. 'Better for family life,' he explained. 'Got three grown kids now, and five grandwees.'

'Five?' Elise seized the opportunity to steer the conversation firmly away from her own life. 'That's wonderful. What ages?'

Kev's weathered face softened as he spoke about his grandchildren. The oldest was ten, the youngest just six months. He pulled out his phone to show her photos of a gap-toothed boy on a bike, girls in matching dresses, a baby with a shock of ginger hair.

'They're adorable,' Elise said. 'You must be very proud.'

'Best thing I ever did, having kids. Though I didn't appreciate it properly until they gave me grandchildren.' He chuckled. 'That's how it works – you're too busy worrying when they're yours, then you get to enjoy it properly the second time around.'

Elise smiled, ignoring the hollow feeling in her chest. At thirty, with no relationship prospects and a career that consumed most of her energy, children seemed an increasingly distant possibility. She told herself she was happy just being Auntie Elise to her brother's three kids, and in many ways, she was. But sometimes, in reflective moments, she wondered if she'd missed some invisible window. She'd never been good at letting people close – never learned how to trust that love wouldn't come with strings or expectations she couldn't meet. That kind of trust had been chipped away early, when being pretty meant being noticed for all the wrong reasons. Intimacy had always felt more like a performance than a connection. And the idea of bringing a child into that mess – of trying to be a mother while still piecing together who she really was – felt selfish at best, dangerous at worst.

Gabe was seated at a table across the room with Aidan, Lilah, and Scarlett. Kev continued to talk about his grandkids, and Elise listened, but her focus kept shifting to their table. Lilah was laughing with Aidan, possibly trying to boost up Scarlett. But Gabe wasn't participating in their conversation. He was looking directly at Elise, those blue eyes finding her across the busy dining room as if drawn by a magnetic force.

She dropped her gaze, focusing on her plate with unnecessary intensity. She couldn't let this get any more heated... or dangerous. But a prickling sensation at the back of her neck made her sure he was still watching.

'... and then wee Jamie says to the ref, "That's not a penalty, that's daylight robbery!" Bold as brass, he was. Gets that from his grandmother's side, not mine...' Kev laughed.

'He sounds like a character,' she said, trying to piece together her fragmented attention and make appropriate noises of interest, but there was no stopping her wandering mind. Against her better judgment, she risked another glance across the room.

Gabe was still looking at her. One corner of his mouth lifted in what might have been the beginning of a smile, but it was challenging. Almost intimate. Heat rose in her cheeks and simultaneously pooled in her core.

She looked away again, taking a large gulp of her wine.

'You ok?' Kev asked.

'Fine. Yeah.'

Kev followed where her gaze had been across the room. 'That man there, isn't he the one who does those nature shows? My daughter watches him.'

'Yeah. *Wilder at Heart*,' Elise said. 'Environmental activism and awareness stuff. He became something of a local celebrity during lockdown.'

'That's the one. What's he doing on a coach tour, then? Doesn't seem his kind of thing.'

It was the same question Elise had been asking herself. 'He's with the group who won the tickets.'

'Ah yes,' Kev said, 'strange choice for a holiday when he could probably be filming in the Amazon or something.'

'Yeah. It's odd.'

A movement caught Elise's eye. A middle-aged woman had approached Gabe's table and was talking animatedly to him, a look of star-struck enthusiasm on her face. Gabe was smiling politely, signing something.

'Looks like he's got fans.' Kev grinned.

'Mmm.' Elise tried to sound disinterested as she cut into her main course, which had arrived during their conversation. The fish was perfectly cooked, but she barely tasted it.

The woman eventually moved away from Gabe's table, clutching her signed paper like a treasure. Elise kept her eyes firmly on her plate, determined not to look his way again. This... whatever it was... had to stop. She was a professional. She had a job to do. And Gabe Wilder was a complication she neither needed nor wanted.

But her resolve lasted only until the dessert course. As she listened to Kev describe his youngest daughter's new house, her eyes betrayed her, drifting across the room of their own accord.

Gabe was watching her as if he'd known she would look again and had been waiting for it.

Their eyes locked, and something passed between them – something electric and completely inappropriate. His gaze dropped deliberately to her mouth, then back to her eyes, the message unmistakable. Heat bloomed deep inside her, spreading outward until she felt flushed from head to toe.

This wasn't the open dislike they'd shared for years. It wasn't even simple attraction. It was something much more explosive. Across the crowded dining room, with dozens of people between them, Gabe Wilder was doing wicked things to her with his eyes. The intensity of it stole her breath. She couldn't look away, couldn't break the connection, and worst of all, she didn't want to.

CHAPTER EIGHT

Gabe

Gabe tried not to stare as Elise rose from her seat across the dining room, but since he'd spent the entire meal exchanging glances with her that were definitely not appropriate for a man who was supposed to dislike her on principle, he didn't hold out much hope of stopping now.

'We were thinking of going for a walk after this.' Lilah glanced at Scarlett, who hadn't spoken during the whole meal. 'Down to the harbour.'

'Fancy it?' Aidan looked at Gabe. A nighttime stroll would normally appeal to him, but…

'I think I might give it a miss,' he said.

Aidan looked at him. 'You sure? We won't mind, if that's what you're thinking.'

'I know.' Gabe raised his glass to his lips. 'But you should have some time to yourselves.'

'Do you want to come?' Lilah asked Scarlett.

'Na. I'm ok.' She looked anything but.

Gabe sympathised with her, and while spending the evening drowning his sorrows with her in the bar wouldn't be his first choice of activity, he would do it if it helped. But neither his heart nor his mind would be in it – they'd already leapt several steps ahead and were now lurking in a very dangerous place: right outside Elise's bedroom door. The way she'd been looking at him told him she was having just as many unholy thoughts as he was.

But Christ, it was wrong. So wrong.

Heat crept up his neck as he glanced at Aidan. Lusting after his best mate's ex was madness. But it wasn't like he wanted to marry her. Or even date her.

What if they just scratched an itch?

One that had been growing all day – maybe even longer, though Gabe refused to entertain that thought. It was much easier to stick to his go-to line that he couldn't stand her.

That was still true.

Wasn't it?

It bloody well had to be – just as it always had.

'I think I'll go to my room.' Scarlett pushed her barely touched drink away. 'I've got a headache coming on.'

'Are you sure?' Aidan asked.

'Yeah.' She got up and wandered away.

'Oh dear,' Lilah said. 'I'm really worried about her.'

'Me too,' Aidan agreed. 'It's these god-awful men who treat her like shit. I'd like to pulverise the lot of them.'

Gabe signalled a waiter for coffee.

Lilah sucked on her lower lip. 'I'm not sure if it's best to give her some space or go after her. Sometimes she can be moody anyway, though not as bad as she used to be. She was horrible to me when we were at school. And remember when we first met?' She beamed at Aidan. 'She accused me of wrecking your mum's stall at the craft market.'

'Like I'll ever forget.'

They shared a sappy look that both warmed Gabe's heart and made him want to shove his fingers down his throat.

'She's only warmed up to me in the past year,' Lilah went on. 'And... Well, sometimes it's a lot, almost like she doesn't have a lot of other friends, though she was really popular at school.'

'I think she scared a lot of people off.' Aidan let out a sigh. 'With her mood swings. God knows, I get annoyed with her. But I get her more now. And I see it's not her fault. She's constantly getting treated like shit.'

'She seemed like she was in a much better place.' Lilah cocked her head with a sad smile. 'But then Leon came on the scene and dragged her under again.'

Gabe exhaled with a low whistle. 'Not a nice place to be. Does she get help for it?'

'Mum's suggested seeing someone before,' Aidan said. 'But I don't think Scarlett ever has. Then again, she doesn't exactly confide in me, so she might have done, and I just don't know about it.

No doubt Scarlett's love life would be a hot topic this week. If nothing else, it served as a distraction from where his mind wanted to go.

Aidan and Lilah headed up to their room after dinner to get their jackets before their walk, planning to check on Scarlett before they left. Gabe decided he might go for a walk himself after they were gone, but he didn't want to look like he was deliberately avoiding going with them – even if he was. Encroaching on their space all the time made him feel creepy. He could grab a drink first, then go out for some fresh air after.

As he crossed the dining room, the weight of several pairs of eyes landed on his back like hot coals. He didn't need to turn around to know who they belonged to – the group of women who'd approached him during dinner, armed with questions and asking for his autograph. He quickened his pace slightly, hoping to slip out before any of them could intercept him. Being stuck on the coach with a group of fangirls hadn't been something he anticipated. It made his untimely attraction to Elise all the more complicated. Even if he could get past her history with Aidan – a big if – any interaction between them wouldn't just be between them. It would be fodder for people like these women, who'd be watching his every move and possibly not discreetly.

He shook his head, trying to clear it, and made his way towards the bar. It was a cosy space with low lighting, already half-full with other guests. He found a stool at the far end and signalled the bartender.

'Whisky, please. Neat.' He paused, considering. 'Make it a Talisker. When in Rome, and all that.'

The bartender, a young man with a neatly trimmed beard, nodded and reached for a bottle. 'Good choice. Local stuff.'

Gabe was grateful for the simple interaction – no questions, no recognition, just a straightforward transaction. He paid for his drink and took a sip, feeling the smooth burn of the whisky against his tongue. It tasted of smoke and sea salt.

He rotated slightly on his stool, taking in the rest of the bar's occupants. Couples leaning in close, a few solo travellers like himself, a group of hikers still wearing their boots and comparing notes about the day's adventures. No sign of his fangirls. Thank god.

He traced the condensation on his glass with one finger, drawing aimless patterns that vanished almost as quickly as they appeared – much like his resolve to stay away from Elise.

What was it about her? He took another sip of whisky, letting the smoky heat of it linger in his mouth. He knew where Elise's room was. He could go and talk to her. Just talk. Clear the air.

'Do you sell bottles of wine to take away?' he asked the bartender.

'Sure. Red, white, or rosé?'

Good question. What did Elise prefer? He had no idea. 'Red.' She was fiery, and he could imagine her rocking a red dress with her figure and hair colour. 'Something decent, but not too fancy.'

The bartender returned with two bottles, explaining the merits of each. Gabe chose one and handed over his card.

The bartender slid two wine glasses across the bar. 'Is two enough?'

'Yeah, definitely.' He gathered the wine and glasses and headed for the hallway.

Moments later, he stood outside Elise's door, not entirely sure how he'd got there. It wasn't too late to turn back. He could return to his own room, drink the wine himself, and pretend this moment of madness had never happened.

But then he remembered the way Elise had looked at him across the dining room and, before he could talk himself out of it, he raised his hand and knocked on the door.

He counted to ten in his head as he waited, shifting his weight from one foot to the other, the wine bottle growing slippery in his increasingly damp palm. Just as he was beginning to think she might be asleep – or not in her room at all – the door swung open, and there she was dressed in grey PJ bottoms and a loose white T-shirt, her dark hair coiling in loose waves around her face.

She blinked at him, then at the wine and glasses in his hands. 'What are you doing here?'

'I, um, brought wine.' He held up the bottle. 'I thought we could talk.'

Her eyebrows rose higher. 'Talk? At' – she glanced at her watch – 'half-past nine?'

'Is it that time already?' He tried for a charming smile. 'I lost track.'

She leaned against the doorframe, arms crossed, not inviting him in but not shutting the door in his face either. 'And what exactly did you want to talk about that couldn't wait until morning? Do you have a problem?' She eyed him over. 'Apart from the obvious. I assume this is professional?' A glint in her eye suggested she knew exactly why he was there, but she was going to make him work for it. Fair enough.

'No,' he said simply.

'No?' she repeated, her eyebrows lifting.

'I'd say it's completely unprofessional, but kind of necessary.'

'I think you've had too much to drink.'

'One whisky, that's all. I'm clear-headed enough to know that the way you've been looking at me all day isn't the way a tour guide normally looks at a passenger.'

A faint flush crept up her neck. 'I haven't been looking at you any particular way.'

'Liar,' he said softly, not curbing the smirk that was growing on his lips.

'Says you.' She leaned a little closer, her dark eyes searching his face. He held her gaze, though it was like being struck by a taser. 'You've done nothing but stare at me since you got on the coach.' She narrowed her eyes. 'Like what you see, do you? Fancy a bit more? Because if you do, you can forget it. I'm not that stupid.'

He took a deep breath and drew back. 'Yeah, it would be stupid. But for the record, I think it would be bloody explosive.'

Her fingers tightened on the door until her knuckles went white, her eyes never leaving his.

'Get in.' She indicated with her head for him to come inside and she snapped the door shut behind him.

He stepped inside, giving her a crooked smile.

'Are you suggesting we hook up?' She folded her arms.

'Sure, why not?'

'Why not?' Her tone was incredulous.

'Yeah. I know.' He put the wine and the glasses down on the vanity unit. The room was similar to his own, but Elise had already put her stamp on it. A laptop was open on the small desk. A half-empty cup of tea sat beside it. Her tour guide jacket hung neatly over the back of the chair, and a book lay open on the bedside table.

Unlike his chaotic room, where clothes had already migrated to every available surface despite his being there less than a day, hers was tidy. The only sign of relaxation was the unmade bed, the duvet pulled back as if she'd been sitting under it when he knocked.

'Were you working?' He nodded towards the laptop.

'Just checking the weather forecast for tomorrow.'

'I see.' He lifted the wine bottle. 'Shall we?'

'You really are insane.'

'Is that a yes?'

'Fine. Have you fallen out with Aidan or something?'

'Course I haven't.' He uncorked the wine using the corkscrew on the tray and poured it out. 'Why?'

'It's the only reason I can think of that you'd want to be here with me.'

'Wrong.' He handed her a glass. 'I'm here because I can't stop thinking about you... And all the wicked things I'd like to do with you.' There. He'd slammed the words into her court, and she could do what she wanted with them. 'Can I sit?' He gestured to the edge of the bed, all too aware he was in Elise Reid's hotel room, about to share a bottle of wine with the woman he'd hated for years.

'Go ahead.' She blinked, watching him before she sat down next to him. 'Are you sure you aren't drunk?'

'Positive.'

She raised an eyebrow, then took a large gulp of wine. 'I prefer white. For future reference.'

'Noted.'

They lapsed into silence, sipping their wine, the tension between them charged, almost crackling. Their eyes met over the rims of their glasses, and a surge of energy punched Gabe in his lower belly, pulses travelling all the way to his groin.

'So where do we stand?' He topped up their glasses.

'Nowhere. We sit drinking wine in my hotel room,' she replied. 'Which is already completely inappropriate.'

'It doesn't have to be inappropriate,' he said, though they both knew that was a lie. 'Not if we're discreet. It could just be two people who find each other attractive, enjoying a bottle of wine together.'

'Who said I found you attractive?' She traced the rim of her glass with one finger.

'Your eyes told me.'

She snorted. 'You're a passenger on my tour. I'm working. There are professional boundaries.'

'True.'

'And then there's our history. It's a mess.'

'Also true.'

'And I'm not looking for anything right now,' she continued. 'My life is complicated enough.'

'So's mine. And I'm not looking for anything past tonight either... After that, we bugger off back to our old lives and never darken each other's doors again.' He held her gaze.

Elise looked away, out of the window where the sky still held onto the summer evening light. 'Well, you better swear that's the truth of it. You better not be here so you can get me into trouble. If this is a setup.'

'I'll swear on anything you like.' He raised his hands high, still holding his glass.

The silence stretched between them again. Gabe watched her profile, the way the light cast shadows on her face, highlighting the elegant line of her jaw, the curve of her lips. He wanted to lean over and kiss them.

'I've made so many mistakes,' she said finally. 'Things I can't take back or fix. The last thing I need is to add another one to the list.'

'Who says it would be a mistake?'

Her eyes found his again. 'Wouldn't it?'

'Yeah, probably,' he said. 'I'll go. Sorry.'

Elise took a deep breath, then threw back her wine in one decisive swallow, then took hold of his arm before he could stand up. 'Both of us have a reputation for being able to handle ourselves – you're the king of short flings. And you've always been quick to point out my relationship failings.'

He winced internally though he knew he deserved it. She moved closer.

'Ok then.' She put down her glass with a thump.

'You want to?'

'Yes... Or are you chickening out now?' she whispered, her lips close to his. 'Can't take the heat?'

'Oh, I can.' He gazed into the depth of her warm espresso coloured eyes.

'This is insane.' Her eyes dropped to his lips. 'Because I don't even like you.'

'Mutual,' he murmured.

The tension between them was a living thing, electric and volatile. One touch and he'd combust. Already his chest swooped, and his groin throbbed.

She slipped her hand around his cheek, the contact almost eliciting a gasp from him. The first touch of her lips on his sent a torrent of desire through his veins. She tasted of wine, her mouth warm and insistent against his own. He pulled her closer, one hand sliding up her back to cradle the nape of her neck, feeling the silky strands of her hair.

She made a small sound in her throat – half sigh, half moan – and it nearly undid him. Her body pressed against his, soft curves meeting hard angles. He smoothed his large palm over the back of her soft top. The kiss deepened, her tongue meeting his, exploring, tasting, demanding more. He gave it to her, gently dragging his hand around to cup her breast. A pebbled nipple met his fingertip through the fabric of her top.

When they finally broke apart, they were breathing hard, their foreheads pressed together.

'Well,' Elise said, her voice slightly unsteady, 'so much for sensible decisions.'

Gabe laughed. 'I think we've established that neither of us is particularly sensible.'

'Clearly not.' She pulled back just enough to look at him. 'We just crossed a line.'

'Yeah, but not far enough. For me anyway. Do you want to stop?' he asked, his hands still on her waist, his thumbs tracing small circles against the thin fabric of her T-shirt.

'No. You haven't even begun to scratch my itch yet.'

Her eyes searched his face, and he smiled. 'Is that what we're calling it?'

'Call it what you want. But let me see what you're made of.'

'You won't regret it.'

'Oh, I'm sure I will... But let's find out.' She pulled him back to her, capturing his mouth in another kiss that was somehow both tender and fierce. Gabe responded in kind, his hands sliding under the hem of her T-shirt to find the warm skin beneath. She shivered at his touch, her body arching into his.

'God, Elise,' he murmured against her mouth, then along her jaw, down the elegant column of her neck. She tilted her head to give him better access, her eyes fluttering closed, her breath coming in short gasps that made his blood sing. This was already hotter than anything he could have imagined, and it had only just started.

Chapter Nine

Elise

Gabe's mouth moved against Elise's, hot, hungry, and unrelenting. A deep, primal jolt fired through her, bypassing thought, bypassing all the usual barriers she kept in place. As they perched on the edge of her hotel bed, her bones felt like they were dissolving. His hands cradled her face with surprising tenderness, then slid down to her shoulders, fingers tracing fire along her neck before skimming her spine and finding the hem of her t-shirt. When his fingers met her bare skin, she shivered – not from fear or resistance, but from something deeper rooted and more fragile: the shock of wanting, without armouring herself first.

She wasn't used to this. To giving in without performing. Without pretending. Gabe didn't look at her like a trophy or an ideal. He didn't even like her, did he? Not really. Which meant, for once, she didn't have to impress anyone. Didn't have to be poised or polished or perfect. There was a strange freedom in that. A safety in the fact that he already knew the worst of her – or thought he did. So when his hands moved lower, and she arched into his touch, it wasn't calculated. It wasn't controlled. It was raw instinct. Her walls, always so carefully reinforced, gave just a little. And in that tiny surrender, she felt something she hadn't in years.

Here sat Elise Reid. Stripped bare. Unguarded. Real.

'Can I?' he whispered.

She nodded, and he lifted the thin cotton over her head. The air kissed her bare skin as the fabric slid away, and suddenly she was exposed – completely, achingly present. His gaze dragged over her chest like a caress, and her nipples tightened in response, betraying how desperately alive she felt beneath his eyes.

For a beat, she almost curled in on herself. She'd perfected the art of being admired without being seen – posing just right, using angles and control like a shield. But Gabe wasn't looking at her like a man dazzled by an image. He looked like a man seeing *her*. The raw, unscripted version.

'Christ,' he breathed. 'You're so beautiful.'

The words hit something deep in her chest – because they didn't sound rehearsed. And Gabe Wilder wouldn't do flattery with her.

Before she could speak, his mouth found hers again, hungrier now, as if he too had allowed something to slip free. She let herself fall back onto the bed. A breathless laugh caught in her throat; the mattress soft beneath her spine. Gabe followed, bracing on his forearms, the crisp buttons of his shirt cool against her flushed skin. The contrast only heightened her awareness of every place they touched – and all the places they didn't yet.

His lips left hers to blaze a trail down her jaw, her neck, the hollow of her throat. She clutched his shoulders, fingers curling into the fabric of his shirt. It had been so long since she'd *wanted* this – really wanted it. Not just done it because she felt like she should. Like it was a duty. With other lovers, she'd always kept part of herself hidden, waiting for the moment she'd need to retreat. But now she didn't feel the urge to disappear. He already knew her mess, and he was here anyway. *Still looking at her like that.*

When his mouth reached her breast, he paused, gaze lifting to hers. The eye contact was molten. Almost too intimate to bear. He didn't demand – he asked. And that made her feel something rare. Safe.

She gave a small nod.

He took her nipple into his mouth, and she gasped, her back arching off the bed. Pleasure streaked through her, hot and clean, and instead of shutting it down, she let it flood her. For once, she didn't pull away from the sensation of being wanted – not just for her body, but for *all* of her. It was terrifying. And it was bliss.

He took his time until she was squirming beneath him, her body a live wire under the slow, deliberate sweep of his hands and mouth. When his fingers dipped to the waistband of her grey pyjama bottoms, her breath caught. He tugged them down her legs, leaving her completely naked while he remained fully clothed. The imbalance should have made her self-conscious – it had with others – but now it only fuelled the aching thrill building in her belly. Gabe's gaze wasn't judgmental or greedy. It was reverent. And it made her feel powerful and utterly undone at once.

When his mouth found her inner thigh, her hands fisted the bedsheets, her breath came faster, shorter, trembling on every exhale. This was Gabe Wilder – her long-time nemesis – about to do something so intimate, so unthinkable mere hours ago, and yet right now it felt like the most natural thing in the world.

And god, she wanted it.

She tried to keep her eyes open, to watch him, to cling to the reality of what was happening, but the sensation overwhelmed her. Her head fell back, a broken moan spilling from her lips as the pleasure crashed over her, hot and blinding.

When she caught her breath, she dragged him up by the shirt collar, and brought him in close, the weight of him grounding and thrilling at once. Her fingers fumbled with his buttons, her breath quickening. She'd never imagined herself undressing *Gabriel Wilder*, not consciously in any real, waking moment. And now here she was, peeling him open like a gift.

He caught her wrist mid-button and brought her hand to his mouth, kissing her palm slowly and deliberately. A jolt rocketed straight to her core. 'Let me.'

He made swift work of the remaining buttons and shrugged out of his shirt, tossing it aside.

Elise's breath caught. She'd known, objectively, that Gabe was fit. But this? This was a whole new level of unfair. Lean muscle carved his torso, every line and plane honed from real work, not gym vanity. A light trail of dark hair dusted his chest and arrowed down his stomach, disappearing into the waistband of his jeans.

Her hand moved without thought, following the dip between his pectorals. The heat of him, the shift of muscle under her touch – it was addictive. His eyes fluttered closed, his breath hitching in his throat.

'You're a hot bastard as well as an arrogant one.' The words slipped out on a breathless laugh.

He smirked, eyes opening slowly, a spark of challenge dancing in their depths. 'Like a bit of dirty talk, do you?' He nipped at her bottom lip, just enough to make her gasp. 'Well then, let's see if you're a good girl – or if I need to make you beg for more.'

Her heart thumped, hard and fast. His teasing should've made her bristle. But before she could process the chaos of her thoughts, he was kissing her. He guided her hand down, over his abdomen, to the button of his jeans. She took the hint. With shaky fingers, she popped it open, then slid the zip down.

'I need my wallet.'

'You don't have to pay me. I haven't fallen that low.'

'Ha. Very funny. I have condoms.'

'Someone came prepared.' She aimed for teasing, though her voice came out rougher than expected.

He gave a half-shrug as he extracted a foil packet. 'Always best to be sensible.'

That earned a snort from her, though it died when he shoved off his shoes and socks, then stood to strip away the last of his clothing. Elise propped herself on her elbows, watching him – completely, gloriously naked, unashamed and utterly aroused.

She was still staring when he returned to the bed. Her body moved before her brain caught up, pushing at his shoulders until he lay back against the pillows. She swung one leg over him, straddling him. Gabe's hands settled lightly on her hips, his thumbs drawing slow, grounding circles against her skin.

She hesitated.

Not because she didn't want this – god, she did – but because it had stopped feeling like an escape and started feeling like something else. Something dangerous. Enjoyment and pure indulgence. Her hair was a mess, her mouth swollen, her voice shaky with need, and Gabe looked at her like he'd never wanted anything more.

His thumbs stilled, his gaze never leaving hers. 'We don't have to,' he said softly. 'We can stop.'

A flicker of panic rose – because he meant it. He wasn't trying to push or control. He was giving her an out. And she didn't want to take it.

'I don't think so.' Her fingers tore open the wrapper, and Gabe's breath caught as she rolled the condom onto him. His grip on her hips tightened, just a fraction.

'You're killing me,' he muttered, his voice thick.

'Good. That sounds more appropriate for you and me than anything we've done so far.'

He let out a hoarse laugh, and something inside her loosened. She didn't need to be in control of everything. Maybe this time it was safe to just *feel* – to let this happen.

She shifted forward, positioning herself above him, the heat between them pulsing, magnetic.

'Ready?' she asked.

His answer was a nod, his throat working as he swallowed.

Elise lowered herself slowly, taking him in inch by inch.

'You ok?' Gabe asked.

'More than.' She rocked her hips gently, finding a rhythm that matched the pulse between her legs. Gabe's eyes never left her face, as though he didn't want to miss a second.

'You're so beautiful,' he murmured, one hand sliding up to cup her breast, thumb brushing her nipple in a slow, lazy stroke.

She should have laughed or deflected, but the words lodged somewhere deep. They didn't sound fake or practised. If anything, they disarmed her more than the act itself. One-night stands weren't supposed to *mean* anything. But her senses were overloaded by more than just the physical. His gaze was so intense, his touch so careful.

Gabe didn't push. He matched her pace, their breathing syncing, hands steady on her hips, grounding her as they moved in that slow, deliberate rhythm. There was no rush. No pressure.

Just a kind of quiet intensity that made her feel like he was really seeing her, understanding what she wanted, and giving it to her without needing anything in return.

Maybe she shouldn't surrender like this – not with him. But her body, her heart, and her soul didn't listen. They couldn't.

When she picked up the pace again, Gabe met her thrust for thrust, his hands everywhere, finding every place she needed him most.

She tightened around him, trembling, her climax threatening.

And then he sat up, wrapping her in his arms, burying his face in her neck. The sudden intimacy of it was overwhelming.

'You are so fucking beautiful,' he said again, his voice raw.

That did it. Her head fell back, a cry tearing from her lips as her climax tore through her. Somewhere, distantly, she registered that the walls probably weren't thick enough for discretion. She didn't care.

He held her tight as he thrust up once more, his face contorting with pleasure as he followed her over the edge. She almost laughed at the sheer intensity of it all and collapsed against his chest, her breath coming in ragged bursts. His arms banded around her, his big hands warm against her back.

Her body hummed, sated in a way she hadn't been in years.

A dangerous thought.

Because this was Gabe Wilder.

And nothing about this was supposed to matter.

Consciousness gradually returned to her. She was still curled into Gabe's chest, her head on his shoulder, their skin fused with sweat.

'I think you broke me,' she said.

She felt more than heard his chuckle. 'If it's any consolation, I'm not sure I remember my own name right now.'

She lifted her head to look at him. His face was relaxed, his usual intensity softened. His blue eyes, normally so sharp and piercing, were hazy.

Elise had never been particularly spiritual. She didn't meditate, didn't do yoga, didn't read books about mindfulness or inner peace. But what she'd experienced when she'd come apart had felt like... something close to transcendence. A suspension of time and self. A quiet obliteration.

Again, she blamed his eyes. They made her feel things – things she didn't want to feel. It made everything too *real*.

He shifted beneath her, and Elise took it as her cue to move. She climbed off him, immediately missing the warmth of him. Alarm bells should surely be ringing, telling her not to get used to it. Not to think it meant anything.

The hotel room felt cold now, reality seeping back in around the edges of their bubble.

Gabe headed to the bathroom to deal with the condom.

Elise slid under the covers and pulled the sheet to her chest. The transcendent moment was already slipping through her fingers, like a dream she'd woken from. Maybe it *hadn't* been any different from other times. Maybe her body had just wanted it more than usual because she hadn't done it in a while. Simple biology.

Only... her chest felt oddly hollow. She wasn't supposed to feel hollow. She wasn't supposed to feel *anything*.

Gabe returned and sat on the edge of the bed, his back to her. His shoulders were tense again, the relaxed intimacy of moments ago already replaced by distance.

'So...' He glanced back over his shoulder.

'Yeah,' she agreed before he could finish, already guessing the script. The one where no one said too much, just enough to close the door quietly.

She *should* want him to leave. Should be grateful for the clarity. But something inside her curled up at the thought of being alone again.

'I guess we did what we agreed,' she said. 'Got it out of our systems.'

'Right. Yeah. We did... and we did.' His tone was light, but the words came out slower now. Like maybe he didn't fully believe them either.

He stood and reached for his clothes, pulling on his shirt without meeting her eyes. 'Well, then...' He put on his trousers. 'I, um, will see you in the morning.' For a moment he looked at her, then bent over and kissed her on the cheek. His lips were warm and gentle, but chaste. 'Sleep well.'

'Yeah. See you.'

The door clicked shut behind him.

Elise lay back on the rumpled sheets, the scent of him still clinging to her skin. She stared at the ceiling, her throat tight, her chest weirdly heavy.

She wasn't sure if she wanted to scream or cry or sleep for a hundred years.

Instead, she closed her eyes and did none of those things.

She just lay there, hoping the ache inside her would fade faster than the memory of his hands on her skin.

Chapter Ten

Elise

Elise must have dozed off at some point, because the next thing she knew, the alarm on her phone was blaring and sunlight was streaming through the gap in the curtains.

Six thirty.

Breakfast started at seven, and the coach was scheduled to leave at half-past eight. She had exactly ninety minutes to pull herself together and try to present a fresh face – not the haggard one staring back from the bathroom mirror of someone who'd been awake for half the night.

She applied concealer to the shadows under her eyes and tried to stop herself from constantly yawning. Her limbs felt heavy, her head even more so, and her body... well, her body ached in ways she didn't have the luxury of processing right now.

Last night was supposed to have scratched an itch. One-and-done. No lingering anything.

So why was her chest still tight?

By the time she got downstairs, the breakfast room was already beginning to fill. The smell of coffee hit her first, followed closely by the murmur of conversation and the clink of cutlery. She paused just inside the doorway, eyes automatically scanning the space until they landed on *him*. Gabe stood at the buffet, plate in hand, looking annoyingly well-rested and unfairly good in a navy Henley that made his eyes seem even more piercing than usual. Her stomach performed an unwelcome flip. Was this going to happen every time she saw him for the rest of the week?

But it was no joke. His eyes did something to her.

She squared her shoulders and headed over. He glanced up from selecting his breakfast as she approached, a flash of something crossing his features before his expression settled into a casual smile.

'Morning,' he said in a low voice.

'Hi.' She reached for a plate, her hands feeling oddly disconnected from the rest of her. Gabe cleared his throat, stepping slightly to the side to give her room at the buffet.

'Sleep well?'

'Not really,' she admitted. 'You?'

He shrugged. 'Well enough.'

Of course he had. She stabbed at an egg, irrationally annoyed, and the yolk burst out, making a mess of the serving plate. Damn it. Here she was, operating on approximately an hour of broken sleep, while he looked like he'd spent the evening in a spa retreat rather than between her legs.

'Listen...' She eyed the buffet, pretending to survey the selection of pastries. 'About last night.'

Gabe glanced around, presumably checking if anyone was within earshot. 'What about it?'

His tone wasn't cold, exactly, but it wasn't warm either. Matter-of-fact. Like they were discussing the weather or the day's itinerary rather than the fact that less than twelve hours ago, they'd been naked and tangled together on her bed.

'I just wanted to make sure we're... ok.' She internally cringed at how needy it sounded.

'Yeah. We're all good.' Gabe selected a croissant. 'We're adults. We had some fun. No big deal, right?'

No big deal.

The words landed like a stone in her stomach. Which was ridiculous, because that had been the agreement from the start. One night, to get it out of their systems. She had no right to feel disappointed that he was taking it exactly as intended.

'Right,' she agreed. 'I just wanted to make sure we're on the same page.'

'We are.' His eyes met hers, and for a moment, Elise thought she saw something flicker in their depths – a hint of the intensity she'd witnessed last night. But it was gone so quickly she might have imagined it.

'Good.' She reached for the tongs to select a croissant of her own. 'That's... good.'

Gabe glanced over at his table, where Aidan, Lilah, and Scarlett were seated. 'Well, see you about.'

'Sure.' Elise nodded. She watched him walk away, trying and failing not to notice the breadth of his shoulders beneath that blue top, the way his jeans hugged his taut backside. She'd had her hands on those shoulders, those hips. Had traced the muscles of his back as he thrust inside her.

Christ, she had to stop this.

A wave of heat crept up her neck, not from desire but shame. Not because of the sex – they'd both wanted it – but because of what it stirred in her. How exposed she'd felt at the end. No games, no walls. Just her. Raw and open. And he'd walked out, like that kind of intimacy didn't touch him at all.

She hated that. Hated how it echoed the things she'd worked for years to bury. The way people looked at her, even when she was too young for it. As if what they wanted from her mattered more than who she was.

Why the hell had she given in so easily?

She plastered on a smile. She could charm her way through the day as usual. Keep it light. Distracted. Professional.

The real her could stay hidden, where it belonged, and away from Gabe bloody Wilder.

Balancing her overloaded breakfast plate in one hand and clutching a mug of desperately needed coffee in the other, she scanned the dining room for somewhere to sit. She was just about to claim an empty table by the window when a flutter of movement caught her eye. Three middle-aged women had descended on Gabe's table like seagulls on an abandoned sandwich. The Gabriel Wilder Fan Club was in session, it seemed.

'We just love *Wilder at Heart*,' the first woman gushed, a bottle blonde in her fifties with an elaborate floral scarf draped artfully around her neck. 'The episode about sustainable farming practices changed my whole outlook on food shopping.'

Her voice carried across the room. Gabe smiled, the expression not quite reaching his eyes. 'That's kind of you to say so. I'm glad you've found the podcast helpful.'

'More than helpful.' She splayed her hand on her chest. 'Transformative.'

Elise shook her head, but a twang of something else struck her, tightening the muscles around her heart. Almost like she felt sorry for him.

'Would it be terribly forward of me to ask for a selfie?' the woman went on, already fishing her phone from her handbag, her two friends nodding eagerly. 'The girls back home will be green with envy.'

Gabe's smile grew more strained, but he nodded. 'Of course.'

An awkward dance ensued, each woman positioning themselves close to Gabe, determined to get the perfect angle that showed both his face and their own best side.

He hated this. The realisation struck Elise. He was acting a part and he tolerated it because he cared about his cause, because it helped spread his message, but he didn't enjoy it. He just wanted to eat his breakfast in peace, though the women would never have guessed. He was a master performer – Elise knew one when she saw one.

The knowledge should have pleased her – here was a chink in his apparently impenetrable armour. Instead, she felt a surge of protectiveness. She knew only too well what unwelcome attention felt like. Should she march over and "rescue" him? Invent some urgent tour guide business that required his immediate attention?

No. That was ridiculous. Gabe was a grown man who could handle a few enthusiastic fans. And why should she care if he was uncomfortable? It wasn't her problem. They weren't friends. They weren't anything.

Still, she found herself moving towards them, coffee in hand.

'Good morning, ladies.' She put on her best tour guide smile. 'I hope you're enjoying your breakfast. Just a reminder that we're leaving sharp, so don't leave it too long to grab yourself something cooked from the buffet.'

The women stepped back reluctantly. 'Oh, yes. We should go. But we'll catch you later.' The woman patted Gabe on the shoulder, and he gave her a vague smile, then he glanced at Elise and mouthed, *Thank you.*

'No problem.' Elise swished past him, sat down, and began eating her breakfast. Her gaze fell on Scarlett, who was hovering near the buffet, looking like she might throw up. Her bright red hair hung limp today, her usual punky accessories notably absent. There were shadows under her eyes that makeup couldn't conceal.

She looks even worse than me.

When Elise finished her breakfast, Scarlett was still hanging around like she wasn't sure what to do. Elise got up and headed towards her. There had been a time, when Elise was dating Aidan, that Scarlett had almost revered her, occasionally to the point of being annoying, but Elise felt a twinge of sadness for her. She'd always been an insecure kind of person, and this breakup must be agonising for her self-esteem.

'Scarlett,' Elise said, 'how are you doing? I know yesterday must have been difficult.'

Scarlett gave her an almost quizzical look. 'I'm fine.'

The response was automatic, unconvincing. Elise's heart went out to her. 'It's ok if you're not.' Elise kept her voice low enough that people at nearby tables couldn't overhear. 'What happened with Leon was unfortunate.'

Scarlett's mouth twisted. 'That's one word for it. "Unfortunate." Like rain at a picnic.'

'Ok, you're right. It was more than unfortunate. It was awful, and I'm sorry it happened.' She met Scarlett's eyes directly. 'I'm especially sorry that it's impacted your holiday.'

'It's not your fault he's a dick.' She glanced over Elise's shoulder and blanched slightly. 'I better get some food. And you'll be wanting to speak to *him*.'

With a frown, Elise looked over her shoulder, her pulse quickening, expecting to see Gabe. Had Scarlett maybe seen him leave her room? *Shit*. Had they been rumbled? But the only person behind her was Lloyd, the smartly dressed man with glasses, from the coach. He was with his mother. Elise was sure she'd seen her somewhere before but couldn't place her. Was she someone from Glenbriar? The memory wasn't forthcoming however, so she abandoned it and smiled at the two of them.

'I hope you slept well.'

'I never sleep well in strange beds,' the woman said. 'That's why I need a single room. Didn't want to share a twin with Lloyd as I'd have kept him awake. I like to get up and read when I'm not sleeping.'

'Oh... Well, I hope the reading kept you relaxed.'

'Not at all. Susan Hill's books are quite terrifying.'

Lloyd gave Elise a half smile that seemed to be an apology for his mum's slightly negative manners.

As she nodded at him, her eyes caught on a familiar figure at the buffet. Gabe was back for seconds, piling his plate with more bacon and eggs. But rather than focusing on his food, he was watching her, a strange intensity in his gaze that suggested he'd been listening to her conversation.

Their eyes met across the room, and an invisible wire crackled between them again, almost combusting with the heat.

Elise forced her focus down to check her watch: eight-fifteen. Time to wrap things up and get everyone moving to the coach.

Despite the sleepless night and emotional whiplash of the morning, she had a job to do.

Outside, the morning air was crisp and clear, the sky a brilliant blue that promised perfect weather for the Fairy Pools. Elise took a moment to breathe deeply, trying to centre herself. From the hotel's position on the hillside, she looked over the colourful buildings of Portree harbour below, fishing boats bobbing in the gentle swell.

Kev was already at the coach with a flask in hand.

'Everything ok?' she asked. 'I didn't see you at breakfast.'

'I was in early before the passengers arrived. Just been for a little walk and some peace before we're stuck with them for the rest of the day.' He chuckled. 'Such a nice morning.'

'Ah good. As long as you're not ill.'

'No, not at all.' He smiled. And actually, it was a sensible move, grabbing some peace while he could.

Passengers began trickling out of the hotel, some bright-eyed and eager for the day's adventures, others yawning and clutching travel mugs of coffee. Elise greeted each one as they boarded.

Scarlett came out looking marginally better than she had at breakfast. She'd applied fresh makeup and added a few of her usual accessories – a studded choker, several rings, and a small pin on her jacket that read 'NOT TODAY, SATAN.'

'Nice pin,' Elise said.

Scarlett gave a small smile. 'Felt appropriate.'

'Very.' Elise nodded.

'Thanks.' Scarlett shifted a little. 'For not being... you know. Judgy.'

'It's fine,' Elise replied. Because, hell, didn't she know what that felt like?

Behind Scarlett was Gabe. He gave her half a lift of his eyebrow as he passed by. Her eyes lingered on his broad forearms as he grabbed the side rail and hoisted himself onto the bus. How good had it felt being held in those arms?

That was a question she needed to bury. Along with many more. And never bring them up again. For now, there were the Fairy Pools to see, a group to guide, a day to get through. Stifling a yawn, she climbed on the coach and lifted the microphone. One step at a time. That was the best she could do right now.

CHAPTER ELEVEN

Gabe

Beautiful landscapes rolled past the windows beneath a glorious blue sky. Gabe should be drinking in every bit of it, but all he could focus on was the sound of Elise's voice coming through the speakers. Every inflection sent unwelcome heat coursing through his body. He shifted in his seat, annoyed at his own reaction. It had been one night – one impulsive night that shouldn't still be occupying his thoughts twelve hours later.

'And if you look to your left,' Elise said into the microphone, 'you'll see the Black Cuillin mountains in the distance. They're among the most challenging climbs in Scotland.'

How was she managing to stay so controlled? Nothing in her tone suggested she'd been writhing against him less than twelve hours ago, her fingernails leaving imprints on his back. Gabe swallowed hard and forced his attention to the view.

Last night meant nothing. Two consenting adults scratching an itch. Holiday flings happened all the time.

So why couldn't he stop thinking about it?

The coach hit a bump in the road, and Scarlett, sitting across the aisle, jolted awake from a nap.

'Are we there yet?' She pushed her bright red hair out of her eyes.

She looked exhausted. Unsurprising after yesterday's events.

'I think we're nearly there,' Gabe said.

Scarlett nodded and fished her phone from her pocket, stifling a yawn. Maybe it was just Gabe's imagination, but she didn't appear to be focused on the screen. Her eyes had settled on the man with glasses in the seat in front of Gabe. She had a kind of glazed look, like she wasn't really concentrating on anything. No doubt she was full of regrets and conflict about this whole trip after Leon's departure.

Gabe's mind drifted back to Elise. She'd stopped talking, and he closed his eyes for a moment. His body responded to the memory of her pressed against him. His fingers twitched with the phantom feeling of her skin.

This was ridiculous. He'd had one-night stands before. Plenty of them. They didn't normally leave him this distracted.

The coach slowed as they approached the car park, and Elise spoke again. 'We're arriving at the Fairy Pools now,' she said. 'Please make sure you take everything you need with you as the coach will be locked while we're gone.'

The car park was already filling with early bird tourists when they arrived, but nothing compared to the crowds that would descend by midday. Gabe stepped off the coach and breathed in the crisp air, grateful to be free of the enclosed space.

'The path to the Fairy Pools is about a mile and a half,' Elise explained, gesturing towards a well-trodden trail leading away from the car park. 'It's relatively easy walking, but there are some uneven sections and a couple of stream crossings. The pools themselves are a series of crystal-clear rock pools along the Allt Coir' a' Mhadaidh.'

Gabe tried not to notice how the breeze caught strands of her dark hair, tugging them free of her ponytail, or think about how much he'd like to stroke them back in.

'I've never actually visited before,' Elise continued with a smile, 'but I've done my research. The pools are famous for their crystal-clear blue water and the natural waterslides between some of them. The brave among you might attempt dipping your feet, but I'd advise caution – the water is always cold, even in summer.'

'You planning to take a dip?' Aidan asked Gabe quietly, nudging his arm.

Gabe shrugged. 'Yeah, why not?'

'Let's head off.' Elise led the way. 'You're free to explore at your own pace. Just be back at the coach by eleven-thirty.'

The group began moving along the path, with Elise still at the front. She stopped to talk to a few people and pointed up to the surrounding hills.

The path wound gently uphill, following the course of a stream that occasionally came into view through gaps in the landscape. Looming in the distance were the Cuillin mountains, their peaks disappearing into wisps of morning cloud.

'The weather's being kind to us.' Lilah lifted her face to the blue sky. 'I packed for constant rain.'

'It's amazing,' Aidan replied with a smile.

Gabe nodded absently.

'You're quiet today.' Lilah observed curiously. 'Usually you'd be giving us a full lecture on the ecosystem by now.'

'Just taking it in.' Gabe smiled. 'Sometimes even I need to shut up and appreciate nature without analysing it to death.'

Aidan laughed. 'That'll be the day.'

They continued walking, the path occasionally crossing the stream via stepping stones. At one crossing, an older woman hesitated, clearly nervous about the slightly slippery stones.

'It's perfectly stable,' Elise reassured her, reaching out. 'I'll help you across.'

The woman took Elise's offered hand, and she helped her over.

After about twenty minutes of walking, the path opened up to reveal the first of the Fairy Pools. A collective murmur of appreciation rose from the group. The pool was small but perfectly formed, a natural basin of startlingly clear water fed by a narrow waterfall. The morning light caught the ripples, sending sparkles dancing across the surface.

'The first pool,' Elise said. 'This is just the beginning – there's a whole series of them further up the glen. Feel free to explore. Just remember to stay on the paths where possible to minimise

erosion, and of course, take nothing but photos and leave nothing but footprints.'

The group began to disperse, some pausing to take pictures of the first pool, others continuing up the path towards the larger pools ahead. Aidan and Lilah moved towards the water's edge, hand in hand.

'Coming?' Aidan called back to Gabe.

'In a minute.' Gabe pulled out his phone. 'Just want to take some pics and check something.'

Aidan nodded and turned away, leaving Gabe standing alone on the path, phone in hand. He pretended to be engrossed in his messages, but his eyes tracked Elise as she spoke to a few stragglers from their group. She was pointing out features of the landscape and laughing. Wow, when she smiled, she was radiant.

He shook his head. This was getting ridiculous.

The last of the tour group moved away, heading further up the path, leaving Elise standing alone by the first pool. She took a moment to herself, shoulders relaxing slightly now that she wasn't performing. She tucked a strand of hair behind her ear and gazed at the water, seeming genuinely appreciative of its beauty.

Gabe pocketed his phone and walked over.

'Not bad for someone who's never been here before,' he said quietly, coming up beside her.

'I told you, I did my research.'

'You did.' He glanced around. They were relatively alone – the rest of the group had moved further up the path, out of earshot, though still visible at a distance.

'Shouldn't you be taking artsy nature photos for your Instagram?' she asked. 'I think you've got several more followers from this group already.'

'In a minute.' His eyes held hers for a beat too long. 'Walk with me?'

'Where to?'

'Over here.' He strolled slightly off the track, so they were hidden by a massive rock. 'I've been thinking about you all morning.' Up close, he saw flecks of gold in her brown eyes, the slight hint of freckles across her nose that her light makeup didn't quite conceal.

'That's a you-problem,' she said, but her eyes dropped briefly to his lips.

He placed one hand flat on the rock and sighed. 'Not an us-problem?'

'Nope. Unless you mean that someone might see us.'

'Adds to the thrill, doesn't it?'

She rolled her eyes. 'You're unbelievable,' she said. 'Yesterday you could barely stand to look at me, and now—'

'Now I can barely stand not to touch you.'

'You what? I mean... You said one night. And that's what we did. It's out of our systems. Done. Finished.'

'Does it really feel finished to you?'

Their eyes locked, and for a moment, Gabe thought she might storm off. Then her lips parted slightly. But voices drifted towards them from the path, breaking the spell, and Elise straightened, moving slightly away.

'This is completely inappropriate,' she said. 'I'm working, and you're—'

'I'm what?' He shrugged. 'We're just talking.'

'I mean… Why do you want to see me again? You don't like me, and we did what we agreed.'

'Because we had a good time, didn't we? For what it's worth, I enjoyed it anyway.'

She sucked on her lip like she wasn't sure what to say. 'It was… Ok.'

'Ok?' Was she for real?

She let out a breathy laugh. 'Maybe slightly better than average.'

With a quick glance around, he lowered his voice, 'Why don't we revise our agreement?'

Elise stared at him. 'Have you gone completely mad?'

'Hear me out.' He held up his hands. 'We're stuck on this tour together for the next five days. Five days in one of the most beautiful places in Scotland. We clearly have chemistry; last night proved that.'

'Last night was a mistake,' she said.

'Was it?' Gabe challenged. 'Because I remember it being pretty good for both of us.'

A flush crept up Elise's neck, and she checked around to make sure no one was within earshot. 'Keep your voice down!'

'Ok fine.' He moved back towards the path.

'What exactly were you suggesting when you said we could revise the agreement?'

'Just that we make the most of the situation. A no strings, no expectations fling, just a bit of fun to make the week more... enjoyable.'

Elise's eyes narrowed. 'And what happens when we get back to Glenbriar? We pretend none of it happened?'

'Exactly,' Gabe nodded. 'What happens on Skye stays on Skye.'

'That would be ridiculous,' she said. 'And completely unprofessional.'

'I wasn't suggesting we sneak off during your working hours,' he clarified. 'Just... after hours. Like last night.'

Elise let out a short laugh. 'You're unreal.'

'Thanks,' he replied with a grin.

'And what about Aidan?' she asked quietly. 'Your best friend, remember? The one whose honour you've been defending all these years?'

Gabe flinched. 'Aidan's moved on. He's happily married to Lilah now.'

'That's not the point, and you know it.' She sighed. 'This is exactly why last night was a mistake. It's complicated things.'

'Ok, that's fine, though it doesn't have to be complicated. It can be simple attraction. Chemistry. Two people enjoying each other's company for a few days, then going back to their normal lives.'

For a moment, he saw hesitation in her eyes, a flicker of consideration. 'No,' she said. 'I have a job to do here, and getting involved with you would be a distraction I can't afford.'

'Fair enough.'

She gave him a sharp look, then walked away. She didn't turn around, but he caught a slight shake of her head before she approached another group from their tour, seamlessly slipping back into her professional persona.

With a resigned sigh, he turned and headed further up the path. He hadn't really expected anything else, but he'd deemed it worth a shot.

Aidan and Lilah weren't far off, sitting at the edge of a pool dangling their bare feet in the water. Scarlett sat perched on a boulder nearby. Gabe plastered on a convincing smile and headed towards them. So Elise had rejected him – big deal. There were plenty of other women in the world who'd be more than happy to have a fling with him. The fact that he couldn't stop thinking about the one who'd said no was just wounded pride. Nothing more.

'There you are.' Aidan waved him over. 'Thought you'd got lost.'

'Just taking my time.' Gabe stepped carefully over the rocky ground to join them.

'It's absolutely gorgeous,' Lilah said. 'I can't believe how beautiful it is.'

Gabe pulled off his socks and shoes and sat down beside them, plunging his feet into the refreshingly cold water. The shock helped bring him back to his senses.

They spent some time just enjoying the pools and relaxing before they continued along the path. The landscape truly was spectacular – the crystal-clear water flowing between dark rocks, creating natural pools and cascades. Another time, he'd like to come back here without the tour group and just exist in his own bubble. No Elise. No complications.

'You ok?' Aidan said.

'Fine.'

Aidan studied him for a moment. 'You seem a bit out of it. What's eating at you?'

'Nothing.' Gabe shrugged. 'Just enjoying the peace.'

Twenty-five years of friendship meant Aidan could read him too well, and he obviously didn't believe him. Gabe needed to take care... Which was something he'd never been that good at.

CHAPTER TWELVE

Gabe

'I'm thinking something fishy.' Lilah glanced up, smiling as Gabe tried to draw his focus to the lunch menu and rein in his thoughts, which hadn't quite caught up with what was happening either at this moment or in his life in general.

'The burger looks decent,' Aidan replied.

'Everything's so bloody expensive.' Scarlett flipped the menu over as if hoping to find cheaper options on the back. 'Twenty quid for a fish that probably came from the harbour we're looking at.'

'It's tourist pricing,' Aidan said with a shrug.

Gabe slouched in his chair, picking at something on the edge of the outdoor table while Aidan, Lilah, and Scarlett debated the lunch options. The morning at the Fairy Pools had been fun. Gabe had taken some good pictures, but being with all these other people was claustrophobic. And the sense that many eyes were watching him made him want to go somewhere and hide. It went with the territory, but it could be tiring.

The hotel garden was perched on the hillside above Portree and offered a postcard-perfect view of the village below. The colourful buildings lined the waterfront in blues, pinks, and yellows. Maybe he could sneak down there for a walk later.

'What about you, Gabe?' Lilah asked. 'What are you having?'

He pulled his gaze from the boats bobbing gently in the harbour below and glanced at the menu. 'Oh, uh... the macaroni.'

'Are you ok?' Aidan frowned at him.

'Fine, yeah. I'm just... I don't know...' He straightened in his chair. 'I'm not used to this kind of tour. Normally when I travel, I'm doing active stuff, you know, hiking or kayaking or something. This is fun, but I'm just a bit out of it.'

The idea of a relaxed tour of Skye with his friends had sounded perfect a few weeks ago. But with hindsight, he hadn't really considered exactly what it would entail. And that was before he knew Elise would be leading it. Before last night had thrown his emotions into disarray.

'I am happy being here with you guys,' he clarified. 'I'm just taking time to adjust.'

'It's the control freak in you,' Aidan said.

'Yeah. You're not wrong.'

A waitress approached their table, and they placed their orders, temporarily halting the conversation. Gabe listened and sipped his drink while they waited for the food. When it came, the delicious smell of the macaroni sent every thought out of his head. He devoured it.

If anything could get him out of bad moods, it was food.

As he ate, his gaze drifted to the hotel's large windows. Through the glass, he caught a glimpse of Elise in the lobby, talking to a member of staff. Her posture looked a little deflated, her professional smile briefly slipping when she turned away from the conversation.

'Is yours good?' Aidan asked.

'Yeah, it's delicious.' Gabe forced his attention back to the table. 'Yours?'

'Excellent.'

When he was finished, he drained his water glass and stood up. 'Just nipping to the loo. Back in a min.'

He made his way through the hotel lobby. The midday sun streamed through the large windows, turning dust motes into floating constellations.

Elise's voice caught his attention. 'I completely understand your concern, but as I explained—'

'I don't think you do understand,' a sharp voice interrupted. It sounded both posh and peevish at once. 'We paid good money for this tour, and we shouldn't have to put up with that sort of language or... or appearance.'

Gabe slowed his pace, glancing towards the source of the confrontation. Elise stood near a cluster of armchairs in the corner of the lobby, facing two older women. Both were expensively dressed in sensible walking shoes paired with designer outdoor jackets.

With a jolt, he recognised them as two of the women who'd approached him at breakfast, gushing about his environmental podcast and asking for selfies.

'I appreciate that everyone has different standards of comfort,' Elise was saying. 'But she's a paying guest on this tour, just as you are.'

'It's those terrible t-shirts she wears.' The second woman tapped a manicured finger against her collarbone. 'Such vulgar slogans on them. And she had a necklace with a very rude word on it.'

'And her language! I distinctly heard her use the F-word several times.'

Gabe winced, knowing they were discussing Scarlett.

'I understand,' Elise nodded, 'but her personal style and vocabulary choices aren't something I can control. She's not a minor, and she's not breaking any laws or tour policies.'

The women exchanged affronted glances, clearly expecting more accommodation of their complaints.

'Well, I think you should at least speak to her,' the first woman insisted. 'Tell her to tone it down. She's spoiling the experience for the rest of us.'

Elise's shoulders tensed, though her face remained composed. One of the woman caught sight of Gabe and her expression transformed.

'Oh! Mr Wilder!' she exclaimed. 'How lovely to see you again.'

Elise's head snapped around, her eyes widening slightly at the sight of him. He gave her a small nod before stepping forward with his best public-persona smile.

'Hi... Um, how did you ladies enjoy The Fairy Pools?'

'Oh, absolutely breathtaking,' the first woman said.

'Though so many young people taking selfies instead of appreciating the natural beauty is very silly,' the second added.

Gabe kept his smile fixed in place, despite the irony of this complaint coming from a woman who'd nearly dislocated her shoulder trying to get the perfect angle for a selfie with him at breakfast.

'That's the double-edged sword of social media,' he said diplomatically. 'It brings more people to these beautiful places, which is great for tourism and awareness, but can sometimes impact the experience.'

'Oh, absolutely.'

'We're just heading into the village. Perhaps you'd like to walk with us.'

Gabe hesitated for a split second as he scrambled for an excuse. 'I've arranged to do something with my friends.'

'Of course, well, we'll see you around.' The women waved as they headed off.

'Bye.' Gabe watched as they bustled away towards the stairs.

Once they were safely out of earshot, he turned to Elise, who was eyeing him.

'You didn't have to do that,' she said.

'I didn't do anything.' He shrugged. 'I was just a distraction, I suppose.'

Elise shook her head, but her shoulders relaxed. 'Well, thank you anyway. That was an unpleasant little conversation. Did you hear what they were saying?'

'Yeah.' Gabe rubbed the back of his neck. 'For what it's worth, you were handling it really well. I mean, it's a bit low making attacks on people's appearance.'

'Thanks.'

They stood in awkward silence for a moment.

'Anyway,' Gabe said finally, 'I'll leave you to your work.'

'Right.' Elise nodded.

Their eyes locked for a beat too long, and that familiar magnetic pull gripped him. It wasn't just lust this time – though that still burned beneath his skin – it was something deeper, harder to define. A current surged through him, urgent and unsettling, as if his body wanted to move closer to her while his brain scrambled for a reason not to. The connection buzzed in his chest, raw and insistent, demanding something, though he wasn't sure exactly what.

'I hate this job.' She let out a sigh. 'Not working for Highland Horizon, that part's fine. I'm good at the behind-the-scenes stuff, the planning and logistics. But the actual guiding? Being everyone's personal concierge and emotional punching bag? It's not for me anymore.'

'Then why are you doing it?'

'Because no one else could. This is the company's inaugural tour from Glenbriar. The branch is brand new, but the guide pulled out at the last minute. My boss was frantic. The whole opening fell flat because the person she'd employed as manager also didn't take up the position. The boss is covering that role herself.' Elise rubbed at her temple. 'She made a good deal with me, so I couldn't refuse. I just have to get on with it now. Just a few more days, then back to my normal job and someone else can deal with demanding passengers.'

'You look like you need to escape for a bit. Take a time out.'

Elise gave him a wary glance. 'What are you suggesting?'

'Not like—' He backtracked slightly, 'I just mean a break. Some fresh air and something that doesn't involve shepherding sixty tourists around a beauty spot.'

'That's a nice thought,' she replied with a sigh, 'but I'm on duty all day. Even on my breaks, I'm on call.'

'So tell them you're helping a guest,' Gabe suggested. 'Me, specifically. I could have... got lost on the way to the village and you need to personally guide me.'

She laughed. 'No one would believe that.'

'Why not?'

'Because you can see the bloody village from here.'

'Details.' He flapped his hand. 'But who cares? I'm a paying guest too, and I'm giving you a valid excuse to get some time away from these people. A half-hour walk to the village and back. That's all.'

She studied him for a long moment, brown eyes searching his face. 'Ok.' She fiddled with the neckline of her top. 'Let me just grab my jacket and tell the hotel manager I'm helping you with a special request.' She glanced at her watch. 'One hour, that's all I can spare.'

'One hour is great. Meet you at the side entrance in five?' He winked and headed for the loo, then sent a quick message to Aidan, saying he was nipping out and would catch them all after.

Five minutes later, the door opened, and Elise stepped out into the sunshine. She'd changed from her formal tour guide uniform into jeans and a lightweight blue sweater. Her hair fell in loose waves around her shoulders, pinned back from her face with large sunglasses. Absolutely stunning. Flames licked in Gabe's gut.

'Ready?' He pushed away from the wall he'd been leaning against.

'As I'll ever be.'

They fell into step together as they walked down a path through some trees. The afternoon sun filtered through the branches, casting dappled shadows across the path. The further away from the hotel they got, the more Elise's posture loosened. She breathed more deeply, as if consciously letting go of tension.

'So,' Gabe said as they descended the path, 'apart from demanding tourists and impossible bosses, how are you finding Skye?'

'When I get glimpses of it between work responsibilities? It's stunning,' she said. 'I've always wanted to visit properly, but somehow never made the time. I'd like to come back without all the pressure.'

'Weird. I was thinking exactly that earlier.'

'Great minds.'

He smiled and caught her eye. She beamed back, and they both started laughing. No need to explain what she was thinking. He would never have thought the day would come when Elise Reid would be calling him a great mind either.

The path to Portree was steep in places, winding down through patches of gnarled trees. As they walked, the harbour grew larger in their view, boats bobbing on water that shifted from navy to teal depending on the light.

'What made you go into the travel industry?' he asked.

'Don't laugh at this, but I've always loved maps,' she said.

'Why would I laugh at that? It sounds cool to me.'

'I think so too, but some people think it's odd. Even as a kid, I'd pore over atlases, planning imaginary journeys. My parents love travelling too and they always took my brother and me on fancy holidays. I guess I got the bug from them. After university, I fell into guiding for a tour operator, and it just... fit.'

'But you're not so into the guiding now?'

'I grew out of it, and I got fed up with some aspects of it, though I still love travelling. Just not with so many people to babysit.' She gave a wry smile. 'I'm more of a behind-the-scenes person now. Planning itineraries, sorting logistics. I like solving problems, not... performing.'

'Is that how you see it? As a performance?'

'That's what it is. It's about putting on a face. I've known actors who have doubled up as tour guides when they can't get theatre or film work. And they do a great job because this is like learning a part and being the face people want to see.'

Gabe knew what that was like. He had a camera face, and it wasn't really him either. When he'd started out making podcasts from his own home, he'd never thought it would grow to the point where people would approach him when he was out and about. Why had he thought a trip like this would be different? If anything, it was worse. So many eyes on him. 'I hear you.'

'I have to be "on" all the time, you know? Cheerful, helpful, unflappable. The customer is always right.'

'Yeah. It's exhausting. I totally get why you don't enjoy it.'

'And if things go wrong, I still have to keep the face on, try to make everyone happy, even when I know I can't.'

'You seem like you're doing great to me. You haven't cracked anyway.'

'Haven't I?' She glanced around. 'Hooking up with you last night was a pretty big crack.'

A grin tugged at his lips. 'Yeah, I guess. But we're kind of in the same boat. This tour isn't really a good fit for either of us. You were forced into it. I came along without properly thinking it through. What we did together was a good distraction. It definitely made the week more exciting.'

'Risky, you mean.'

'That too.' He huffed out a laugh.

'So, tell me about you… Environmental podcaster isn't exactly a conventional career path. What even made you think of that idea?'

'It wasn't planned.' He ran a hand through his hair. 'I studied environmental science, did some field research, worked for a conservation charity. The podcast started as a side project during lockdown, just me ranting about climate issues from my flat. Then it caught on, and suddenly I was getting calls from all over. I've had *Wilder at Heart* on E-Broadcast Scotland for years now.'

'The reluctant celebrity.' Elise waggled her eyebrows, though her wry smile told him she got where he was coming from.

'Very reluctant. It's not me at all.' And he wanted out. He was done with it. What he'd thought was burnout was possibly a lot more. Maybe it was a change he needed and not just a holiday. But how to give up without looking like a failure? And what would he do?

'Guess we have something in common then.'

'A lot more than we would ever have imagined. We definitely both know how to put up a front.'

She looked at him, then she nodded. 'Exactly.'

They reached the edge of Portree, where the path merged with a proper road leading down to the harbour. Colourful buildings lined the waterfront – the iconic view that featured on countless postcards and social media feeds.

'People often mix this place up with Tobermory on Mull,' Elise said. 'It has the painted houses too.'

'Yeah, at first glance, they're similar towns.' Gabe scanned around. 'I like Mull.'

'I've never been there either,' Elise said. 'I've done more travel abroad than in my own country.'

'I'm the opposite.'

Tourists meandered along the harborside, taking photos and browsing the shops.

'Fancy an ice cream?' Gabe nodded towards a small shop with a queue spilling out onto the pavement.

'Why not?' Elise raised an eyebrow.

The ice cream was locally made. With flavours including Highland whisky and sea salted caramel, it was worth the wait in the queue. They walked along the harbour, cones in hand, pointing out particularly picturesque boats or interesting architectural details on the buildings. Conversation flowed easily now. Gabe nibbled on his cone, not entirely sure why he'd spent so many years determined to dislike this woman. She really wasn't bad at all... As long as he steered his mind away from her history with Aidan. Christ. He really couldn't let himself think about that now. What would Aidan make of this if he could see what he was doing?

'We should probably go soon.' Elise checked her watch. 'My hour of freedom is almost up, and we still have to walk back.'

'Ok.'

They started up the path, often turning to look at the sea, the coloured buildings, the boats, and the sweep of hills surrounding the town.

'It's beautiful,' Elise said.

'This weather definitely helps.'

'It really does.' She watched him for a moment, a slight smile playing on her rosy lips. 'Thanks for doing this. Your company hasn't been entirely terrible.'

'High praise.'

The air between them seemed to crackle, charged with the same electricity that had drawn them together last night. Elise didn't back away, her eyes meeting his.

'What the hell are you doing to me?' Her hand came up to cup his cheek.

'I'm not doing anything.'

'Oh, you are. You might not be meaning to, but you are.'

He leaned a little closer. 'Probably exactly the same thing that you're doing to me.'

'I need you to tell me to stop.'

'Stop what?' he whispered.

'From making a mistake I'm going to regret.' Her thumb grazed his cheekbone. 'But I can't not do it... I just can't. Why do I have no discipline when it comes to you?'

'I don't know. But if it's any consolation, I feel the same. My restraint has jumped into the sea and gone back to the mainland.'

She let out a little laugh. Then he closed the final inch between them. Their lips met in a gentle kiss. He slipped his hands around her waist and backed her carefully towards a large oak tree at the edge of the path, never breaking the kiss.

Her back met the trunk, and he braced one hand against the rough bark beside her head, the other staying at her waist, pulling her closer. She tasted of the salted caramel ice cream, and he devoured it. Her fingers tangled in his hair, tugging slightly, sending heat coursing through his body.

When they finally broke apart, both breathing hard, Gabe stayed close, his forehead touching hers.

'Still think this is a mistake?' he asked.

'One hundred per cent.' Her hands remained on his shoulders, keeping him near. 'But I'm having trouble remembering why right now.'

He grinned, running his thumb along her lower lip. 'That's the thing about chemistry. It doesn't really care about all the reasons it shouldn't exist. And sometimes the more reasons there are, the more explosive it becomes.'

She laughed. 'Is that your professional environmental science opinion?'

'Absolutely.' He nodded solemnly. 'I'm very knowledgeable about... natural phenomena.'

'I bet you are.' She raised an eyebrow.

He tilted his head and sealed his lips over hers, more deliberately this time, one hand sliding into her hair while the other remained braced against the tree trunk. She responded with equal fervour, her body arching against his.

When they separated this time, Gabe kept his hand in her hair, gently tucking a strand behind her ear. 'So...' He trailed his fingers lightly along her jaw. 'What do you say now to continuing our holiday fling? No strings, no drama, just... this.' He brushed his lips against hers again in a feather-light kiss. 'This is what you'll be missing if you refuse... But I won't do it again if you say no. Not unless you beg me.'

'Bugger off.' She prodded him in the chest. 'And stop being such a drama king about it.'

Gabe blinked, then threw his head back and laughed. Elise joined in. 'Drama king?'

'Absolutely.' She slid out from between him and the tree and tossed her hair over her shoulder. 'I won't be begging for anything from you... You on the other hand.' She looked him up and down. 'You can get on your knees and beg if you like.'

He raised his brows, still grinning. 'You bet I will... If that's what you want.'

Voices were approaching on the path from above.

'Bollocks,' Gabe muttered.

'What?' Elise followed his gaze. 'Oh.'

Aidan and Lilah came around a twist in the path, walking hand-in-hand. They hadn't spotted Gabe and Elise yet, absorbed in their own conversation.

But there was nowhere they could go to hide.

Aidan saw them first, his hand lifting in greeting. Too late to attempt an escape. Gabe raised his own hand, forcing a casual smile.

'Hey,' Aidan said.

'Just heading back from my walk,' Gabe replied quickly. 'I, um, bumped into Elise in town.'

'Nice.' Aidan nodded, his focus straying vaguely to Elise.

The strength of their shared history burned into Gabe's soul. Why was he wasting time with this woman when he knew how much she'd hurt Aidan? And Aidan's cousin...

Am I next?

'I'll see you all at dinner,' Elise said with a polite smile. 'Enjoy the rest of your afternoon.'

She continued up the path, maintaining her brisk, professional pace, not once looking back at Gabe. He watched her go for a moment longer than was strictly necessary before turning back to Aidan and Lilah.

'I didn't know this was where you were going,' Aidan said. 'Or we could all have gone together.'

'Na. You need a bit of space from me too,' Gabe said. 'And I don't mind being on my own.'

'Though you managed to find some company,' Lilah said.

'She was on her break, I think.' Gabe cleared his throat. 'Just crossed paths with her.'

'Was she ok?' Lilah's brow furrowed. 'I'm never sure how to take her and I know you don't like her.'

'Um... Yeah, she seemed ok.'

'She's mellowed a lot. I mean, we made our peace a while ago, but we'll never be friends.' Aidan frowned over his shoulder. 'Her being here just makes things so awkward.'

'I'm sure she feels the same.' Lilah patted his arm.

'I guess.'

'Do you want to come back to the village with us?' Aidan said. 'Or have you had enough?'

'Um... yeah, I'll come back with you.' Gabe fell into step beside them. He had no desire to hang around the hotel, so staying out would be good as long as he could keep off the subject of Elise. At least if he was away from her, he could avoid his eyes betraying him...

For now.

Chapter Thirteen

Elise

'She's a really promising footballer. Lovely to see girls getting involved in the sport these days.' Kev was in full flow about his grandkids again – almost like twenty-four hours hadn't passed – picking up from where he left off and making sure Elise knew every detail from their after-school clubs to their dinner preferences. To be fair, she didn't mind. He was a nice guy and obviously proud of his family. Keeping him talking also meant she didn't have to speak and helped keep her mind off other things.

She sipped her wine, images of Gabe threatening to break into her head, but as she looked around the dining room, that wasn't the only thought threatening. The women who'd been complaining about Scarlett weren't far off. They were sitting with Rita Miller, Lloyd's mother – who Elise had nicknamed "the man with glasses" in her head, even though several people on the tour had glasses. Lloyd didn't seem to be in the room, but Rita had her head together with the other women and they looked like they were spinning the gossip wheel at a hundred miles an hour.

Why the hell did they keep glancing over? Elise tried not to catch their eyes. Were they still angry about her perceived lack of action about their complaint? She took another gulp of wine. Why did she get the oddest sensation that it was something else? Something worse. Her stomach churned a little like she was hovering on the verge of a dangerous cliff and any second now, someone would shove her over.

'Did you have a good afternoon?' Kev asked.

'Oh... Yeah. It was ok. I went for a walk with... a passenger who needed assistance.'

'It's been a lovely day for it. Are you joining the quiz night this evening?'

'I'll look in, but I'm not joining in.'

'Same.' Kev put down his glass. 'I might take a wee stroll if it stays nice, but I'm happy with the telly.'

'Good idea.' Though Elise had no plan to do the same. She needed to at least show face at the quiz night, and who knew how long it would go on for? If she went to her room, she'd worry that hell would break loose downstairs. Maybe it was irrational, but it felt like something was brewing. Or maybe it was just her conflicting thoughts about Gabe.

Though she didn't think so.

Laughter and giggles cut through the ambient noise, snagging Elise's attention. Aidan and Lilah were both covering their mouths as though stopping themselves from howling at something. Neither Gabe nor Scarlett was with them, which seemed odd. A horrible, fleeting image danced into Elise's brain of Gabe and Scarlett hooking up. Surely he wouldn't do that with Aidan's sister... But then he'd done it with her, and before yesterday, that would have seemed just as unlikely.

Her gaze landed on Aidan and Lilah again. They looked so happy, so complete in each other's company. It stung to see it. Not because she wished them ill – not now. Maybe she'd been guilty of that in the past, but now her soul wept alone. That was the bed she'd made for herself. All the smiles she put on for the guests were just a cover for a lonely individual. She didn't deserve the kind of love and happiness Aidan and Lilah had. She'd had her chances and ruined them.

She watched Aidan brush a stray curl behind Lilah's ear, his touch gentle and intimate. Elise picked up her phone and opened it. 'I haven't checked my emails all day.' She pulled a face at Kev.

'I wouldn't worry about it. Doubt there'll be anything in them that'll change the world.'

'True.' But she screwed up her nose when she saw one from Gill Campbell.

'Everything ok?' Kev asked.

'There's an email from Gill. I hope it wasn't urgent.'

'Na. She would have called if it was.'

'I guess.' Elise tapped the message open, her eyes scanning it quickly.

Sorry to bother you while you're away, but I really need some clarification on whether you want to go ahead with the Glenbriar job. I'm still covering, and it really isn't working. It makes so much sense for you to be here. Your familiarity with the town, your experience. I really need to press you to accept.

Elise sighed. Patience was not a virtue Gill possessed.

'You ok?' Kev frowned at her.

She ran her fingers through her hair. 'Gill is desperate for me to take up the manager position at the Glenbriar branch.'

'Is she? That's good, isn't it? Didn't you say you come from there?'

'I do, yes.'

He nodded, then peered forward. 'I don't get the impression you're very happy about the idea though.'

'I'm not really.'

'Do you not like living there?'

'I did.' She sat back, knitting her fingers together, then flexing them. 'It's a lovely little town. My friends still live there.' And she missed them, especially Genevieve and Hayley. But they were so closely connected to Aidan and Finlay that everything had got too messy. Hayley was Finlay's sister and Aidan's cousin. Genevieve had married Finlay. Elise's part in those two men's lives had cemented her as the villain. She'd all but cut contact with her two best friends. How could she face them? Even if they said nothing openly, things would never be the same again.

'But?' Kev raised his eyebrows.

'Ah, just stuff. Things got messy with an ex-boyfriend.' Two, to be precise. And one of them was just across the room. Neither fact was one she wanted to share with Kev, nice as he was.

'Oh dear. And is it bad enough to keep you away?'

She gave a little shrug. 'I feel like I'm in the spotlight when I'm there.' Rather like she did here. Only she felt like everyone in Glenbriar wasn't just looking at her but judging her – and often unfairly. She'd never thought herself blameless, but sometimes they didn't seem to take anything else into account. Aidan hadn't exactly been perfect himself, though what she'd done to Finlay had been cruel. She couldn't bear thinking about it without making herself feel sick. Revenge wasn't worth toying with someone's feelings. And Finlay was one of the good guys. He didn't deserve to be messed around.

'Sometimes it feels like that,' Kev said. 'Especially if we've made mistakes. It's like all the eyes are on us, ready to scorn us or pounce on our failings. But I think those feelings come more from the demons inside than actual facts.'

A smile formed on her lips as she watched his kindly face. He had a slightly rough edge to his look, but he was a gentleman and a wise one too. 'You make a good point. And I'm sure you're right in some ways. The inner critic is always the worst.'

'You hold your head high, no matter what you choose to do. There are always people out there who are quick to judge, but I've yet to meet the perfect human and I'm sixty-three.'

She chuckled and gave him a grateful nod. 'Thank you.'

After dinner, Elise helped the hotel staff set up for the quiz night. She glimpsed Gabe in the bar just off the dining room, where he was having a bar meal rather than the full dinner, which explained why she hadn't seen him. He was on his own. Her chest lifted a little to know that Scarlett wasn't with him. That was a stupid idea now that she thought about it. Scarlett had just had one of the messiest breakups ever – she was unlikely to jump straight into bed with her brother's best friend a day later.

Most of the passengers hadn't returned to their rooms after dinner but were either in the bar or outside, making the most of the lovely summer evening. The hotel owner had left the patio doors open, and she stood by them, telling everyone the quiz was about to start. Slowly the room filled up again. Gabe came out of the bar with a small tray of pints and put them down on a table. Lilah and Aidan joined him, and they put their heads together, talking. Elise couldn't know for sure, but she suspected they were wondering where Scarlett had got to.

Gabe's 'fan club' settled at a table along with Rita, who had a huge glass of violet-coloured something – gin, Elise assumed – with a cocktail stirrer and a slice of lime on the side. Rita glanced up and narrowed her eyes at Elise. For a second, Elise had that sense again that she knew this woman from somewhere, but it passed quickly, giving way to a sinking sensation in her tummy. Why the hell was the woman staring at her like that? She hadn't been one of the ones who had some beef with Scarlett, so what was with the nasty looks?

Or am I just being too sensitive?

Like Kev had suggested. Perhaps it was the inner voice whispering all sorts of lies when really the woman had possibly just had too much to drink and wasn't meaning to stare at all.

Elise sat down at the side of the room, trying to avoid meeting anyone's eyes as the owner started talking and telling them how the quiz would work. As soon as they were settled, she was getting out of here. But despite being tired, she was restless. Maybe she should go for another walk, though she didn't really want to do that alone either.

The email had unsettled her. It was something she wanted to think about, perhaps talk over with someone. But who? Ringing her old friends out of the blue seemed out of the question. She'd left it so long, she wasn't sure what their reactions would be. And why did she think they'd be interested in her issues? It would look like she only called when she needed help. She had to be strong. Going to pieces didn't help.

Her parents were away in Australia on a three-month trip and weren't really the kind of people who would see something like this as a big problem. They tended to leave their children to their own devices. Elise's brother, David, and his wife, Amanda, would listen, but Amanda would spout off so many solutions that Elise's head spun just thinking about it. None of them seemed the right people to confide in.

She'd just have to figure it out on her own.

Her heart sank. Everything she did these days was lonely, and that seemed to be her lot in life. Of course, there was a willing distraction if she wanted to forget about the email – and everything else. But that was a dangerous road to go down – even if it was the one that lit up her mind and made her insides dance.

Chapter Fourteen

Elise

As soon as the quiz night was in full swing, Elise got up and strolled into the hotel foyer. Outside, it was still bright, and she went out through the main doors, not with any particular plan, just following her nose.

Her knowledge of Skye came mostly from research done online. She wasn't familiar with the Scottish islands, but there was an alluring charm about Skye, an oddly wild and untouchable sensation. The breeze was cooler now. That was something she'd learned quickly. Even when the sun was out, the air could be fresh and chillier than she was used to even in Glenbriar, though it wasn't unpleasant.

She nipped back inside, headed up to her room, and grabbed a jacket. Sitting outside for a bit appealed to her, but she wanted to be warm. Back outside, she walked across the lawn to where she saw a bench near a large flower bed. She sat down, glancing over her shoulder to where the front room of the hotel was all lit up and full of guests enjoying the quiz.

Elise turned her attention to the view beyond of the sea and hills. So beautiful. A place where she could be at peace. But whenever it was quiet her brain leapt into action. Gill Campbell was probably sitting at home furious that Elise hadn't given her an answer about the Glenbriar job. Elise just couldn't decide what to do about it.

The soft crunch of footsteps on gravel made her turn. Gabe stood a few feet away, silhouetted against the fading light, two wine glasses dangling from one hand and a bottle in the other. His dark hair was tousled by the evening breeze, and he wore the same jeans from earlier but had changed into a black Henley – his favourite brand of casual wear, it seemed.

'Thought you might want company,' he said.

Elise raised an eyebrow. 'Did you?'

'Well, I'm a very thoughtful person.' A crooked smile played across his face as he approached.

She shifted on the bench, leaving space for him to sit. Their thighs didn't quite touch, but warmth radiated from him.

'White this time.' He held up the bottle.

'Well remembered.' She accepted the glass he poured for her. The wine was crisp and cold, washing away the taste of anxiety that had lingered in her mouth all afternoon.

'Well,' Gabe said after a moment, 'you won't believe what's happened now.'

'Oh god, what?' She stared at him.

'Scarlett apparently heard you "shagging Lloyd" – whoever he may be – last night.'

Elise almost choked on her wine. 'What?'

Gabe looked around. 'Clearly it wasn't him...' He pulled an innocent face. 'It was me. But... Scarlett was apparently accosted earlier by the same women that approached me this morning and were complaining this afternoon. They were having a go at her and this Lloyd's mother appeared. Scarlett, in her rage, decided to grass him up... And you.'

'You are having me on.'

'Nope. Wish I was.'

'So they think I've been sleeping with passengers?'

'Which technically you have.'

'Don't you dare do that. You promised me you'd be discreet.'

'Hey.' He put his hand on her arm. 'I was joking. Though it was in bad taste. I assume Lloyd, whoever he is, has told his mother it wasn't him.'

'He's the man with glasses whose knee I fell on yesterday. He seems nice, but I noticed he wasn't at dinner. Maybe he's too embarrassed to show face if rumours like this are flying around. This is not good. I probably shouldn't even be out here with you, or they'll all be gossiping.'

'I think they all went upstairs. The quiz is finished.'

She let out a sigh and pressed her fingers into her forehead. 'I really don't need this on top of everything else.'

'What else has happened?'

'My boss gave me an ultimatum.'

'Oh?'

'She's determined for me to take the managerial post in the new Glenbriar branch.' She swirled the wine in her glass. 'I just don't think I can.'

'Why not?'

'People in Glenbriar have long memories.'

He took a deep drink from his glass. 'I see.'

The alcohol warmed her veins, loosening the knot in her chest and her tongue. 'I miss it though,' she admitted quietly.

'Glenbriar?'

'Yep. My friends – Hayley and Genevieve. But they're so wrapped up in everything that happened. I can't face them.' Elise closed her eyes briefly. 'I know what I did to Finlay was wrong. I've known that for a long time. I shouldn't have used him to get back at Aidan. But you weren't there. You didn't see how Aidan just... left. One minute we were making plans for the future, and the next he was off to Canada with some vague promise about coming back "when the time was right".'

Gabe stared ahead, swirling the wine in his glass. 'Yeah. Yeah...' He sighed. 'I know he wasn't completely innocent. He knows it himself.'

'He didn't even ask if I wanted to go with him or give me any indication of when he'd be back. Just expected me to wait indefinitely.'

'He was so cut up about his dad dying. He wasn't thinking straight.'

'I know that. And we've made peace since. Neither of us were blameless. But I feel that everyone still blames me. It's amazing how even in modern society, women are always held more culpable than men. Just look at any woman who ever accidentally gets pregnant. I guess I just felt used. Like he didn't really care. So, I went looking for someone else... And yes, I picked someone that I knew would hurt him. It wasn't right. I know that. Finlay's a nice guy. Really nice. He didn't deserve me using him like that. God.' She huffed out a sigh. 'I've messed up so much.'

Gabe nodded and tossed back his remaining wine. 'Listen, I'm sorry.'

'For what?'

'I've been horribly hard on you. I have no excuse. Aidan was so gutted after his dad died, I felt like I had to stand by him, and hating on you was part of that. But it wasn't fair. I see that now.'

The admission surprised her. 'Thanks, but what difference does it make?'

'I misjudged you.'

'I'm not sure you did. Some of the stuff I did is...' She shuddered. 'I didn't even go to Finlay and Genevieve's wedding. It was too awkward.' She covered her face with her hands. 'I feel so bad.'

Gabe gently pulled her hands away. 'Hey. It's ok. You've just made a bit of a mess.'

'A bit?' she said dryly.

'We're all messes in our own way.' His thumb traced small circles on her wrist where he still held it. 'Some of us just hide it better than others.'

The touch sent small electric currents up her arm. 'Is that what you do? Hide your mess?'

His eyes found hers in the gathering darkness. 'Expertly.' He took another sip of wine. 'My family situation is a dumpster fire.'

'Really?'

'Hell yeah. My father and I don't get on. Haven't for years. I walked out as a teenager, after he broke me, and my mother's heart. I stayed with Aidan and his dad for a while. That's partly why I felt so guilty when Aidan's dad died. Mine is still alive, and it just seemed so unfair. I've tried to persuade my mother to leave him, but she can't. It's not in her to do it. She lives in fear of the man but in more fear of leaving him and there's damn all I can do about it.'

'Wow... I had no idea.'

'It's not something I shout about. Why would I? He could be hurting her right now. Probably not physically, that's not his style, but verbally and emotionally, he's there wearing her down. She's a wreck.' He threw out his hands. 'But I can't change that. I've tried, but she won't hear me out. Doesn't even want to talk about it. Sometimes I feel like she can't even accept my reasons for not wanting to see him.'

'We really are a pair.'

'Aren't we just?' A muscle twitched in his jaw. 'I used to envy Aidan so much,' he continued, almost to himself. 'He had everything, but he was also my best friend. It wasn't my place to envy him, just to stand by him, especially in tough times.'

'Which meant berating me.'

He nodded. 'I've been a real prick.'

He refilled their glasses with the last of the wine. 'Right, I think that's enough of my daddy issues.'

She let out a little giggle.

'Let me get another bottle. Looks like we need it.'

Elise waited on the bench as he disappeared inside. The sky over Skye was finally darkening now and a slight chill had crept in. Thank goodness she'd put on her jacket.

Gabe returned with another bottle and topped up their glasses. 'Everyone's gone to bed, I think. I didn't see any of my fans anyway.'

She huffed out a laugh. 'That's something. Because I'm sure they'd have plenty to say about us sitting out here getting plastered.'

'Just a bit.'

Night had fully settled now, wrapping the garden in a blanket of darkness broken only by the lights from the hotel windows and the distant streetlamps in Portree. Elise's skin felt hypersensitive, aware of every point where she and Gabe touched – shoulder to shoulder, thigh to thigh. The wine had left her in that peculiar state of heightened awareness where everything seemed both sharper and softer at the same time. His scent – woodsy cologne mixed with something lemony – filled her senses each time she breathed in.

She turned to look at him, finding his eyes already on her.

'What?' she asked, her voice barely above a whisper.

'Nothing.' He took her hand, his thumb tracing slow circles on her palm. 'Just thinking.'

'About?'

His gaze dropped to her mouth, then back to her eyes. 'About how much I want to kiss you right now.'

'Then do it. I want you to.' And she did. So much for telling herself this was a bad idea. But there was something about him. Something that made her drop all the pretence. Something that had her aching for contact with him – physically and emotionally. Even just talking to him like this had taken a weight off her shoulders.

He leaned in slowly, his free hand rising to cup her cheek, fingers threading into her hair. Their lips met and a hot bolt fired into Elise's tummy. She sighed into the contact.

The kiss deepened gradually, his tongue tracing the seam of her lips until she opened them for him. He slid his hand from her cheek to the nape of her neck, thumb stroking the sensitive skin there in a way that made her shiver.

Elise's head swam with the combined effects of wine and desire. She turned more fully towards him, her hand finding his chest, feeling the steady thud of his heart beneath her palm. He was solid, warm, sexy.

'This is a bad idea,' he murmured against her mouth. 'We've had too much to drink.'

'I'm the mistress of bad choices.'

His low chuckle vibrated against her skin and his lips returned to hers, the kiss growing more insistent. She shifted in his embrace, seeking closer contact.

For a long moment, they traded increasingly desperate kisses, hands exploring through clothing, bodies straining towards more intimate contact.

Elise finally pulled back, placing a restraining hand on his chest. 'Actually.'

His hand stilled immediately. 'Too much?'

'No, but you were right...' She tried to gather her scattered thoughts. 'We've had a lot to drink, and...' She sighed, resting her forehead against his shoulder. 'And if we keep going, I'm not going to want to stop. But I'm exhausted and tipsy, and we have an early start tomorrow.'

Gabe pressed a kiss to her temple. 'Ok.'

She looked up, frowning. 'You're ok with that?'

'Of course I am.' His smile was crooked in the darkness. 'I may be horny, but I'm not an arsehole. Besides,' he added, his voice dropping to that low register that made her stomach flip, 'when we do this again, I want you fully present. Not half-asleep and wine-soaked.'

The 'when', not 'if', sent a fresh wave of heat through her. 'You're very sure of yourself.'

'I'm very sure of our fling.' He brushed his lips against hers. 'Aren't you?'

'It seems to be happening.'

'Only if you want it to.'

'I do… Just not tonight. I have to be sensible.'

'Ok.' His voice was barely a whisper. He wrapped a strong arm around her and for a second, she wished she could sleep right here. And she would if she were in his embrace. That might be the weirdest thought of her life. But it was accurate.

He helped her to her feet. The world tilted slightly as she got up, confirming that her decision to stop had been the right one. He steadied her.

'Alright?'

'Just a bit dizzy.' She smiled ruefully. 'Told you I was a light-weight.'

'I feel a bit dizzy myself. Come on, then. Let's get you to bed.' He paused. 'Your bed. Alone. That's what I meant.'

She giggled. 'You're nuts.'

'What about them?'

'Stop it.'

He kept his hand on the small of her back as they made their way along the garden path towards the hotel entrance, still chuckling.

The lobby was deserted but a low light was on.

They stumbled up the stairs. When they reached Elise's door first, she paused, key in hand. 'Well. This is me.'

'So it is.' Gabe stroked her hair. 'Get some sleep. I'll see you tomorrow.'

'You too.'

He leaned in, and for a moment, she thought he was going to full-on kiss her again. Instead, he pressed his lips to her cheek. 'Goodnight,' he murmured against her skin.

'Goodnight.'

She watched him walk to his own door further down the corridor. Only when he disappeared into his room did she let herself into hers.

The room was cool and dark. Elise kicked off her shoes and sat on the edge of the bed, touching her fingers to her lips.

'Just physical,' she reminded herself. But as she got ready for bed, she couldn't think about anything else. And worse. All she really wanted was him beside her. Not for sex. Not really for anything physical. Just for company. Someone who saw her and understood her... Which was insane, because Gabe Wilder had never been on the same page as her. But over the last couple of days, she'd discovered they had a lot more in common than she would ever have believed.

She'd strayed into dangerous territory. Would she be able to keep out once the wine wore off and her head cleared?

Chapter Fifteen

Gabe

The coach rolled to a stop beside the secluded sea loch. Gabe squinted against the morning sun, gazing out over the water stretching before them like polished glass. One thing he couldn't complain about this week was the weather. He'd thought it looked a bit overcast when he'd woken up far too early, perhaps even a little drizzly, but that had blown off on the Skye breeze leaving another sunny morning.

'Right then, everyone,' Elise's voice crackled through the coach's speakers. 'We're here. We've got water activities available for the adventurous souls, and for those who'd prefer to keep dry, there's a lovely café and walking trails.'

Aidan nudged Gabe's shoulder. 'You're coming in the water, right?'

'Try and stop me.' Gabe grinned back at him. This was much more up his street than sitting in a café. The coach erupted into movement as passengers gathered their belongings and filed into the aisle. Gabe's eyes landed on Elise – as he knew they would. He'd given up trying to stop himself. Looking didn't do any harm. Not any more than he'd done already. His body and soul ached for her. When they'd gone their separate ways yesterday, he'd spent most of the night lying awake wishing she were next to him. Not through lust, but just a deep desire to be close to her. He'd quite liked to have talked some more. A sensation he knew was totally bizarre and alien to him – but it existed nonetheless.

He gave her a brief nod before stepping off the coach into the crisp morning air. The scene before them was straight out of a tourism brochure – impossibly blue water, green hills rising in the distance, and a smattering of brightly coloured canoes dotting the shoreline.

'Are you coming too?' Lilah asked Scarlett.

Gabe blinked and gave himself a mental shake. He'd almost forgotten Scarlett was there; she'd been so quiet. She hadn't been at dinner last night and had come in late for breakfast looking flushed and harassed. Cruel how she'd not only been dumped but now seemed to be under close scrutiny from several judgy people. Though telling people she'd heard Elise with Lloyd was insane – typical Scarlett, no filter, and completely cringe at times, acting like she was sixteen, not twenty-five.

She'd been trailing behind them with her phone in hand, and she looked up with a half-hearted shrug. 'I suppose. Yeah.' Her eyes flitted around the group, landing on the woman Gabe now guessed to be Lloyd's mother, and quickly looking away again. No wonder she was embarrassed. Spreading crazy rumours when you were in such proximity to all these people was madness.

Gabe raised an eyebrow. Definitely not a smart move after what had already happened to her this week, though maybe it was all part of her reaction to that.

Aidan put his arm around Lilah. 'Well, let's get going. I miss Maya in places like this.'

'She'd love it,' Lilah agreed.

'I'll message Mum later and see how she is.'

Gabe grinned at them. Their dog was their baby. One day he might get one too. That might be exactly the kind of companionship he needed.

They made their way down to the water's edge, where a young man in shorts and a t-shirt was helping visitors. Up close, the options looked more limited than Gabe had hoped – just a handful of canoes, but not that many people had chosen to come down. Most had gone off on the walking trail or made their way into the nearby café.

'Welcome,' the instructor said. 'Any of you done this before?'

'I have,' Gabe said, at the same time as Aidan. Lloyd and a few others also nodded or raised their hands.

'Great! That'll make things easier. We should be able to get you all something, though you might have to share.' He gestured to the boats.

Aidan immediately wrapped an arm around Lilah's waist. 'We'll happily share.'

'Perfect.' The instructor pointed to a blue canoe. 'That one's all yours. I'll get you sorted with buoyancy aids.'

Lloyd was standing nearby. He adjusted his glasses and frowned, possibly at Scarlett, who was in front of him. Gabe held his breath. *Please, not another scene!* If Lloyd decided to confront Scarlett about her accusations, this could get unpleasant.

'Anyone else want to share this canoe?' The instructor looked around.

Scarlett glanced at her feet, then up at Gabe and around to Lloyd.

Gabe opened his mouth to say he would do it, but Lloyd spoke first.

'I'll share with you, if you want.' He gave her a vague smile.

'Yeah... sure, ok.' She beamed back at him like he'd just told her she'd won the lottery.

Gabe raised his eyebrows with growing confusion. Ok, that made no sense. Not unless Lloyd wanted to get her alone in the canoe so he could have a go at her with no one else listening. But he didn't seem like that kind of person. He'd been quiet, private, and mild-mannered from what Gabe had seen of him so far.

Just like my father.

Gabe grimaced. Outsiders would never believe the other side of Mr Wilder senior. What if Lloyd was exactly the same?

It wasn't his place to stop Scarlett going if she wanted to, and she'd already agreed.

'Are you sure?' Gabe frowned. Maybe Lloyd hadn't heard the rumour, or he was being remarkably forgiving.

'Yeah.' Scarlett shrugged.

The instructor handed her a buoyancy aid, which she pulled on with a grimace. 'These things are hideous.'

'Better hideous than drowned,' Lloyd replied with a quirk of his lips, and Scarlett actually smiled back.

What the hell was going on? Gabe couldn't even say anything to Aidan and Lilah as they'd already gone. But this was weird. He could always keep close to them.

But two other couples went next, and Lloyd and Scarlett had already gone some distance. It would be hard to catch them. Gabe found himself left with a canoe all on his own, which wasn't a problem. He'd always been comfortable alone – preferred it, even.

But something about watching the others pair off tugged unexpectedly at his heart.

'Just you then, mate?' The instructor handed Gabe a paddle.

'Yep, all by myself.' As he strapped himself into his own buoyancy aid, he caught sight of Elise standing a little way off, talking to some of the passengers who'd opted to stay dry. She was smiling, but it didn't quite reach her eyes. Last night's conversation played through his mind again, how they'd opened up to each other, and everything had been unexpectedly chill. They were actually ok together.

The cold water seeped through Gabe's trainers and the edges of his three-quarter combats as he waded in knee-deep before climbing in, but he wasn't really bothered. The sun was warm enough to ensure he'd dry quickly.

He pushed off from the shore, digging his paddle into the clear water. Each stroke put distance between himself and the others. He wasn't sure where Lloyd and Scarlett had got to. Most people had headed towards scattered islands in the bay and were paddling around them.

After twenty minutes of paddling, his arms burned pleasantly with the effort. He paused to catch his breath, letting the canoe drift, still not seeing Scarlett and Lloyd or Aidan and Lilah. Back on the shore, Elise stood at the edge of the café's outdoor seating area, a paper cup clutched in her hand. Something about her solitary figure made him change direction.

He made his way back to the pebbly beach. The canoe scraped against the stones as he dragged it ashore.

Elise hadn't noticed him yet. She was still gazing out at the loch, occasionally sipping from her cup with a distant look. Her dark hair was pulled back in a neat ponytail, emphasising the elegant line of her neck.

'Enjoying the view?' He approached her with a smile.

She turned towards him with widened eyes. 'Oh... yes, it's lovely. How's the water?'

'It's great,' Gabe grinned. 'You should give it a go.'

Elise shook her head. 'I'm working.'

'Yeah,' he said, 'pity.'

'I have to be available if anyone needs assistance.'

He glanced around at the peaceful scene. 'Though it doesn't look like anyone's in dire need at the moment.'

Elise bit her lip. 'You'll be the end of me.'

He tipped her a little wink and turned to a couple who were passing. 'Excuse me. Quick poll – do you think our tour guide should be allowed to enjoy the loch too, or should she stand on shore watching all day?'

'Gabe!' Elise hissed, her cheeks flushing. 'What are you doing?'

'Get in the water.' The woman chuckled.

'You've earned a break,' the man added.

'Thank you.' Gabe turned back to Elise with a triumphant smile. 'Democracy has spoken.'

She shook her head, but he could see she was fighting a smile. 'This is coercion.'

'This is permission,' he countered. 'From your charges. Who apparently think you deserve a bit of fun.'

Elise looked at the water, then back at Gabe. 'I'm not wearing a wetsuit,' she warned. 'And I'm not getting in anything tippy. I'll look ridiculous enough without being soaked.'

'Canoes are good and steady, and you don't need a wetsuit.'

'Ok, but just half an hour.'

They walked together towards the water's edge.

'I haven't done anything like this in years,' Elise said as they approached the instructor.

'It's like riding a bike.' Gabe raised an eyebrow. 'Except wetter if you fall off.'

That earned him a genuine laugh.

The instructor looked up as they approached. 'You ok?'

'I've convinced another victim to try the water.' Gabe nodded towards Elise.

'Great! Let me get you set up with a buoyancy aid.'

As they followed him to the equipment rack, Gabe caught sight of Aidan and Lilah further down the shore. The instructor handed Elise a bright orange buoyancy aid, and Gabe eyed her as she turned it over in her hands, looking at it like it was an alien artefact.

'It goes on like a waistcoat,' Gabe said.

'I know how it goes on.' She screwed up her face. 'I'm just appreciating how fantastically unflattering it's going to be.'

'Ah, no one will mind.' Gabe dragged the canoe towards where Elise stood struggling with her buoyancy aid. She'd got it on, but the zip caught halfway up, and her frustrated attempts to force it only made it worse. Her cheeks were flushed, fingers fumbling with the stubborn metal tab.

'Need a hand?' Gabe dropped the canoe paddle onto the pebbles.

'It's stuck.' She yanked at it.

He stepped closer. 'Let me see.'

Elise dropped her hands to her sides, a gesture of surrender, and Gabe focused intently on the zip, trying to ignore the faint scent of her perfume that kicked him straight in the groin.

'You've got to...' he muttered, fingers working to free the trapped fabric. 'Hold still a moment.'

He tugged her closer. Their eyes met and his heart jolted. The zip finally came unstuck, and Gabe dragged it upwards, pulling Elise forward with the motion. For a heartbeat, they were close enough that he could dip in and kiss her – which he absolutely must not do this close to so many people.

He cleared his throat and stepped back. 'There you go. All sorted.'

'Thanks.'

Together, they carried the canoe to the water's edge. The wind had indeed picked up, creating small waves that lapped against the shore.

'You get in and I'll pull us out.' Gabe held the canoe steady.

Elise climbed in and Gabe dragged the canoe into the water before jumping in himself.

For a few minutes, they paddled in silence, finding their rhythm.

'You didn't see Scarlett come back, did you?' he asked.

'No, I don't think so. Why?'

'She went off with Lloyd which seemed odd to me, but they seemed happy about it.'

'Bizarre.' Elise glanced back at him over her shoulder. 'This is actually nice. Thank you for thinking of me.'

'No worries. I'm used to being alone; it suits my lifestyle, and I could see you were feeling the same, despite being surrounded by people.'

'That's exactly it. I'm always around people, but I still feel...'

'Apart,' Gabe suggested.

'Yes.' She resumed paddling.

'Being alone can be straightforward. You know where you stand.'

'And where's that?' she asked. 'Lonely?'

'It's a fine line, isn't it? Between alone and lonely.'

'Sure is. I needed to be alone,' she said. 'After everything that happened with Aidan and Finlay... it seemed safer. Less complicated.'

'Even now?'

'Even now. Though, yes, it can be lonely.'

The candour in her voice made something shift in Gabe's chest. 'I know what you mean. We're more alike than I thought.'

Elise half-turned, careful not to destabilise the canoe, and gave him a little smile.

They were approaching a small, rocky outcrop that jutted into the loch, creating a natural cove sheltered from the wind. Gabe guided them towards it, his paddle cutting cleanly through the increasingly choppy water. A pair of oyster catchers picked their way along the stony beach, their bright orange bills striking against their black and white plumage. Gabe pointed them out to Elise like he was doing one of his podcasts. A gust of wind pushed the canoe slightly out of the cove, back into the main body of the loch. Looking up, Gabe realised they had drifted closer to where Aidan and Lilah were now paddling.

His stomach clenched. He wasn't sure he wanted them to see him with Elise. 'We should probably head back. It's a bit breezy.'

'Good idea.'

The wind had picked up considerably by the time they approached the shore, pushing small waves against the canoe's side and making their final approach more challenging than Gabe had anticipated. Aidan and Lilah had already landed and stood watching from the pebbly beach. Great... Just what he needed. There was no way he could hide from them. A handful of other tour members who'd finished their water activities or their coffees were also observing.

'Oh hell,' Elise muttered under her breath. 'Do they have to all be watching?'

Gabe didn't like to say this was how he'd felt this whole trip – what with his 'fans' prying on his every move.

'Easy does it,' he called over the sound of water slapping against the hull. 'Let me steer us in.'

The canoe lurched slightly, and Elise gripped the sides, her knuckles whitening.

'Almost there.' The shore loomed closer, the canoe scraping against submerged pebbles as they entered the shallows.

The instructor waded out to meet them, grabbing the front of the canoe to steady it. 'Good timing. The weather's turning a bit.'

Elise exhaled with visible relief, her shoulders dropping as the canoe stabilised. She shifted her weight, preparing to stand. The instructor maintained his grip on the front, but the canoe still rocked ominously with her movement.

'Careful,' Gabe said.

Elise rose unsteadily to her feet. For a moment, it seemed she would make it without incident. Then a larger wave hit the side of the canoe, tilting it just as she was taking her first step towards the shore.

Elise's arms windmilled frantically, her body contorting in ways that defied physics as she fought to stay upright. She lurched left, then right, but somehow, miraculously, she managed not to fall completely, though her left foot plunged into the water up to her knee.

From the shore came the unmistakable sound of stifled laughter.

Gabe glanced up to see Aidan with his hand over his mouth, shoulders shaking, while Lilah had turned away. Several other onlookers weren't even trying to hide their amusement.

Elise finally found her footing, half-stumbling onto the pebbly shore with her left side thoroughly soaked.

Gabe scrambled out of the canoe. 'You ok?' He reached for her arm.

She jerked away from his touch. 'I'm fine.' She didn't meet his eyes. Her wet trousers clung to her leg, water dripping from the hem.

'Elise—' he started, but she was already moving away, squelching towards the path that led back to the coach.

'I need to get dry.'

Reluctantly, Gabe made his way over to where Aidan and Lilah stood, now joined by Scarlett, who was sipping from a takeaway cup with a bemused expression.

'Did I miss something good?' she asked.

'Just Elise doing her best impression of a drunk flamingo.' Aidan set off another round of giggling from Lilah.

Gabe felt his jaw tighten. 'It wasn't that funny.'

Aidan raised an eyebrow. 'It was pretty funny.'

'She was embarrassed,' Gabe said.

'Since when do you care so much about her?' Aidan narrowed his eyes. 'You've spent years taking the piss out of her. What were you doing in the canoe with her anyway?'

'Nothing,' he muttered. 'We had to share. We should all just be nice.'

Aidan raised an eyebrow, which Gabe took to mean: that's rich coming from you.

Lilah's face dropped, and she placed a hand on her husband's arm. 'He's right, we shouldn't have laughed. I didn't realise she was actually struggling. I thought she was acting. It just looked so funny, but I feel terrible now.'

Gabe sighed and ran his fingers through his hair. He didn't exactly feel great himself. A squirming sensation in his gut niggled away at him. Aidan was not going to like it if he found out what Gabe and Elise had got up to, if he was this weirded out about them spending half an hour in a canoe together. Gabe screwed up his face and shuddered into the oncoming wind, but that wasn't the force threatening to pull him apart. His insides were being pulled every which way, as his loyalty to Aidan battled with his crazy desire for Elise.

Chapter Sixteen

Elise

Elise squelched her way back to the coach, her left side soaked up to the knee. She'd managed to make a fool of herself. Not for the first time. In fact, it felt depressingly representative of her life as a whole – stumbling from one shitshow to the next, always just about holding it together on the surface while everything underneath teetered on collapse.

Laughter still echoed behind her, and she tried to tell herself it didn't matter. That it was harmless. But that old, hollow feeling twisted in her gut. Maybe it should've been refreshing – at least people weren't whispering behind her back this time, not pretending to be polite while quietly judging her. Not reducing her to someone they could comment on or leer at without consequence. No, this time they'd just laughed to her face.

Better? Or worse?

Heat burned in her cheeks, not from embarrassment, but from that old, familiar brew of shame and fury. She hated feeling exposed. Weak. The loss of control scraped at something raw inside her — the part of her that often came over as aloof, made people think she didn't care even when it wrecked her.

She dug her nails into her palm and kept walking.

Her trousers clung uncomfortably to her ankle, and her deck shoe was utterly soaked. Thankfully she always had spare clothes on the coach. She'd learned to do that years ago after a passenger had vomited on her. That was a lot worse than this. At least this was only water. She'd packed a pair of walking boots and socks too, in case she'd needed to go on one of the trails. So she'd be fine. But the humiliation couldn't be cast off as easily as the wet clothes.

As she approached the coach, she spotted Kev leaning against the door, arms folded across his chest, grinning at his phone in the sunshine. Probably sharing messages with his family. He had on his proud grandad expression.

'Oh, hello.' He glanced up, pushing away from the coach as she approached, and put his phone into his shirt pocket. 'Are you ok?'

'Yeah.' Elise sighed, pushing a strand of hair from her face. 'I was persuaded to go on a canoe, and I got wet when I was getting out.'

'Oh dear.' Kev scrunched up his nose as he looked down at her sodden shoe.

'Could have been worse. I saved myself from falling in, but in such a stupid way I had half the coach laughing at me.' She rolled her eyes. 'Talk about humiliating.'

'Ah, don't stress about it. You'll not have to see these people again after the next few days and if that's all they remember about their holiday, then give yourself a pat on the back for being so memorable.'

She tossed him a wry smile. 'Thanks, Kev. You always know how to cheer me up.'

He saluted her with a cheesy grin.

'Can you let me on so I can change into some dry clothes?'

'Aye, sure.' Kev pulled out the key fob, and the door hissed open. 'You're very sensible to have extra stuff with you.'

Elise climbed the steps and pulled out her backpack from the storage area near her seat.

'I'll lock you in and stand guard outside.'

'Thanks, Kev.'

'No bother at all.' He closed the door.

Alone in the coach, Elise fished out her spare clothes. She peered out the window. No one could see her in here as the windows were blacked on the outside, and Kev was the only person there anyway, standing close to the door looking at his phone, but she still didn't like the idea of stripping off like this.

Moving to a seat a little further back, she ducked down and pulled off her shoes, socks, and trousers. 'For God's sake,' she muttered, nearly losing her balance again. Thank goodness no one could see her half-naked and flapping around like a caught fish.

She quickly dried her foot off with a part of her trousers that wasn't wet, before pulling on the spare pair of plain black trousers and her walking socks and boots.

After she'd tied the laces, she sat back in the seat and threw her head back on the rest. This tour was barely holding together at the seams. First Leon, then the people complaining about Scarlett, now Scarlett's crazy rumour-mongering... and, of course, Gabe. He was the icing on the crap-show cake, stirring up all these complicated feelings she'd rather not examine.

She let out a long moan. Just a few more days to get through and then she was never doing another tour again.

Her Glasgow job should have been perfect. Behind the scenes, away from Glenbriar and all its memories and judgement. A fresh start. Wasn't that what she'd needed? To leave behind the girl who'd made such a mess of things with Aidan and Finlay?

But she missed Glenbriar so much. Glasgow was an interesting place to live, but too stressful. The pace of life in Glenbriar suited her so much more. It was what she was used to. Could it ever be the same though? What about Genevieve and Hayley? Her heart ached every time she thought about them, but the longer she left it to contact them... wouldn't that make it so much worse? And she'd left it so long already.

Now there was a job opportunity right there in Glenbriar waiting to be snapped up. Was she a fool not to jump at it? She deliberately hadn't gone for it in the first place because of her history in Glenbriar and those reasons still stood. This time, it felt like Gill was bullying her into taking it. If things had been different, it would be ideal, but going back to the town filled her with conflict, her love for it soured by fear of judgement.

She sighed, pulling a brush from her bag and attacking her hair with it. Each stroke felt like punishment for her indecision.

Was the Glenbriar job actually a step backwards instead of forwards? The pay rate might be almost the same, but was managing a small-town branch better than project managing at the HQ? Did it even matter? Who really cared about stuff like that? If only she could run it by her friends. They'd always been there to help her through times like this, but she was on her own this time.

She laid the wet trousers over the handrail of the coach steps – hopefully they'd dry there – then she checked her reflection in her compact mirror, grimacing at the state of herself.

She stepped off the coach. The sun was still out, but a gentle breeze rustled through the trees that lined the path back to the loch. She had a job to do, duties to attend to, and couldn't hide in the coach all day – no matter how tempting that might be.

'All sorted?' Kev asked.

'As good as it gets,' she replied with a small smile. 'Thanks for standing guard.'

'Part of the service.' He winked at her with a grin.

'Are you coming down to the café for lunch?'

'I'll have a look in later. I'm happy just getting some peace in the sunshine. There's a wee picnic table down there. I've been sat there reading for a while. I might go back for a bit.'

'Ok. Well, I'll catch you later. I better get back and see if anyone needs anything.'

'Right you are.'

With a nod, Elise turned and began walking back along the path towards the cafe and shore. The path curved through a copse of trees, dappled sunlight creating patterns on the ground. Distant laughter from the loch filtered up on the wind. Hopefully, whoever it was had found something more amusing than her crazy balancing act to chuckle at.

She rounded a bend in the path and saw Scarlett coming in the opposite direction. Her head was down, shoulders hunched, and she still looked completely lost. When Elise had dated Aidan, Scarlett had been bright and feisty. Now, she was a shadow compared to that. So much vibrancy sapped from her. She must only be about twenty-five. How cruel that men and relationships had done this to her.

'Hey,' Elise said, mostly to make her presence known as Scarlett would possibly walk right into her.

Scarlett looked up, and Elise was startled to see her eyes were red-rimmed. Even her trademark flame-red hair looked like the colour had been desaturated.

'Oh... Hi,' Scarlett muttered, attempting to move past.

Elise hesitated. Every instinct told her to keep walking, to ignore Scarlett, or even to be mad at her after the rumours she'd been spreading. But Elise knew better than anyone how people lashed out when they were wounded. She'd done exactly the same when Aidan had hurt her. And turned to his cousin. She'd picked Finlay to hurt Aidan, just as Scarlett had attacked others when her defences were low. Best not to take it personally.

'Are you ok?' Elise stopped in front of her.

Scarlett didn't meet Elise's eyes. 'Yeah. Fine.'

It was clearly a lie, and for a moment, Elise considered accepting it and continuing on her way. Scarlett wasn't her problem, not unless she was directly affecting the tour. Maybe the rumours had ruffled some feathers, but whatever was going through Scarlett's mind, she was clearly upset, and Elise couldn't in all conscience ignore her.

'Hey,' Elise said. 'I know this trip has been awful for you. I can't begin to imagine how you must feel.'

'Why do you even care?' Scarlett finally looked at her, defiance flickering briefly across her features, before crumbling again. 'It's not like I've been nice to you. I said some stuff about you yesterday. I shouldn't have, and I know now it wasn't true.'

Elise sighed. 'Listen, I heard about it, and it's fine.'

'I'm sorry. I hope you didn't get into trouble because of it. I don't know why I said it. I just thought you were in the room next to me and... Oh god, I shouldn't have been listening, but the walls aren't very thick.'

Elise hoped the heat in her face didn't make her look like a tomato. 'Yeah, well, it wasn't me and Lloyd.'

'I know.' Scarlett hid her face. 'I don't even know why I thought it really. Just when Leon pushed you and you landed on his knee. I'm so dumb sometimes. My head just leaps to conclusions.'

Elise glanced away, trying not to smile. She shouldn't find Scarlett's predicament funny, but sometimes she was so ridiculous. Her reasoning was beyond insane, but possibly not any crazier than Elise actually having been with Gabe.

'Just let it go,' she said. 'Hopefully the gossips had fun chatting about it.' And more to the point, she hoped Lloyd had stamped out the rumours to his mother. Poor man getting caught up in this.

Scarlett stared at her for a long moment, then her face crumpled. 'I don't know what I'm doing anymore.' The words tumbled out in a rush. 'With anything. I thought this trip would be fun. A chance to get away, spend time with my boyfriend.' She wiped at her eyes angrily. 'But now Leon's gone, and I'm... Well, I don't know. It's all so confusing.'

Elise wasn't sure what to say, but in this moment, she understood some of Scarlett's turmoil.

'Breakups can do that anyway, but the way it happened to you was particularly harsh. I mean, with everyone watching and then being trapped on a coach. You've done well to stick it out. Most people would have given up and left the tour.'

'Yeah.' Scarlett wiped her eyes with the back of her hand. 'I'm glad I stayed... I think.' She squinted over her shoulder towards the loch. Elise looked too. Someone else was coming up the path, and it was obvious in a second who it was.

Gabe. Looking edible as always in his navy short-sleeved Henley, open at the neck just enough to show his tanned chest.

Scarlett quickly wiped away the last traces of tears. 'I—I should go.'

'But—' Elise began, but she'd already dashed away towards the wooden toilet cabin set back among the trees.

'Is she ok?' Gabe gestured towards Scarlett. 'She looked upset.'

'She's just having a rough time.'

'That Leon has a lot to answer for.'

'He really does.' Elise frowned after her. 'But it's not really my place to say more.'

'You want to walk down and see if she's ok?'

'Yeah, let's do that.' They headed down the path.

'She's always been a bit of a mess,' Gabe said. 'Kind of unpredictable. And this week isn't going to help her mentally.'

'I hope she's got friends who stand by her.'

He let out a long sigh. 'I'm not sure. It sounds cruel to say this, but she's broken up with so many people over the years – friends and boyfriends. You know how awful she was to Lilah at school and when Lilah first started seeing Aidan.'

'I guess that's all forgotten now.'

'Lilah's a very kind and generous person. She saw a way to forgive Scarlett. And Scarlett's lucky because Lilah's a good friend to her now. Possibly one of the few she has left.'

Elise bit her lip. She understood Scarlett even more now. Sometimes it was easier to cut and run, but not always nicer.

'Poor girl.'

'Yeah. It can't be easy without friends.' He glanced down at her. 'I don't know where I'd be without Aidan.'

The way he looked at her made something flutter in her chest, but she sensed his conflict. Everything he desired with her would hurt the friend he was so loyal to.

They'd reached the little toilet block, and Elise went into the ladies' side. Both cubicle doors were open and Scarlett wasn't in either of them.

Elise returned to Gabe. 'She's not there.' Another path led through the woods back towards the shore.

'Maybe she went down there. Let's go see.' Gabe ran a hand through his hair. 'By the way, I was looking for you for a reason.'

'Oh?' Elise raised an eyebrow. 'Has something else happened?'

He huffed out a laugh. 'Not exactly.'

'Well, spit it out.'

'A few of the guests approached me... My "fans".' He air-quoted. 'They asked me to lead some sort of impromptu wildlife hunt this afternoon.'

'And you don't want to?'

'I half thought that if I did it, maybe they'd lay off a bit. Though that could backfire completely.'

'I see what you mean.' She nodded. 'If you give them an appropriate time to talk to you, they might not bother you as much at other times.'

He gazed back at the loch for a moment. 'Exactly. But I don't want to step on your toes. You're the guide, after all.'

Elise blinked. That was his concern? 'I don't mind,' she said. 'If the guests want it, and you're willing, I don't see the problem.'

'Well...' He shifted a little. 'I'm not actually... that confident with groups.'

She couldn't help the small snort of laughter that escaped her. 'Really? I find that hard to believe.'

'Honestly.' His bright blue eyes met hers with an almost pleading look. 'With the podcasts, it's just me and a microphone. I talk about the things I love, the research I've done. But I'm not interacting with real people in real time.'

Elise studied him. Was that genuine vulnerability beneath his confident exterior? Kind of disarming and strange.

'I don't know what to do with a group,' he continued. 'How to keep them engaged, how to manage different interests and personalities. That's your strength, not mine.'

'You think?'

'I know. I've seen you doing it for the past few days. Maybe we could do it together? Combine our strengths?'

Elise pulled a face. 'I'm not exactly a nature enthusiast.'

'But you're a brilliant guide,' he said. 'You know how to read people, how to keep them interested. How to make them feel included.'

Her cheeks warmed at the praise, but not just from pleasure. There was something almost sharp in the way it landed – like an unexpected prod to a bruise. *Brilliant*. That word didn't quite sit right. Not when it described the carefully curated version of her she presented on these trips, always confident, cheerful, and composed. It was the professional mask she'd polished over years of faking it. Because people liked that Elise. They listened to her and didn't look too closely – didn't try to get past the surface.

'I don't know about "brilliant",' she said lightly, though her throat had gone a little tight.

'Well, I do,' he said. 'You've handled everything this week perfectly.'

She managed a smile. 'Except for the way I've behaved with you.'

'All consensual and I won't breathe a word.'

'Thanks.' She swallowed, the word catching as it went down. It was kind of him to say so, but always felt a little strange, being seen for the performance and not the person beneath it – the person who didn't always know what the hell she was doing in her personal life, who ruined things when they got too real. The one who didn't trust people to see her without the act, even though he'd had a glimpse of it, and was still saying these things. Analysing it would make her head spin. It was already a little overwhelming.

'What exactly would this wildlife hunt involve?' She steered the conversation away before her feelings tangled any further.

'Nothing complicated. Just a walk around the loch edge, pointing out native species, maybe some tracks if we're lucky. I can handle the information part. I just need you to...'

'People?'

'Exactly.' He returned her smile, and something warm flickered in her chest.

'I suppose we could give it a go.' She stopped, shielding her eyes and looking around. 'If that's what people are looking for. I aim to please after all.'

'You certainly do.' He gave her a little wink.

'Though I warn you now, if anyone asks me a question about wildlife, I'm pointing them straight to you.'

'Deal.' His smile widened, and he stepped forward, wrapping his arms around her in a bracing hug.

The contact was unexpected, and Elise froze for a moment, caught off guard by both the gesture and her body's response to it. He was warm and solid against her, his arms strong around her shoulders. She moved her hands around him and held on. The heat of the embrace filled her from the soul out, nourishing dormant parts of her and reminding her she was more than just a façade. She had emotions, spirit, heart. All of them awoke in this hug and she felt more alive than she had done in ages.

And more than that – something in the way he held her felt genuine. Like he wasn't holding the version of her that charmed tourists or kept conversations flowing with surface sparkle. He was holding *her*. The real her. And he wasn't flinching from it.

But would the feeling last if she let go? Because she couldn't stand here forever. And for all she knew, this hug might be a one-off.

Chapter Seventeen

Gabe

Gabe waited at the edge of the loch while the coach party finished their lunch at the lochside café. He had agreed to this nature walk – voluntarily – which still shocked him slightly. Elise wandered over, her dark hair catching the light. She raised an eyebrow at him.

'You're either brave or crazy volunteering for this.' She nudged a small stone on the ground off the path with her walking boot.

'The latter, I think.' Gabe grinned, nodding towards the outer deck of the café where his three fans were lifting bags and jackets like they were getting ready to leave and head over.

'Well, I hope your little gamble pays off and they won't be on your case for the rest of the week after this.'

'Me too.' He crossed his fingers.

'Did you ask Aidan about Scarlett?'

They hadn't found her when they came back down the path. Gabe had checked with Aidan and Lilah. Neither of them were coming on the walk. They were going to take a canoe out again after lunch.

'Lilah said Scarlett had texted, saying she was walking the other way around the loch with a couple of other passengers.'

'Who?' Elise frowned.

'I'm not sure. Aidan's going to call her and check she's ok. But she sent some photos to Lilah and apparently she seemed ok.'

'I thought she seemed on the verge of a breakdown,' Elise said.

'Remember she went off with Lloyd in the canoe earlier? Maybe she's got pally with him.'

Elise raised her eyebrows. 'Can you think of a less likely duo?'

Gabe smirked. 'Us?'

She laughed. 'Hmm... Nope, I think they would still take the cake.'

'Well, Aidan reckons the real Gabe Wilder has been abducted and replaced with someone else. The genuine article would never voluntarily go anywhere with Elise Reid, let alone spend an afternoon showing his adoring fans the local wildlife.'

'Is that what he said?' She raised an eyebrow.

'Yup. He thinks I've suffered a minor brain injury or possibly been hypnotised.' Gabe tapped his temple. 'Can't blame him, really. Until a few days ago, I'd have agreed with him.'

She gave a little laugh, glanced around the space, then whispered. 'What's happening to us?'

Gabe took her hand and squeezed it. 'I don't know, but god, I want you,' he murmured. 'It's driving me mad. I never thought I'd see the day you and I needed each other like this.'

She withdrew her hand. 'Yeah, it's wild.'

'Isn't it?' He craned his neck, watching the approaching fans. 'Can I see you again, then?'

Elise's expression fell. 'We need to be careful, Gabe. This is how people get burned.' She looked away. 'And I would know. I've done the burning before.'

'I'm a big boy, Elise. I can handle a holiday fling.'

'That's what everyone thinks – until they can't.' Her eyes met his again.

'I'm an activist.' He tipped her a wink. 'I like a bit of danger.' He peered over her shoulder. 'Though not with this lot.'

Elise seamlessly transformed into the consummate tour guide.

'Perfect timing,' she said brightly to a couple who'd arrived at the meeting point from the café. 'We're just about to get started.'

More people were making their way over. The woman he now knew to be Lloyd's mother marched up to them with determined strides.

'I hope this walk isn't too strenuous,' she said. 'Lloyd's gone off for a hike, which is way beyond me these days, and I don't want this to be something unsuitable too.'

'It's a gentle route, Rita,' Elise assured her. 'Mostly flat paths with beautiful views of the loch.'

Rita peered at her and pursed her lips. Perhaps she still wasn't one hundred per cent convinced Elise hadn't been sleeping with her son. The idea made Gabe smirk, though it probably shouldn't.

Gabe spotted his self-proclaimed fan club approaching and mentally braced himself.

'There he is,' the tallest one tittered. 'He's so handsome.'

Gabe cringed. That was clearly an attempt at a low voice, but everyone on the island probably heard her. He caught Elise's eye and saw her press her lips together to suppress a smile. He narrowed his eyes at her in mock threat.

A few more people joined the group and Elise stood on a patch of higher ground and looked around. 'I think that's everyone who wanted to come. Sixteen altogether. Perfect.' She clapped her hands once to get everyone's attention. 'Welcome to this lochside nature walk!' she began. 'We're very lucky to have a celebrity with us on our trip' – she gestured towards Gabe – 'Gabriel Wilder, the well-known activist and eco blogger. We've all seen his podcasts, *Wilder at Heart*, and know about his love of wildlife and the outdoors. He's kindly agreed to share his expertise with us today.'

Gabe gave a little wave at this rather gushing introduction.

'Just a friendly reminded that Gabriel is also on holiday, so once this walk is done, it's only fair to give him his personal space. If you have burning questions or anything you'd like to chat to him about, this is the place to do it, then he can enjoy his break like the rest of you.'

He watched her with a slight quirk of his lip. None of that was strictly necessary, but Gabe felt a rush of warmth towards her for even trying.

'Before we set off, just a few quick safety points,' Elise continued. 'We'll be staying on marked paths, but some sections might be a bit muddy or uneven, so take care. And let us know if you need to stop for any reason.'

She turned to Gabe with a smile. 'Anything you'd like to add before we start?'

'Just that this area is home to some incredible wildlife.' He slipped into his own professional tone. 'We might spot red deer, otters, and various bird species if we're lucky, not to mention a lot of insects, including dragonflies. The key is to move quietly and keep your eyes open.'

A woman with a large camera perked up. 'What about eagles?'

'It's possible,' Gabe nodded. 'Golden eagles and white-tailed sea eagles hunt in this area. No guarantees, but we'll keep watch.'

Elise led them onto the path that wound around the loch. Gabe fell into step beside her at the front, hyperaware of her presence just inches away, fighting an urge to reach for her hand.

'You're good at this,' he murmured, low enough that only she could hear.

'So are you,' she replied, her eyes fixed ahead on the path. 'Very professional.'

The path curved gently alongside the loch, offering spectacular views of the water and the mountains beyond. Under different circumstances, Gabe would have been fully absorbed in the landscape, pointing out interesting flora and watching for wildlife. Instead, he found his attention divided between his surroundings, the presence of Elise beside him, and the growing awareness that his fan club was manoeuvring to get closer to him.

They managed it within ten minutes, somehow sliding past an elderly couple and Rita until they were directly behind Gabe and Elise.

'Gabriel,' one woman said, slightly breathless from the effort of catching up. 'What got you interested in nature initially?'

It was a question he'd answered hundreds of times in interviews, but he gave his standard response. 'I grew up in a small town surrounded by beautiful countryside. I was the kid always coming home with frogs in my pockets and mud in my hair.'

'How charming.' Another woman chuckled. 'You must have been an adorable little boy.'

'I think my mother would use different words.' Gabe laughed.

'Do you have any children yourself?' The third woman asked.

'No.'

'Not married?'

'Nope.'

'Girlfriend?' The first grinned. If she was hopeful, she was also out of luck.

'I'm very focused on my work.' Gabe turned to Elise and pulled a face only she could see, then pointed towards a stand of trees. 'If you look over there, those silver birches are home to woodpeckers. You might hear them if we're quiet for a moment.'

A transparent attempt to change the subject, yes, but thankfully Elise picked up on it.

'Let's pause here and listen.' She held up her hand, bringing the group to a halt.

They fell silent.

After about thirty seconds, the first woman, who had on very large sunglasses, leaned closer.

'What's your favourite animal to spot, Gabriel?'

'Probably otters. They're a lot of fun, playful but shy. It's always special to see them.'

'Just like you.' The woman gave him a wink that made him want to disappear into the undergrowth.

Elise made a small choking sound beside him, which she covered with a discreet cough.

'Should we continue?' she suggested.

Gabe nodded, and they resumed walking. The path narrowed slightly, forcing the group to spread out in a longer line. His fan club fell back a few paces, giving him a moment to breathe.

'Enjoying yourself?' Elise murmured.

'Immensely,' he replied dryly. 'Nothing I love more than being compared to an otter.'

'Could be worse,' she said. 'At least otters are cute.'

'Is that what you think of me?'

Her eyes met his briefly. 'Among other things.'

The electricity between them crackled, hopefully invisible to everyone else but impossible for him to ignore. He wanted to pull her off the path and finish what they'd started earlier, but instead he pointed out a heron standing motionless in the shallow water just off the shore.

The path veered away from the loch's edge and into the dappled shade of woodland. Elise moved to help an elderly gentleman over a protruding root. Gabe smiled. He'd always seen her as sharp-edged and calculating – an impression formed largely through Aidan's post-breakup bitterness and his own stubbornness to even consider there might be other sides to the story – but she wasn't really. Not deep down.

'Gabriel, what's this?' A woman called, pointing at something on the ground.

He moved closer, instantly recognising the distinctive print pressed into a patch of mud. 'That's a deer track.' He crouched for a better look. 'A roe deer. See how it's heart-shaped?'

The group gathered around, peering at the indentation. Camera Woman knelt beside Gabe, snapping close-ups.

He stood up, brushing dirt from his hands, and found Elise watching him. He smiled at her before they started walking again.

They soon came to a small stream cutting across the path. It wasn't wide – perhaps two feet across – but slippery stones and muddy banks made it tricky to cross for some of the less sure footed of the group.

'Careful here,' Elise said. 'Take your time crossing.'

Gabe automatically positioned himself in the middle of the stream, offering a hand to each person as they crossed. Most managed with little trouble, though Camera Woman nearly lost her balance when she tried to cross one-handed while protecting her expensive equipment.

When it was Elise's turn, she pulled a face. Her walking boots were clearly new.

'Not your natural habitat?' Gabe extended his hand, and Elise took it.

'Definitely not.'

The now familiar spark from the contact jolted him. Her hand was smaller than his, but her grip was firm as she placed one foot carefully on the first stepping stone.

'I've got you.'

Elise glanced up, meeting his eyes. 'I know.' She crossed the remaining distance with his guidance, but neither of them immediately let go once she reached the other side.

When he refocused on the group, he saw Rita eyeing him with an unfriendly expression.

He held up a hand for silence, then pointed. About thirty yards away, a roe deer stood motionless in a shaft of sunlight, its tawny coat glowing against the dark green backdrop. Its large ears twitched, alert for danger.

The group froze collectively. Even his fan club managed to contain their excitement to hushed gasps.

The deer stepped delicately through the undergrowth, pausing to nibble at a low-hanging leaf before disappearing into the trees.

'That was so cute.' Elise stared at the spot where the deer had been.

'It never gets old,' Gabe said, though they were pretty common really, even around Glenbriar; it was amazing how many people had rarely seen them or noticed them.

The path curved back towards the loch as they neared the end of their circuit. 'This looks like a good view,' he said. 'A little bay perfect for otters, sheltered, with plenty of fish.'

'Will we see one?' Camera Woman asked.

'No guarantees,' Gabe said. 'Sometimes you can sit out for hours watching for them and they never appear. Other times you get lucky.' His eyes met with Elise's again and something tugged in his chest, not lust, something deeper, like affection. Which was weird... And very dangerous. He'd been an affectionate child and look at what had happened. The two people he used to love getting hugs and kisses from had grown distant. His father was an arsehole, and his mother had so many barriers that, even if he did hug her, her emotions were so trapped inside, he felt little warmth. She made every excuse under the sun for his father, her favourite one being, 'At least he's not a cheat.' Which seemed to give him carte blanche to be a prick in every other area.

Gabe led the group to a grassy bank overlooking the small bay. The water was calm, reflecting the surrounding hills like a mirror. A fallen tree created a natural barrier where they could sit or lean without being too visible from the water. His eye caught something promising, fresh marks on a muddy section of shore. He pointed them out to Camera Woman, who nodded appreciatively and aimed her lens in that direction.

Minutes passed in silence. Even his fan club was absorbed in the quiet intensity of wildlife watching. Gabe used his binoculars to scan the water's edge methodically, moving from one end of the bay to the other.

Beside him, Elise stood so close their arms brushed now and then, each fleeting touch sparking heat across his skin. When he handed her the binoculars, their fingers met – quite deliberately. Whether by accident or intent, he kept edging closer, answering the pull inside him that wanted nothing more than to close the distance.

'Look along the far shore,' he whispered, his lips close to her ear. 'By that cluster of rocks.'

She adjusted the focus, leaning into him as she steadied herself. 'I don't see. Oh!'

Gabe smiled. Even without the binoculars, he saw the ripple in the water, a V-shaped wake moving steadily across the surface. A sleek, dark head emerged.

'There...' Gabe whispered, pointing for the benefit of the others.

A collective intake of breath swept through the group as the otter surfaced fully, twisting sinuously in the water before diving again with barely a splash.

'It's fishing,' Gabe said as they waited for it to reappear. 'They can hold their breath for up to four minutes but usually resurface much sooner.'

Sure enough, the otter popped up about thirty seconds later, this time with something wriggling in its mouth. It swam to a flat rock jutting from the water and hauled itself out, the fish still thrashing in its jaws.

'Aw, look at it,' Elise said, still watching through the binoculars.

The otter finished its meal and slipped back into the water, disappearing with barely a ripple. Everyone waited, hoping it might return, but after several minutes of watching, Gabe suspected the show was over.

He glanced around at the group, noting their rapt expressions. Even Rita looked interested. His gaze lingered on Elise, who was still scanning the water hopefully, the binoculars raised to her eyes.

While everyone's attention remained fixed on the loch, Gabe gently touched Elise's elbow.

'Can I talk to you for a second?' he murmured.

She lowered the binoculars, looking at him questioningly, but nodded and followed as he stepped back from the group, moving just far enough away to be out of earshot while still keeping the others in view.

'What is it?' she asked. 'Did you spot another one?'

'No, I wanted to ask you something.'

A slight furrow appeared between her brows. 'Ok?'

'Um... Do you...?' He ran his hand through his hair, not at all sure what it was he wanted to ask. There seemed to be questions hovering in his mind, but he couldn't catch one. 'Can I see you later?'

She raised an eyebrow. 'Didn't we already agree to that?'

'You didn't give me a proper answer.'

'Then yes, you can.'

Gabe rubbed the back of his neck. 'Good.'

'Is that all?'

It wasn't. Not by a long shot. But the words wouldn't come – how could he explain feelings that barely made sense to himself?

What he did know was this: some things were worth fighting for. Even if he couldn't put a name to it, even if all it bought him was a couple more days, this – *she* – was one of them. And right now, that felt like enough.

Chapter Eighteen

An early night called. Or so Elise had told Kev. She may be in bed early, but not to sleep.

Sitting down on the edge of the mattress, she let out a long, slow breath. Was she being completely ridiculous? Part of her knew she was, but the desperation and hunger for Gabe was real. It burned from the inside out like a craving she couldn't satisfy. What if she still went on feeling like this once the tour was over?

Well, she'd have to put herself on short rations again. She could have him in the here and now, and that must be enough. Just this once, she could let herself want something without apology.

Today had gone surprisingly well, despite getting wet after the canoeing. Hopefully her little spiel to the 'fans' would stop them pestering him anymore, though she wasn't convinced.

A soft knock at the door made her heart leap. She got to her feet and opened it.

'Hey.' Gabe smiled as he slipped in. His trademark black Henley hugged his chest, and his dark hair was damp and smelled of tangy shampoo.

She closed the door behind him. 'Have you recovered from today?'

'Yeah.' He ruffled up his hair. 'The fan club didn't bother me at dinner time, so I think your little speech might have worked.'

'I hope so, though they probably hate me for it.' Well, she was used to being the 'baddy', so it wouldn't exactly change her life. But for once, it hadn't felt like a performance. She'd spoken up for someone else, and it had meant something.

'Their loss then,' he said.

'Says you, who has spent years hating me.'

'Exactly. And that was my loss.' His hand found her waist, warm through the thin fabric of her black-and-white short sundress. She looked up, meeting his eyes, seeing the heat there.

'And now, I need to make up for lost time. Instead of hating you, I'm going to worship you.'

'I definitely like the sound of that more.'

He claimed her mouth, and she rose on her toes, pressing closer, hands skimming the firm planes of his chest. The kiss deepened, tongues tangling, sparks igniting in her veins. His hands slid to her bum, pulling her tight against him – and the hard evidence of his desire sent a heady rush of power through her.

'I've been thinking about this all day,' he murmured against her lips.

'About what?' She nipped lightly at his bottom lip.

His hands tightened on her. 'About what I'm going to do with you.' He walked her backwards until her legs hit the bed. His fingers found the thin straps of her sundress, sliding them down her shoulders. The fabric dropped to her waist, revealing her black bra. His laser-blue eyes darkened as they swept over her.

Elise smiled and reached for the hem of his Henley, tugging upward.

He helped her remove it, tossing it aside. She placed her palm against his sternum, feeling his heartbeat beneath her hand.

'What else have you been thinking about?' she asked.

He answered with another kiss, easing her dress down. It pooled at her feet, leaving her in just her bra and knickers. He mapped her sides, her back, and the curve of her waist with gentle touches.

'That you're beautiful,' he breathed. 'And not at all like the person I thought you were.'

For a heartbeat, Elise froze. Her first instinct was to laugh it off, to joke or deflect – but the sincerity in his voice held her still. Could he really see past the mask? Past the walls she'd built to keep herself safe? The ache in her chest was almost unbearable – because she wanted him to see her. Not the version she performed, but the messy, guarded, craving heart beneath.

Elise worked at his belt. 'How does this come off?' she muttered.

He chuckled, helping her with the buckle, then the button of his jeans. 'Impatient.'

'Tomorrow is the last day,' she reminded him. The week had flown despite how much she'd dreaded it. Soon, these stolen moments would end. 'We have to make the most of it.'

'Yes, we do.' He shifted onto the bed, taking her with him, a tangle of limbs and half-removed clothing, mouths seeking, hands exploring. His jeans were gone, then her bra, then his boxers. Skin against skin, the delicious friction of it making her gasp into his mouth.

'Oh god,' she moaned.

He slowed, his palms and fingertips skimming over her skin in teasing, circling movements. His mouth left hers to plant slow, deliberate kisses along her neck, down to her collarbone, then lower, to the swell of her breast. Each touch was fire, each kiss a brand.

And all the time, his eyes kept finding hers, checking, confirming, connecting. Those eyes had a voice of their own. They were having a conversation without words, and Elise responded viscerally with each question asked.

When his mouth closed around her nipple, she arched off the bed. His hand trailed down her stomach, fingers playing at the waistband of her knickers.

As he slid the fabric down her legs, she gasped, the vulnerability oddly welcome now. His mouth continued its journey downward, past her ribs, across her stomach. Each press of his lips sent tingles radiating outward. Her breath caught as his stubble grazed the sensitive skin of her inner thigh. Then his eyes met hers again, steady and searching, and something inside her fluttered.

'Is this ok?'

She nodded. 'Yes, but don't ask me anything else... I can't think straight.'

His smile was slow. 'Good.' He pressed a kiss to her hipbone. 'That's the general idea.'

Gabe settled between her thighs, nudging them wider. Elise felt suddenly, acutely vulnerable – but also safe. And more than that... desired. Wanted. Cherished.

Christ's sake. It was just sex, right? Even if it was the best sex ever, that was all it was. Nothing more.

Her eyes fluttered closed, her head falling back against the pillow. Gabe took his time, finding the places that made her breath hitch and her fingers tighten in his hair. Her hips moved instinctively, seeking more.

He knew exactly what he was doing, reading her reactions. Elise's core clenched, heat spiralling through her – and it went beyond pleasure.

Maybe it was the way he kept glancing up at her, keeping that connection alive. Maybe it was the tenderness mixed into every stroke of his tongue, every firm, focused caress.

Or maybe it was something else entirely... something she couldn't name. Couldn't control.

His hand found hers, their fingers tangling against the rumpled sheet. She squeezed instinctively, and he answered by increasing the pressure, anchoring her with touch and rhythm until all thought fell away.

'Oh god,' she breathed, her thighs beginning to tremble. Gabe's eyes remained locked on hers. Elise felt stripped bare under that gaze. In the past, it would have frightened her.

Instead, it pushed her over the edge.

Intense and all-consuming waves crashed over her. Her back arched, her hand tightening in his, her other hand fisted in the sheets. The exquisite release was almost painful.

When Gabe finally moved back up her body, Elise's limbs were heavy, her mind a haze. He kissed her and gathered her close against his warm chest.

It should have felt strange – sharing this, with him of all people.

But it didn't. It felt right. Natural. As if they'd been doing this for years instead of days.

'I want you,' she murmured against his lips. 'All of you.'

'You have me.'

And in that moment, with her body still thrumming and his weight a comforting presence above her, Elise let herself believe he meant it.

Just for now, it could be real.

She reached between them, wrapping her fingers around him, feeling a surge of satisfaction at his sharp intake of breath. His skin was hot against her palm as she stroked him slowly.

'Jesus,' he groaned, pressing his forehead to hers, then kissed her again, deeper this time. Elise arched into him.

He stopped for a moment, eyes holding hers and he just looked at her. Elise's heart hammered. So much seemed to go on in that look, and all she could do was gaze back.

Then he let go and rolled to the edge of the bed, reaching for protection in his wallet. He wrestled to get it out of the pocket of his discarded jeans.

When he returned to her, condom in place, Elise felt a moment of perfect clarity. This wasn't just physical... Or convenience or proximity. This was something neither of them had expected, something that had taken root despite their history and all the reasons it shouldn't work.

And it was beautiful. It existed completely out of context, allowing them to be what they wanted to be without having to worry about what happened next... Not yet anyway.

He moved inside her slowly, their bodies wrapped in a deep embrace, lips locked in a kiss that felt endless. The pace was unhurried, each measured thrust stoking the delicious, mounting tension between them. When Elise shifted to straddle him, the connection deepened – their mouths still tangled, tongues echoing the same slow rhythm as their bodies.

Then, making her gasp, he sat up and positioned her on his lap. His hands at her waist, he held her, so she was facing him just as he'd done the first time they were together. The position brought them chest to chest, face to face, intimately aligned.

There was nowhere to hide in this position, no way to avoid his focus, to pretend this was just bodies seeking pleasure.

'Is this ok?' He anchored his hands on her hips.

She nodded. Their faces were inches apart, his breath mingling with hers. His pupils were blown out, darkening his astonishingly blue irises. Her arms wound around his neck, drawing him even closer.

'Christ, Elise,' he muttered, his forehead dropping to rest against hers.

For a moment, neither of them moved, adjusting to the sensation, to the overwhelming intimacy of the position.

When she finally began to move, it was a gentle rock of her hips, a testing of the waters. His hands spanned her waist, guiding her, supporting her. The friction was exquisite.

The way he was watching her almost undid her.

Their movements remained unhurried. Every thrust, every roll of their hips was significant, meaningful.

Gabe's hands roamed her back, her sides, cupping her breasts, and touching her where she needed. She returned the exploration, her palms sliding over the firm muscles of his shoulders, down his arms, feeling them flex as he moved with her.

Another peak was building inside her – inevitable, unstoppable. Gabe's eyes, fixed on hers, darkened with intensity, and she knew he was close too. He threaded his fingers through hers, raising their joined hands, and she gripped him tightly. Focusing on him like this felt almost tantric. It was unlike anything she was used to.

A particularly deep thrust sent a shudder through her. She was hyperaware of every point of contact – their locked hands, his chest against hers, his breath on her face, the steady pulse of him inside her.

He leaned forward and kissed her – and it was like a switch had been flipped. She shattered. Release surged through her like a tidal wave, stealing her breath, her mouth slack against his even as he kissed her.

Dimly, she felt his rhythm falter. His fingers clenched hers, almost painfully. He broke the kiss with a muffled groan, burying his face in her neck as his body tensed. Then, slowly, he softened against her, wrapping his arms around her as she trembled through the aftershocks.

When she could think again, the first thing she registered was the strange sense of completeness.

They remained entwined, neither willing to break the connection just yet, their breathing gradually slowing in tandem.

Gabe lifted his head from her shoulder, his eyes finding hers again. The look in them made her chest tighten. He stroked stray hairs from her face and she nuzzled into his palm.

He kissed her again, slow and deep; it felt like a continuation of what they'd just shared rather than the beginning of something new. Elise melted into it, her body still humming with residual pleasure, her mind blissfully empty of everything except the sensations of him against her, inside her, around her.

When they finally separated, it was with reluctance. Gabe helped her lift off him. 'I probably should clean up.'

'Go ahead.' She missed his warmth as soon as he slipped from the bed.

While he was gone, Elise stretched, luxuriating in the pleasant ache of well-used muscles. Would he leave now? Or was there more? She had no idea what time it was, and it didn't seem to matter.

When Gabe came out of the bathroom, he slid back into bed beside her, pulling her close again. His hand drew lazy patterns on her skin, raising goosebumps in its wake. She tucked her head under his chin, listening to the steady thump of his heart. Maybe it would be best not to say anything. She didn't want to mention him leaving in case he took it as a hint and went away. Not that she expected him to stay all night. That wasn't the kind of deal they'd signed up for. But it felt too soon.

'What will you do when you get back?' Gabe asked.

Elise absently ran her fingers over his chest. 'Decide if I want to take the Glenbriar job, I suppose. What about you?'

'I don't really know. My contract with E-Broadcast Scotland is up for renewal. And I'm considering other options too.' His fingers moved to her hair, combing through the dark strands.

She glanced up at him. 'Like what?'

He hesitated. 'Something different. I loved doing the podcasts when they first took off, but I feel like I've said everything I needed to say. And now it's just – expected.'

'So change it. Try something else.'

'Easier said than done.' He gave a soft, humourless laugh. 'There's a fine line between change and giving up. I'm not sure everyone would see the difference.'

Elise frowned, sensing the weight behind his words. 'Anyone who matters would. The rest can sod off.'

He smiled faintly. 'I guess. I've got some family stuff to get out of the way before I decide anything. My parents are going away for a couple of weeks and my mum asked me to house sit. But I hate that bloody house.'

'So, are you not going to do it?'

'I will do, for my mum's sake, though I'm going to camp in the grounds. I can't live in that house. Not even for a day. Not when I know my bastard of a father owns it.'

'That must be really hard.'

'Yup. If it was just my mum, it would be fine. But she's too under his spell. She'll never leave him. I don't want to lose her or cut ties with her but seeing her without him there too is almost impossible. He's so controlling he won't let her go out on her own. I don't even like it when she mentions him – which she does. She can't help herself, but it puts me right on edge. She refuses to acknowledge the disgusting way he treats her.'

'I never get why people stay in toxic relationships.'

'Me neither.'

'I guess lots of people think I'm toxic.'

He pulled her a little tighter. 'You made mistakes, sure. But you faced them. You changed. My mother won't even admit there's a problem. And Scarlett... she just repeats the same patterns over and over. Breaking a cycle takes guts. And you've done that.'

'Not really. I've just stopped trying to have long-term relationships.'

'Maybe that is breaking the cycle. Choosing yourself instead of clinging to someone else. That's not nothing.'

She nuzzled into him as a swell of emotion caught in her throat. She didn't trust herself to speak.

'I'm sorry,' he said quietly.

'For what?'

'For how I was. After you and Aidan split up.'

'You were just being loyal to your friend.'

'Partly. But mostly, I was a judgmental prick who couldn't be arsed to look beyond the gossip. I didn't give you a chance.'

She lifted her head just enough to meet his eyes. 'Apology accepted.'

He pressed a kiss to her forehead, and Elise let herself sink into his arms. The silence between them was soft now, not empty. A shared understanding, wordless and solid, settled over them like a blanket. For the first time in longer than she could remember, she felt steady. Safe. And maybe, just maybe, enough.

She closed her eyes and let the warmth of it lull her toward sleep.

CHAPTER NINETEEN

Elise

Elise hadn't meant to fall asleep. That had been their first rule, no overnight stays, no complicated mornings. But somewhere between their conversation and the comforting cuddles, consciousness had slipped away. Now, morning light was filtering through the gap in the curtains, painting a stripe of gold across the rumpled sheets. And Gabe was still there, his breathing deep and even, one arm flung across her waist as if to keep her from escaping.

She glanced at the clock on the bedside table. Six-forty-two. How had she slept this long without interruption? There seemed no urgency to wake him. Having him here was kind of like a treat. A strand of hair had fallen across his forehead, and without thinking, she reached out to brush it back.

The touch, light as it was, roused him. His eyes opened slowly, and he raised his head from the pillow, focusing on her with momentary confusion.

'Is it morning?' he mumbled.

'Yeah…' she replied, suddenly aware of her morning breath, her tangled hair, and her complete nakedness.

Gabe blinked, glancing towards the window. 'Shit.' He sat up abruptly. 'I'm sorry… I wasn't supposed to do this.'

'We both fell asleep.'

He ran a hand through his dishevelled hair. 'I didn't mean to break the rules.'

The rules.

'It's fine.' She gave a little shrug.

Gabe nodded, but he was already reaching for his boxers, discarded on the floor. 'I'll go. Hopefully no one else is up yet. I'll sneak out before it gets busy in the corridor.'

He dressed quickly, glanced at the door, then leaned forward and kissed her, a gentle press of lips that almost felt more intimate than the sex last night.

'See you at breakfast.'

She watched him as he crossed the room, checked the hallway, then snuck out, the door clicking shut behind him.

Elise fell back against the pillows, her mind in a tangle. They'd broken their first and most important rule. But weirdly, she wasn't as bothered by it as she should be.

She dragged herself out of bed and into the shower, letting the hot water sluice away the physical evidence of their night together. As she washed her hair, she found herself thinking only of Gabe. How much her opinion of him had changed over the last couple of days. Would she go back to her old way of thinking when they got back to Glenbriar tomorrow? Or would he take time to get over?

Today's itinerary was sightseeing, with a lot of on-and-off coach travel. She applied her makeup carefully before heading downstairs for breakfast.

In the corridor, she saw Lilah outside the door next to hers. 'Are you coming?' Lilah asked.

From inside, she heard Scarlett's voice. 'Not yet.'

Lilah frowned, catching Elise's eye.

Scarlett's voice came again. 'I will be soon. You go on. I'll meet you there.'

'Everything ok?' Elise smiled at Lilah, though a faint awkwardness lingered between them. They'd never really been friends – unsurprisingly. Elise hadn't taken Lilah seriously when she first got together with Aidan. She'd seemed too young. Too different from the kind of woman Elise had once convinced herself was Aidan's type – someone like her.

But it was Lilah who had received the love Elise had always longed for.

And the truth she'd never dared admit was that Aidan had probably *tried* to love her like that, back when they were still figuring each other out. But she hadn't known how to let him. She'd held herself at a distance, mistaking self-protection for strength. She hadn't recognised the difference between someone loving her, and her actually *letting herself be loved*.

She hadn't been cold, exactly. Just... unreachable.

And Aidan, for all his patience, had eventually stopped reaching.

'Yeah. Just checking Scarlett's ok,' Lilah said. 'She keeps missing meals. We thought she might sleep in and miss the coach. But it sounds like she's awake at least.'

'Yeah, this hasn't been an easy week for her.'

Lilah nodded, then headed along the corridor to her own room.

The breakfast room was already half-full when Elise arrived, her professional smile firmly in place. She nodded to several passengers as she made her way to the buffet, loading her plate with eggs and toast. Her eyes scanned the room, landing on Gabe, whose large hands were wrapped around a mug of coffee.

He glanced up as if sensing her gaze, his smile flickering briefly before he looked away. Elise's stomach performed an uncomfortable little flip that had nothing to do with hunger. The distance between them seemed too great all of a sudden, after waking up together.

She took a seat at a small table near the window. The coach needed to leave by nine to fit in all three stops before returning to the hotel for the final dinner.

'Morning.' Kev appeared at the table with a loaded plate and a mug of tea. 'Are you ok for me to sit here?'

'Of course.'

'Thanks.' He settled into the chair. 'You sleep well?'

'Actually, I did. Really well.' Which surprised her, given the fact she'd had Gabe in the bed all night. 'You?'

'Aye, not bad. There was some noisy woman ranting in the corridor at some point, but apart from that, it was fine.'

'I must have missed that. What was she ranting about?'

'Not sure. I was a bit too sleepy to concentrate.'

Elise let out a sigh. 'Let's just hope it wasn't about this trip.'

Aidan and Lilah had joined Gabe now, but there was no sign of Scarlett yet.

'This lady doesn't look happy.' Kev frowned at the door. Elise followed his sightline and saw Rita shaking her head as she made her way over to the buffet. 'I heard her yapping yesterday. Apparently she owns that funny wee bookshop on the station platform in Glenbriar.'

'Does she?' Elise gave a slow nod. 'That's why I recognised her. I've seen her there, though I haven't been there for years.'

'She's getting too old to keep it open – her words. So it might be closing down for good.'

'That would be a shame. It's a cute little place.'

Lloyd appeared behind his mother, running a hand through his hair, seeming a little harassed. Rita leaned in, her brow furrowed, almost like she was scolding him. Elise didn't know his story, but he didn't look like someone who should be on this tour – rather like Gabe and Scarlett. A bit of a misfit. Perhaps he was doing it because his mother wanted him to accompany her. But he wore a wedding ring and looked like a man who had kids –

though Elise wasn't sure what made her think that. He just had dad vibes. So why would he leave his wife and family to go on a coach trip with his mother? All very strange.

Scarlett came in, sucking on her lip, and went straight to Aidan's table, bypassing the buffet. She threw herself down and rested her head in her hand. Whatever she was going through, she'd doubtless be thrilled when this week was over.

At eight-thirty, Elise and Kev left and headed for the coach to make sure everything was set up.

Soon the passengers began to arrive, and Kev opened the doors, letting them board.

'Good morning, everyone,' Elise said into the microphone, once everyone was seated 'Today is our final day on the beautiful Isle of Skye. We've got three spectacular stops planned: Neist Point, Kilt Rock, and the Quiraing. Then we'll return for our farewell dinner this evening.'

She launched into details about their first destination as Kev rolled the coach out of the hotel gates.

The drive to Neist Point took them along winding roads past stunning landscapes. Elise pointed out landmarks along the way, filling the journey with information and the occasional anecdote. By the time they reached the parking area for the lighthouse, she'd almost convinced herself she was back to normal. She could do this – get over Gabe. Yes. He wouldn't affect her once they were apart.

'We have one hour here,' she announced. 'The walk to the lighthouse takes about twenty minutes each way, so that leaves time for photos and enjoying the views.'

The passengers dispersed, cameras at the ready, exclaiming over the dramatic cliffs and the distant lighthouse. Elise hung back, making sure everyone understood the directions and timing. From the corner of her eye, she spotted Gabe chatting with Aidan and laughing.

The path to Neist Point was steep in places but offered breathtaking views of the sea. Elise breathed in the crisp air, letting it clear her head. She took a couple of photos for passengers who wanted to be in the frame, answered questions about the history of the lighthouse, and kept an eye on the time.

Doing her job. Being professional. Not thinking about Gabe.

Except she was. But she couldn't get close to him. It hadn't bothered her before, but each moment he was with someone else felt wasted.

An hour later, they were back on the coach, heading towards Kilt Rock. Elise kept her eyes on the passing scenery as she spoke into the microphone. 'We're now travelling along the Trotternish Peninsula, home to some of Skye's most iconic landscapes. Kilt Rock is named for its resemblance to a pleated kilt, with vertical basalt columns resembling the pleats and intrusions of sill forming the pattern.'

Kev stopped the coach, and Elise repeated her safety speech on rote. The group headed towards the viewpoint to look out over the impressive cliff formation and the waterfall that plunged dramatically into the sea below.

Elise kept her eye on the passengers, and everyone seemed happy. Even Scarlett looked slightly better. Beside her were Lloyd and Rita. Maybe the sea air had magical healing properties because there was nothing but smiles.

The day continued in much the same vein at the Quiraing. Everyone seemed in good spirits and nothing untoward happened. Gabe's fan club members were all behaving well, and he seemed to be chatting to them a little bit more relaxed than before, though Elise couldn't see properly as she was at the back of the group.

'Would you mind taking our photo?' one of the older women in the group handed her a phone.

'Of course.' Elise snapped them, her heart swelling. Maybe if she was very lucky she'd grow old with someone who smiled at her the way this woman's husband smiled at her.

Though she didn't have that much hope.

Later on, when the group returned to the coach, everyone looked a little weary. The drive back to the hotel was quiet, a few passengers dozing off. Elise sat silently beside Kev, watching the landscape roll by.

Elise changed into a simple black dress for the final dinner. How quickly this week had gone by. She'd gone from not wanting to be here to not wanting it to end so soon.

The hotel owner had set up the dining room for their farewell dinner with white tablecloths, candles in glass holders, and small flower arrangements on each table. Elise chatted with the owner as the passengers began to make their way in.

'Nice spread.' Kev appeared at Elise's elbow in a pressed shirt that looked slightly too tight around his neck. 'Very nicely done.' He smiled at the owner.

'No problem. You two grab your seats and I'll make sure everyone gets a table.'

Elise and Kev took a table near the wall. From here she could see almost everyone, and she watched as the tables filled.

Gabe entered with Aidan and Lilah, all laughing at something. When he glanced her way, he gave her a brief, almost sad, smile.

'The salmon looks good,' Kev said.

'Mmm,' she replied. 'I was thinking the same.'

At the door, Scarlett had appeared and was wearing a dramatic red dress that matched her hair – and her name. Rita came up behind her with narrowed eyes, shaking her head. She marched up to Scarlett and, in a voice that carried across the whole room, said, 'You have been nothing but trouble. Acting like a... a tart.' She spat out the word and Scarlett stepped back, eyes widening.

Elise leapt to her feet, heading straight for the door. 'Ladies,' she said, 'I think—'

'I don't care what you think,' Rita said. 'This girl has been putting it about, leading my son up the garden path...'

'What?' Elise and Scarlett said together.

'I don't need to listen to this.' Scarlett stormed off. She froze as Lloyd appeared, then sidestepped him and ran up the stairs.

'And you're no better.' Rita turned to Elise. 'I saw that activist man leaving your room this morning. Disgraceful way to behave when you're supposed to be working.'

'Mother.' Lloyd put his hand on her arm. 'Please, stop.' He gently led her away from the door.

Elise stared after them, her pulse throbbing at her temple. This was not the way she wanted the tour to end. Not after the day had gone so well. She half closed her eyes, the pressure in her head almost at bursting point.

What the hell was she supposed to do now? She'd walked straight into this mess, like she always did – no one to blame but herself. The worst part? She could already see the fallout coming, and she had no idea how to stop it. Was she just destined to screw up everything she touched?

Chapter Twenty

Gabe

'What the hell was that all about?' Gabe frowned at Lilah and Aidan before glancing back at the door to where Lloyd had shepherded his ranting mother back into the foyer.

'Don't know.' Lilah shook her head. 'Was she having a go at Scarlett about something?'

'That's what is looked like.' Aidan got up. 'I should go and check she's ok.'

'I'll come too.' Lilah followed him.

Gabe's eyes drifted to Elise, who stood frozen in the doorway, and he scraped back his chair and headed for the door too.

The dining room was ablaze with hushed conversations, the guests leaning towards each other like conspirators.

Aidan and Lilah had disappeared towards the stairs. Gabe closed the distance between him and Elise, tension crackling in the narrow gap that remained. Up close, the rapid rise and fall of her chest was obvious, along with the slight tremor in her fingers as she gripped the doorframe.

'Hey,' he said softly. 'You ok?'

Elise blinked, her eyes focusing on him as if she'd only just noticed he was there. 'I'm fine.'

'You don't look fine.'

'Well, I am,' she snapped, then immediately closed her eyes. 'Sorry. That was, I didn't mean to...'

'It's ok.' He put his hand on her arm. 'I get it. You're rattled, and I'm not surprised. What did that woman say?'

Elise glanced over her shoulder towards the foyer where Lloyd and Rita were still talking. 'I should go and check—'

'No,' Gabe said. 'Let them sort themselves out. You've done enough.'

She snorted. 'That's one way of putting it.'

'What do you mean?'

'I've made a complete mess of things.' She ran a hand through her dark hair. 'This whole trip has been one disaster after another.'

Gabe frowned. 'How is any of this your fault?'

'I'm the tour guide. Everything that happens is my responsibility.' She lowered her voice. 'First Leon storms off, and now this. My boss is going to kill me.'

'That's ridiculous. You can't control how people behave.'

She shook her head, a small, tight movement. 'I can control how *I* behave, and I haven't. Results are what count. And the result is that this inaugural tour has been a disaster.' Her jaw set in a firm line. 'Someone could make a formal complaint.'

Gabe reached out, his fingers brushing her arm. 'You haven't done anything that's jeopardised the tour. You've been professional with everyone.'

'Except you.'

'Everything we did was in our own time.'

She balled her fists. 'I always ruin stuff with my own idiocy.'

'Nothing we did harmed anyone.'

'Not yet. But it might still. Me. My career. And I've only got myself to blame. As usual.' She pulled away from his touch. 'Please, just leave me alone. I'm in enough trouble as it is.'

'Just trying to help.' He held up his hands.

'Then help by sitting back down.' She glanced around the dining room, where several people were watching them. 'You're drawing attention.'

'Fine.' He returned to his table and sat with a sigh. What a bloody shambles this trip had turned out to be. He'd been crazy to think it would bring him the peace he craved. Instead, he'd got caught up in all kinds of drama.

He propped his elbows on the table and dropped his head into his hands, closing his eyes against the bright lights of the dining room. He should have stayed home. The question of his sanity rose to the forefront again. If this wasn't some kind of crisis, he didn't know what was.

'Couldn't wait to jump into bed with someone else. I'm surprised it wasn't... you know, that one.'

Gabe peered through his fingers, following the voice until his eyes connected with a middle-aged woman, speaking in a tone that suggested she was pretending not to gossip while doing exactly that.

'Well, what do you expect?' her friend's reply came. 'Red hair. You know what they say.'

'But Lloyd seems too respectable.'

'Seduced him, didn't she? Men are so easy.'

A titter of laughter. 'Did you see the way she was dressed last night? That skirt was barely there.'

Gabe's hands curled into fists beneath the table. They were obviously talking about Scarlett. These people didn't know the first thing about her. Who were they to judge?

As for her 'seducing' Lloyd... the very thought was ridiculous. She'd barely spoken to the man as far as he knew. And he wasn't exactly the type Scarlett went for. He had to be at least fifteen years older than her for a start. And he wore a wedding ring. These gossips had jumped on the most unlikely scenario and made it into their own soap opera.

'Shameful,' her companion agreed. 'But what can you expect from someone who looks like that? Attention-seeking. I mean, the breakup on the way here was ridiculous.'

'Never seen anything so bizarre, ever. Not even on *Eastenders*.'

They all laughed.

Gabe couldn't listen anymore. He pushed back from the table so abruptly that his chair scraped loudly against the floor, drawing stares. He didn't care. Let them stare. Let them see his disgust.

He stalked out of the dining room, aware of the surprised glances following him but too angry to moderate his pace. In the corridor, he leaned against the wall and took a deep breath, trying to calm the fury coursing through him.

Why were people so bloody nosey? Couldn't they just mind their own business?

'Hey.'

He looked up to see Aidan and Lilah walking towards him.

'Did you find Scarlett?' He frowned.

'She's in her room.' Lilah pinned her curly ginger hair back from her face and shook her head. 'We don't know what's going on. She says she doesn't want food.'

Gabe hesitated, not wanting to repeat the vile things he'd heard, especially not to Aidan about his sister. But they deserved to know.

'People are talking,' he said finally. 'About Scarlett and Lloyd. Saying she… seduced him.'

Lilah's eyes widened. 'What?'

Aidan's expression darkened. 'That's crazy. Lloyd? That guy with the glasses who's here with his mum?'

'Apparently so.'

'That doesn't sound likely,' Lilah said. 'When was this supposed to have happened? She's been with us most of the time.'

Gabe shrugged.

'Wonder what the hell made them say it.'

'Because they love a drama,' Gabe said. 'And if they can't find a real one, they make one up.'

Aidan put a hand on his shoulder. 'Yeah, you're right.'

'We should go back in and eat,' Lilah said. 'We could take something to Scarlett in her room after.'

Gabe hesitated, not sure he could stomach sitting near those people again. But the alternative was going hungry, and he didn't think that was sensible.

They re-entered the dining room, and all eyes landed on them – or it felt like it anyway. He straightened his shoulders and followed Aidan and Lilah back to the table, deliberately avoiding looking at the gossips next to them.

He spent the rest of the dinner eating and watching Elise, who had slipped back into her chair opposite the bus driver. She looked slightly pink cheeked, and he sighed. What a position he'd put her in. *Idiot*.

'You ok?' Aidan frowned at him.

'Hmm... Oh, yeah.' Gabe gave himself a mental shake. 'Just thinking.'

'About her?' Aidan raised an eyebrow, glancing at Elise, obviously having noticed where Gabe's focus had strayed.

'What? Oh... No... I...' He deliberately took a mouthful of food so he didn't have to elaborate.

Dinner wound down like a clock running out of battery – sluggish, stuttering, finally stopping altogether. Gabe didn't hang about for the live music with Lilah and Aidan. Normally he enjoyed this kind of thing, being a bit of a singer himself. But he needed quiet. Maybe some air.

He headed upstairs with a vague idea of getting his jacket. His fingers fiddled with the key as he headed along the corridor for his room. As he passed Elise's door, he stopped. Was she in there? Or was she waiting somewhere else before the music started?

He knocked on the door.

Silence. Maybe she wasn't there. He was about to walk on when it opened a crack, and a brown eye peered out at him. 'Gabe?'

'Hey,' he said. 'I was just... checking if you're ok.'

The door opened wider. 'I'm fine,' she said, then sighed. 'Or not.'

He noticed her eyes were red-rimmed.

'Aw, Elise.' He raised a hand to stroke her hair, gentle and tentative. 'This isn't like you.'

She looked away with a little shake of her head. 'Yes, it is. This is more like me than anything you've seen before. This is who I am behind the façade.'

He stepped inside, closed the door softly, and wrapped his arms around her. 'Then I'm glad you're letting me see it.' His voice was low, steady.

'But I... It's just not ok,' she whispered. 'Nothing about this trip has been ok. That busybody caught you coming out of this room this morning.' She let out a strangled cry and buried her head in his chest. 'She knows we were together.'

'I've got you.' He sat her down on the edge of the bed, stayed beside her, and held her close, pressing a kiss to the top of her head.

'What if she complains? I could lose my job.'

'For what? She doesn't know anything for sure. I could have come in here to return your lanyard or ask a question about the schedule. She's got assumptions, not evidence.'

'She'll twist it. She'll make me out to be some kind of—' Her voice cracked. 'It always happens to me. And I don't help myself. I should never have... done anything with you.'

He drew back just enough to see her face. 'Hey. I'm sorry you feel that way. I hate that this is the fallout for something that felt... good. Real.' His voice caught slightly. 'But I get it. I really do.'

She looked up at him with wet eyes, searching his face as if trying to gauge if she could really trust what he'd just said.

'Try not to worry yet. It might not come to anything.'

She wiped at her eyes with the back of her hand. 'I suppose... I just have so little faith in people.'

'Fair enough. They haven't made it easy. But I'll vouch for you if I need to. And Aidan and Lilah will too. Whatever's happened in the past, they won't deny you've done the job well this week.'

'Thank you.' She rubbed at her face again. 'God, I'm sorry. I don't usually let people see me like this.'

'So? Shocker. You're human after all.'

That earned a little laugh, and she leaned into him again.

'And it doesn't change how I see you.' He let out a quiet breath. If anything, it made him care more. He held her tighter, a fierce warmth spreading through him. A quiet, insistent ache not just to comfort her now, but to stay – and keep showing up for her, no matter what came next.

CHAPTER TWENTY-ONE

Elise

'I need to go downstairs.' Elise pulled back from Gabe and looked up at him. 'I should be there for the music. At least some of it. It looks unprofessional if I don't show.'

She got up from the bed and grabbed her make-up bag. No one needed to see that she'd been crying. It was bad enough Gabe had seen her. But actually, he'd been kind. She'd felt safe enough to be herself. He'd witnessed broken Elise in action and not run away.

Using a wipe, she took off her smudged make-up and quickly reapplied it.

Gabe was quiet for a moment, watching her, and she caught his eye in the mirror as she swiped on her lip gloss.

'I'm not going back down,' Gabe said. 'I might go for a walk to the village or something.'

Elise turned to face him. She'd rather do that too, but her duties were here. 'Listen... When I'm finished down there and when you're back from the walk...' She stopped and took a deep breath. Gabe cocked his head, frowning slightly. 'Would you come back here? I know it's not sensible, but I don't want to be alone.'

He stood up and came over to her. 'Of course.' He took her in his arms again and the wonderful heat and strength engulfed her. But all too soon, she had to pull back. Her presence would be missed downstairs.

She nipped down, already hearing the soft twang of guitar strings and a tuneful female voice. She snuck in and took a seat at the back next to Kev, who smiled and gave her a little wink.

'She has a good voice,' Kev whispered, nodding at the singer.

Elise nodded. 'Yeah, really good.' Her gaze drifted around the room. She saw Lloyd and Rita, seated near the front. Lloyd's shoulders were hunched, his fingers drumming an agitated rhythm on the table that bore no relation to the music. Rita sat ramrod straight beside him, her lips pressed together. Elise ran her thumb along her lip. Surely the rumours about him and Scarlett weren't true. That would be insane. More likely, he was annoyed at the existence of such rumours than anything else.

Everyone clapped as the song came to an end. With only a short pause for a sip of water, the singer launched into a haunting rendition of a Scottish folk song.

Across the lounge, Aidan and Lilah sat close together, his arm draped casually around her shoulders. Elise didn't feel the usual pang of envy. Something niggled her, but not because she wanted to be in Lilah's position. *No.* She could think of better places to be these days.

Scarlett didn't appear to be present. *Poor girl*. Elise's chest constricted when she thought about what a nightmare of a week Scarlett was having. Elise knew so well what it was like to be painted as the villain. Scarlett might have made wrong choices this week and in the past, but no one deserved this kind of kickback.

'Ms Reid?' A voice at her elbow startled her.

She turned to find one of the coach trippers, adorned with a large collection of brooches, smiling at her.

'I just wanted to say how much we've enjoyed the trip. Such beautiful scenery, and the hotel has been lovely. And thank you too,' she added to Kev. 'Wonderful driving.'

'Cheers.' Kev raised his glass to her.

'I'm so pleased to hear you've had a good time,' Elise replied. 'It's been a pleasure having you with us.' Thank goodness some people had enjoyed it.

The band shifted into something more upbeat, and several people clapped along. Elise tapped her knee in sync with the music. How much longer until she could reasonably excuse herself?

Rita caught her eye across the room and gave her a look so cold it could have frosted glass. Elise held her gaze for a moment, smiling, refusing to be cowed, then deliberately turned away.

The song ended, applause rippled through the room, and the singer announced they'd be taking a short break. Conversation swelled to fill the absence of music.

'I'm going to get another drink,' Kev said. 'Want anything?'

'No, thank you. I'm ok.' Elise glanced at her watch. Nearly ten. Surely she could leave soon without seeming rude.

'I'm on the soft stuff tonight.' Kev tapped his glass. 'Safer when I'm driving tomorrow. One more ginger ale and I'll call it a night.'

'Good idea. I see quite a few people have gone up. I might head too. It's been a long day.'

Kev nodded. 'Aye, right you are. You have a good sleep.'

'Thank you. See you tomorrow.'

As he moved towards the bar, Elise surveyed the room one last time. Lloyd and Rita were now in what appeared to be a heated discussion, though their voices remained low. Whatever was going on there didn't look good.

The band returned to their places, the guitarist adjusting his microphone. Elise slipped out quietly.

'Lovely evening,' she said to a couple in the foyer. 'Sleep well, and I'll see you at breakfast tomorrow.'

'You too.'

Elise nodded her thanks, then made her way upstairs. She hovered outside Scarlett's door which was next to hers, then knocked. No reply. She knocked again. 'Hey, Scarlett. It's Elise. Are you in there?'

'Yeah. I'm trying to sleep. What is it?'

'Just wanted to check you were ok.'

'I'm fine.'

'Great. Just give me a shout if you need anything.'

Inside her room, Elise kicked off her shoes. At least Scarlett was safe in her room. Elise padded to the bathroom, peering at her reflection in the mirror.

She looked tired, but her make-up had held. She washed her face and brushed her teeth, then changed from her work clothes into soft pyjama bottoms and a loose t-shirt. Not exactly seductive, but comfortable. And really, this wasn't about seduction, was it? It was about not being alone tonight, about finding comfort with someone who, against all odds, seemed to understand her.

She perched on the edge of the bed and pulled out her phone. 'I've escaped the music night. You still walking, or shall I expect a knock at my door soon?'

She hit send, then lay back on the bed, flat out like a starfish.

Moments passed. She picked up her phone, checking that the message had sent. It had. She put it down again and stared at the ceiling.

Where was he? Had he gone for a longer walk than planned? Had he changed his mind?

A knock at the door made her jump. She leapt to her feet and hurried to get it.

'Hi.' Gabe smiled, adjusting his backpack.

'Hi.' She stepped back to let him in. 'You brought everything?'

He slipped into the room, and she closed the door quickly behind him, hyperaware of the potential for prying eyes in the corridor.

'Figured I might as well.' He set his bags down carefully by the wall. 'We're leaving tomorrow anyway, and it saves sneaking back to my room at dawn.' He ran a hand through his hair. 'Unless you'd rather I didn't?'

'No, no. I want you to stay.'

'Good.'

'How was your walk?'

'Cleared my head.' He shrugged off his sweater and hung it over the back of the desk chair. 'I went down to the shore. You could hear the waves breaking against the rocks. It was peaceful.'

'Sounds lovely. I think I'd have preferred that to the music,'

'Yeah. I like music, I just didn't fancy being stuck in there with all the busybodies. Let me brush my teeth and get ready for bed.'

'Are you going to bother with clothes?' She raised an eyebrow and smiled at him.

'Naughty.' He chuckled.

Elise got into bed while he went into the bathroom. When he came out, he was in nothing but a pair of short PJ bottoms. He slipped under the covers beside her, his fingers seeking hers, interlocking with them and holding tight. The contact sent a current of warmth up to her shoulder and across her chest.

'Do you want to just cuddle for a bit?' he asked.

'Yeah.'

Elise turned off the light, and they shuffled closer. She found her way into Gabe's embrace, and, for a long moment, they lay together without moving.

Gabe's fingers traced the curve of her cheek, and slowly they fell into a kiss, long and decadent. There was no urgency or haste. Even when the kiss deepened and his tongue met hers, it was a slow exploration. He held her so close that she felt untouchable, completely protected from anyone who might want to hurt her.

Time seemed to stretch and compress, moments expanding into eternity before contracting into flashes of sensation – the rasp of his stubble against her skin, the pressure of his hand as it slid beneath the waistband of her pyjama bottoms, the sound he made when she reciprocated, exploring the hard planes of his body with eager fingers.

'Oh god, Elise,' he groaned against her neck. 'I'm done for.'

'Good.' A breathy laugh escaped her.

They helped each other discard their clothes, urgency building with each passing second, their kisses deepening, hungry. When they finally came together, skin on skin, with nothing between them but shared breath and the frantic beat of their hearts, Elise felt a sudden clarity pierce the haze of desire.

This was Gabe. Gabe who'd been Aidan's friend for years. Gabe who'd looked at her with barely concealed dislike for most of the time she'd known him. Gabe, who in the span of a few days, had become the one person she most wanted to be with.

She pulled him down to her again, desperate to feel the weight of him, the warmth, the realness of him.

Everything they did together made her feel whole. Not because he completed her, but because, for once, she wasn't hiding. She was here, fully herself, and she felt alive, cherished, and loved.

Yes. Loved.

The word startled her, made her pulse gallop and some instinct scream to pull away. But she didn't. Not this time. She let it land. Let herself believe it.

And when she did, the feeling was almost too much, a rush of warmth and wonder that swelled through her, both euphoric and unbearable.

Even if it couldn't last beyond this moment, she'd known it – just once.

The breathless awe of being loved as she was. And the heart-stopping beauty of loving in return.

Even if it shattered her when it ended.

'I've got you,' Gabe murmured. His eyes held hers, unwavering, as pleasure built between them like a rising tide. And she believed him. How utterly staggering that someone who'd once been her enemy was now the one person she felt so at home with.

Tears pricked at the corners of her eyes, not from sadness but from the swell of emotions burning inside her.

Gabe kissed her eyelids, her cheeks, the corner of her mouth. His movements grew more urgent, and she matched him.

When her release came, it wasn't just physical satisfaction but an emotional unfurling, as if something long knotted inside her had finally come loose. She breathed out, trying not to be too noisy, her fingers digging into his shoulders, her body arching against his. Gabe followed moments later, her name on his lips, his face buried in the crook of her neck.

They lay tangled in silence, the aftermath of pleasure thrumming between them. Their breaths gradually slowed, heartbeats syncing. Elise clung to him, her nails still pressed into his skin, anchoring herself to the moment. Tomorrow, he'd bear the marks – proof that this had been real. But she couldn't let go. Wouldn't. And he didn't seem to want her to.

'Are you ok?' he asked.

She nodded, her voice breathy and quiet. 'More than.'

But that didn't come close to what she felt. Words would only flatten it – and this feeling was too big, too fierce, to be ruined by a careless whisper.

He pressed a kiss to her temple. 'I'm glad we did this. Gave ourselves this chance.'

'Me too.'

He raised his hand, moving her fingers from his shoulder and bringing them to his lips. 'An unexpected pleasure in what's been a bizarre week.'

'Exactly.' She closed her eyes, relaxing into him, knowing she'd have no trouble sleeping now – not while she was safe with him – though getting up the next day might not be quite so easy.

Morning came too soon. Elise woke with Gabe's arm draped across her waist, his breathing deep and even against her neck. For one suspended moment, she sank into the warmth of him, the unfamiliar comfort of waking beside someone. The undefined nature of her feelings was both thrilling and terrifying, but there was no time to examine them now. What had seemed so clear last night was a lot murkier in daylight – as she'd known it would be. Reality beckoned.

She eased herself from beneath his arm. He stirred, murmuring, 'Hey.'

'No need to rush. You sleep for a bit.'

He murmured something incoherent into the pillow. Elise headed into the bathroom. The shower spray washed away the physical evidence of the night, but nothing could rinse away the memory of Gabe's hands on her skin, his voice in her ear, the way he'd looked at her as if she were something precious. Once she was clean, she put on her uniform. Now she was at least dressed to face the last day – and hopefully it would be drama free, unlike the first.

But a lingering sense of unease clung to her skin. Whatever happened today, it was the end of the road for her and Gabe. Their little arrangement would be over almost the second they stepped out of this room, and Elise would have to go back to how she was before. Something that had seemed a lot easier a few days ago than it did now.

When she emerged from the bathroom, Gabe was awake, propped up on one elbow, watching her with a lazy smile that made her stomach flutter.

'Morning,' he said.

'Morning.' She busied herself with gathering her toiletries. 'I need to go down to breakfast. Make sure everyone's ok.'

'Right.' His smile didn't falter, but something in his eyes shifted – he knew the deal as well as she did. 'I'll stay up here a bit longer. Less suspicious that way.'

She nodded, grateful for his pragmatism. For a second, she considered kissing him goodbye, but that felt premature – even if it was inevitable – and she couldn't bring herself to do it. Instead, she waved. 'See you downstairs.'

'Yeah.' He smiled, but it didn't reach his eyes.

In the dining room, several of her passengers were already at breakfast. No sign of Lloyd or Rita, which was a relief. No sign of Scarlett either, which was more concerning given her state the previous day.

Kev sat alone at a small table with a cup of tea and a full breakfast. Elise poured herself a coffee from the buffet station before joining him.

'Morning.' She slid into the seat opposite.

'Looks like we had the best of the weather this week.' He gestured with his fork to the window, where grey skies threatened rain.

'We did.' She sipped her coffee, wincing slightly at its strength, and keeping half an eye on the room. After the nonsense yesterday, she wasn't sure what to expect. Her phone vibrated in her pocket. She pulled it out, intending to silence it, but froze when she saw the caller ID. Gill Campbell.

'It's a bit early for her, isn't it?' she muttered. It was just after eight.

'Who is it?' Kev frowned.

'Gill. I better take it. Hello.'

'Elise.' Gill's voice was clipped. 'I have literally just sat down at my desk to a very long, very comprehensive complaint email.'

'A complaint?'

Kev met her eyes across the table, and his frown deepened.

'From a passenger who doesn't want to be named, who is alleging unprofessional conduct, favouritism towards certain passengers, and a general lack of appropriate tour management.' Gill's voice grew sharper. 'She specifically mentions finding you in a... compromising situation with one of the passengers.'

Elise closed her eyes. 'That's not—'

'I don't want to hear explanations over the phone,' Gill cut in. 'We'll discuss it in full when you're back in the office. But I wanted to give you a heads-up that this is serious, Elise. Very serious.'

'I understand.' Her voice sounded distant to her own ears.

'Do you?' Gill's tone suggested doubt. 'Because from where I'm sitting, it looks like you've jeopardised the company's reputation on our inaugural tour. The very tour you initially tried to avoid taking.'

'It's hardly my fault—' But then, was it? How often had she been at fault even when not meaning to be? And there was no denying she'd behaved inappropriately with Gabe.

'We'll discuss it tomorrow,' Gill said. 'Just get everyone back safely, with no further incidents.'

Elise balled her fists at the condescension in Gill's tone. 'Of course.'

'Good. See you tomorrow.'

The call ended, leaving Elise staring at her phone, a hollowness expanding in her chest.

'Someone complained?' Kev shook his head like he couldn't believe it. 'What about?'

'Just something silly. Don't worry.' Elise got to her feet. 'It wasn't about you. I need to go and check something. I'll see you on the coach.'

She didn't want to go back to her room in case Gabe was still there. Right now, she couldn't face him – or anyone. She nipped into the toilets off the foyer, closed the cubicle door, put the toilet seat down, and sat with her head in her hands.

How do I always manage to screw up like this?

She took several deep breaths, getting a lungful of the strong rose scented air freshener. She had a job to do, and this wasn't helping. If she didn't get out there and make sure all the passengers were there, the tour would sink further down the drain. She could fall apart later, in private, once all this was over. When she never had to see any of these people again. Including Gabe.

For now, she had to do what she'd learned from her counselling sessions to do – put one foot in front of the other and keep moving forward, even as the ground beneath her threatened to crack open and pull her down under. Above all, she had to keep a professional distance between her and Gabe – like she should have done from the start. This thing between them was over, and she had to accept that.

Chapter Twenty-Two

Gabe

Gabe pressed his forehead against the cool glass of the coach window as the engine rumbled into action. Drizzly rain was falling now, and the colour of the past few days had been sucked out, leaving a dull grey – similar to how he felt. Being with Elise had energised his heart, but that was slowly ebbing away, leaving him with the same flat sensation he'd had a lot recently. In fact, it had pretty much been his reason for coming on this trip at all. Anything to shake the monotony. Which, even inside his head, sounded insane. His whole life was adventurous and wild – he'd built his brand around it – *Wilder at Heart*. Only his heart didn't feel like being wild right now.

'Thank you for your patience, everyone,' Elise said into the microphone. 'We're almost ready to leave. We'll have one stop about halfway for lunch and bathroom breaks, and should arrive back around four this afternoon.'

She made her way to the middle of the coach, doing a head-count. Not a flicker. Not a glance in his direction. Nothing to suggest they'd spent hours wrapped around each other over the past few days. And he couldn't exactly blame her. What did he expect? This was her job. She had to be professional.

The coach rumbled out of the hotel drive and onto the road. Gabe's stomach felt hollow, and not just from the meagre breakfast he'd forced down. For someone who was always ravenous, losing his appetite was worrying.

He slumped back in his seat – the one Aidan and Lilah had occupied on the journey over behind Lloyd and Rita – and tried to make sense of the churning in his chest. It was only meant to be a holiday fling. That's what they'd agreed.

So why did it feel like someone had tied his insides in knots?

'You ok there, mate?' Aidan leaned over the aisle.

Gabe turned away from the window. 'Yeah, all good. You?'

'Yeah. It's gone quickly, hasn't it?'

'Really quick.'

'Even with all the drama.' Aidan made a face to indicate Scarlett in the seat in front of him. Gabe nodded, but Aidan didn't know the half of it. The drama was still unfolding inside Gabe's head, and he wasn't sure how to shut it down. But he must, and soon, for his own good.

Turning back to the window, Gabe looked at Skye and hoped one day he would return – though not on a coach. He'd bring his truck and roof tent. If he'd learned anything this week, it was that coach trips weren't for him. The extra-curricular activities had kept him going, though he wasn't sure they'd helped his mind. And they probably hadn't helped Elise's career.

Gabe closed his eyes, but behind his lids, all he could see was Elise. She seemed to be taking this well. Her professional face was on and no one looking at her would know she'd done anything other than her job – even the ones who listened to the rumours. Maybe she'd reconciled herself to the fact that whatever had happened between them was over.

And that was fine. That was the arrangement. That was what he wanted – wasn't it?

Maybe it was just the island making him sentimental. The magic of Skye that everyone talked about.

He needed to get back to work and make more content for *Wilder at Heart*. But his interest in that was ebbing too. When it started, it was new and exciting. Now, it had lost its shine and people weren't as interested anymore. During the lockdowns, it had been something people had got behind. Kids watched him as part of their schooling and even after the lockdowns, he'd gone on to do chat shows, guest interviews, talks in schools, and conferences on top of the regular podcasts and the series on E-Broadcast Scotland. But keeping up the momentum was hard.

And he felt like a displaced person. He had a flat in Glenbriar, but he was hardly ever there to use it. He lived out of a bag, slept in the open or in a hotel more often than in his own bed – he didn't even think of the bed at his flat as his own. His trusty sleeping bag was his bed. And it was a good one – companies sponsored him big money to showcase their products in the wild.

He opened his eyes and stared at the passing landscape. Somehow, he needed to muster the enthusiasm to keep going because he wasn't sure what he would do otherwise. Going back to his pre-lockdown job as a geotechnical surveyor didn't appeal much either. The long stretches away from home, the relentless cycle of early mornings and late nights on-site, trudging through mud or scaling rocky outcrops just to collect another round of soil samples, was no better than doing the same kind of thing for *Wilder at Heart*, which at least brought him some joy. Add to that the hours hunched over reports, translating field data into technical jargon for clients who barely skimmed the findings and it felt like a pointless, never-ending grind.

And the travel situation wouldn't change... Or if it did, it wouldn't get any better. Mostly it was a string of bleak hotel rooms, service station meals, and weeks spent in places he had no real connection with. At least when he travelled for the podcasts, he could largely pick and choose where he went and when.

He frowned at his faint reflection in the coach window, tilting his head to see his face better. Was he having a mid-life crisis? Surely thirty-five was too young for that. But nothing felt right. He'd arrived at a crossroads, but every direction had a barricade across it and he couldn't see a way to get past any of them.

His phone buzzed, and he lifted it absently. A random message from his mother. He sighed, almost ready to toss the phone onto the empty seat beside him without looking at it, But he better not. He could guess what it was about. This bloody house and pet-sitting gig his mother had roped him into. His father – i.e. the man who held that title in name but nothing else – smoked cigars and Gabe couldn't stomach the smell or the memories that went with them. He'd do his duty by feeding the animals, walking the dogs, and keeping his eye out for whatever issues his mother thought might happen when she was away, but he wouldn't sleep in the house with that smell. Yet another outing for his tent. They had a beautiful garden, extensive grounds, and it wasn't a bad place to spend time – as long as Mr Wilder senior wasn't there.

Gabe checked the message and found his hunch was right. A string of instructions from his mother filled the message in a huge chunk of word soup that he could barely follow. Her texting skills weren't the best, and she'd probably done it at speed, as his father was no doubt whining about her paying too much attention to her phone and not to him.

Gabe's parents' house was a little way out of Glenbriar, and he could easily commute from there to his flat if he wanted to, but really, he didn't want to go to his flat either. It was too small and cramped – rather like this coach – and he craved the open air, big spaces, clear nights and starry skies. And he liked the animals. In an ideal world, he'd visit much more often, help out more, and just be present in his mum's life. But that couldn't happen. Not while his dad was there.

Around him, passengers were either chatting quietly, dozing, staring out at the passing landscape, or tapping at phones. Gabe's head was aching. From directly in front of him, Rita's voice was mumbling something. Gabe couldn't make out the words and wasn't sure it was something he should be listening to anyway. Did she believe all these insane rumours about Lloyd and Scarlett? Gabe glanced over at Scarlett, and his brow furrowed.

She sat hunched over her phone, her bright red hair falling forward to hide her face, which was make-up free – that was almost unheard of for her. And there was a stillness to her that seemed wrong. Scarlett was many things, but still was rarely one of them. Even when she was quiet, there was usually energy humming beneath the surface – a leg bouncing, fingers tapping, something.

Now she looked like she'd been switched off – physically and emotionally. She scrolled through something on her phone, her thumb moving mechanically, her other hand curled tightly in her lap, knuckles white.

She and Lloyd had got in a canoe together the day they'd done water sports, which had seemed weird at the time... But even so, that was just him being friendly, right? Gabe couldn't imagine a duo less likely suited – and not just their ages. She was so spunky and had no filter, while Lloyd seemed buttoned up and mild-mannered. If she was doing anything with him, she probably wouldn't even try to hide it. And would she jump into bed with someone straight after splitting with Leon? With a man who wore a wedding ring? No. It was all too ridiculous.

Scarlett pushed her hair back from her face, and Gabe caught a glimpse of reddened eyes and tightly compressed lips.

Should he say something? He and Scarlett had never exactly been close, but she looked in a bad way. Unease rose in his gut and wouldn't fade, though he wasn't sure it was all related to Scarlett.

At around midday, the coach stopped for lunch. People began to stir, collecting bags and jackets. Across the aisle, Scarlett remained seated, showing no sign of moving. Then, as Gabe watched, she pulled out her phone again, typed something quickly, and stood up so abruptly she nearly collided with an older woman in the aisle.

'Sorry,' she muttered.

'Are you ok?' Gabe asked.

She shrugged. 'Fine.'

Clearly that wasn't true, but she didn't appear to be in the mood to elaborate.

Outside, the air was crisp and clean after the recycled atmosphere of the coach. The party trooped into the café nestled inside a tacky giftshop that was stuffed with every Scottish cliché you could imagine: Nessy toys, highland cow plushies, C-U Jimmy hats, beach towels that looked like kilts when wrapped around your waist, tartan goods, Harris tweed bags, Celtic jewellery and books about history, landscapes, famous Scots, and folktales. A tourist haven if ever there was one.

Gabe and the others avoided it and headed straight for lunch. His eyes scanned around for Elise, but she didn't seem to be there. Aidan and Lilah kept the conversation going over lunch. Scarlett barely ate a thing, didn't look at anyone, and if she wasn't so obvious with her bright red hair, nobody would even have noticed she was there – and Gabe was probably exactly the same. He could barely stomach food or muster the energy to speak.

The sooner he was back home, the better. Even if home didn't really feel like home anymore and hadn't for a very long time now.

Once they were back on the coach, Gabe shoved in his earbuds and closed his eyes, trying to let some of his favourite tracks distract him, but the louder, more upbeat ones made his head ache and the slower, more sentimental ones hurt his heart. This was impossible.

After what seemed like an age, they finally arrived back in Glenbriar. The coach pulled up in the large bus stance where just a few days ago, Gabe and the others had shared their collective disbelief in Elise's being there.

And now they were back.

This was it. The final moment. And no chance to say a proper goodbye to Elise. She wouldn't want him making a scene here. Maybe she didn't want any further contact at all. Well, he could always message her later and say... something. Though god only knew what.

He shoved his stuff into his backpack.

'Right, everyone,' Elise said through the microphone. 'That's us back in Glenbriar. Thank you all for being such wonderful passengers on Highland Horizon's inaugural tour from Glenbriar. I hope you've enjoyed the experience, and perhaps we'll see you on another of our trips in the future.'

There was a smattering of applause, which Elise acknowledged by standing at the front and smiling.

'Can we all also please say a big thank you to Kev, our wonderful coach driver?'

More applause, some cheers, and Aidan whistled.

'Thank you,' Elise said. 'And safe onward travels.'

Gabe hung back, letting others go ahead, watching as Scarlett practically bolted from her seat. She was out the door without a backward glance.

Lloyd and Rita went in front of him and when they passed Elise, Lloyd mumbled a thank you while his mother gave her a brief, rather curt nod. Then it was Gabe's turn.

Her professional smile flickered slightly as their eyes met.

'Thanks for a great trip,' he said.

'You're welcome,' she replied, her tone neutral. 'I hope you enjoyed Skye.'

'More than I expected to.' He held her gaze.

A faint flush coloured her cheeks, but she said nothing else. Not that she could.

'Has Scarlett gone already?' Lilah hopped down and looked around.

'Well, she leapt off the bus almost as soon as it stopped,' Gabe said. 'She looked rough all the way back. I know it's not exactly been a great week for her, but do you think something else has happened? Like maybe Leon got back in touch or something?'

'I don't know.' Aidan let out a sigh. 'We're heading to Mum's to collect Maya. Scarlett should be there too.'

Gabe smiled, knowing how much Aidan and Lilah had missed their dog.

'We'll make sure she's ok.'

'Does she still live with your mum?'

'She does if she's not living with some dodgy boyfriend. And I hope to god she's not gone back to Leon. That would be hideous.'

Indeed, it would. Gabe hoped that wouldn't be the case.

They retrieved their luggage from the hold and set off into the town. As Gabe walked away, he turned around, checking over his shoulder. Elise was at the door of the coach talking to the bus driver, her focus nowhere near him.

Putting his head down, he sighed and kept walking. Now was the time to shove this little holiday fling into the past and forget all about it. Though he suspected that would be easier said than done.

CHAPTER TWENTY-THREE

'Good morning, Elise.' Gill Campbell's smile was as bright – and fake – as ever. Elise knew not to trust that saccharine face for one second. If anything, it was more dangerous than a frown would have been.

Elise smoothed down her pencil skirt and took a seat opposite Gill in the small back office of the new Glenbriar branch of Highland Horizons. Her nerves were jangling so much she could barely focus, but she registered that the setup was actually quite impressive. If she did accept the job – if it was even still on the table – it wouldn't be a bad environment to work in. Glenbriar High Street was full of life and character with an artisan charm. Most of the buildings housed independent shops or cafés. The front office wasn't large, but its wide windows flooded the space with light. The décor followed the company's distinctive branding – purple and blue tones echoing the logo: a stylised hill in violet against a blue sky with a glittering sea in front. Even back here, the office chairs were a vibrant purple.

Gill Campbell sat behind the desk, fingers steepled, her reading glasses perched on the end of her nose. The office was neat, but devoid of personality, presumably because Gill still hadn't recruited a permanent manager.

'I hope you had time to recover after the tour?' Gill's tone remained pleasant, but it was kind of obvious she didn't really care what the answer was.

'Yes, thank you.' Elise nodded. What else could she say? She wasn't going to tell Gill that she'd stayed over at her brother David's house, so she didn't have to go back to Glasgow only to travel in again today. David might have a gorgeous, large, modern house, but it wasn't exactly a restful place. His wife Amanda chattered incessantly about school fundraisers, church events, committees and the children's various activities. Getting a few minutes of peace in the house was near impossible, and Elise was exhausted from just listening to Amanda yapping at them all over breakfast.

'Well, let's get down to business, shall we?' Gill's smile morphed into a pout. 'This complaint.'

The knot in Elise's stomach tightened.

Gill sighed and shook her head. 'Dare I even ask? Did you behave inappropriately with someone on the tour?'

Elise's throat went dry. 'What do they mean by inappropriate? I did nothing that would jeopardise the tour in any way.'

Gill's eyebrows rose. 'The words "unprofessional relationship" were used.'

Elise's heart dropped. 'That's—' she started, then stopped, gathering herself. 'That's not accurate.'

'So you deny having any personal interactions with members of the tour party?'

'I had *professional* interactions with everyone,' she said. 'Though it was a little awkward as there were some people I knew personally on the tour.'

'Oh?' Gill leaned forward slightly.

'An ex of mine was there.' Not technically a lie. 'And some friends. Perhaps the person who complained misinterpreted my interactions as being too familiar. It's difficult when you know people like that. Even when you're being professional, they still see you as a friend.'

'I see.' Gill's expression remained sceptical, and she leaned back in her chair. 'Liaisons with clients are expressly forbidden in your contract.'

A flash of indignation tore through Elise. 'I don't have a contract for doing tours. My contract is for project managing and there's no mention of liaisons with clients. This whole thing was done as a favour.'

Gill nodded, and Elise couldn't miss the steely look in her eyes. She knew exactly what Gill was thinking. Elise hadn't denied the allegation. If she did, it would be an outright lie, but maybe better than the alternative.

'You're quite right regarding the contract. And of course that means that we can't take any action – which believe me, I don't want to – but your position in the company has become problematic.'

'What do you mean?' Elise narrowed her eyes. 'I've done a lot of good work for this company. I'm obviously upset that someone has taken issue with something on that tour, because really, it actually went pretty well otherwise. Considering I didn't want to do it in the first place, and it wasn't a role I was comfortable with. All of which I told you before.'

'All true.' Gill folded her hands on the desk. 'But I can't ignore the needs of the business.'

'I don't get what you mean. Do you want me to resign or something?'

'Absolutely not. Given your very good record with this company, what I really want is for you to take the job here. This is where I need you. And if that's something you think you can do, then I'm sure this silly little complaint will disappear and be forgotten about.'

A dull ache pulsed behind Elise's eyes, the beginnings of a stress headache, and she balled her fists. This was little more than blackmail. And what the hell was she supposed to do about her flat in Glasgow? Where was she going to live if she came back to Glenbriar? She couldn't stomach being with her brother and Amanda for the long term, and they probably didn't want her there either. Though at the back of her mind, a different thought was forming. A more settling idea. Because somewhere deep down, Glenbriar was where she wanted to be.

'Fine,' she said. 'I'll take the Glenbriar position, though could it be on a fixed term, rather than permanent? Someone more suited might come along after all.'

'Alright.' Gill nodded. 'That sounds sensible.'

'And,' Elise added, 'I'll need time to sort out my living arrangements.'

'Of course. We can discuss the details now.' Gill opened a laptop. 'I've already prepared the paperwork.'

Of course she had. If Elise didn't know better, she might think Gill had manufactured this complaint. Except she knew it was too accurate for that. Maybe Elise deserved this as a punishment for breaking the rules.

This wasn't ideal, but she could take this job and start looking for opportunities elsewhere. Wouldn't be the first time she'd run from a tricky situation.

By the time she left Gill's office an hour later, Elise had signed the papers, making her the new manager of Highland Horizons' Glenbriar branch. She stood at the window in the main room, looking out at the familiar High Street, all decorated with hanging baskets and planters, looking every bit the inviting little town that it was. The place she'd once called home was to be her reluctant refuge once more.

And if she was going to be living here again, there were a couple of things she really needed to sort out.

The Glenbriar job started officially the following week, even though Elise was due time back from the coach trip that she intended to take.

'Thanks.' Elise accepted a mug of coffee from Kate Halley, one of the front desk assistants.

Kate smiled at her and tucked a strand of her naturally grey but perfectly styled hair behind her ear. Elise admired women who allowed the natural colour to come through, and Kate really suited it. She was probably in her mid-fifties and looked smart and vibrant. Elise had a feeling she'd met her somewhere before – which wasn't unusual in Glenbriar, though it was slightly un-settling. It was stupid to think everyone in the town knew her business and judged her on her past mistakes, but she couldn't wholly shake the feeling.

'You probably don't remember me,' Kate said. 'But you were at high school with my eldest.'

Uh-oh. Kate was someone who actually did know her... and possibly her history. Elise racked her brains. Kate Halley was the woman's name. Who in her year had that surname?

'My eldest son Jake,' Kate went on, sparing Elise the need to think. 'He dated a friend of yours at school.'

'Oh, of course. I remember now. Georgie Porter.' Elise had all but forgotten her – not for the same reasons she'd been torn away from her other friends, but because Georgie had left the school and gone to play professional tennis. She rarely came back to the town and Elise had lost touch with her now that Georgie had become something of a name.

'Yeah. She broke his heart.' Kate gazed out of the window. 'I heard she retired recently.' Kate pulled a face. 'Nice career that you can retire from at thirty, eh? I think she had some injury. I never followed her career after what she did to Jake. It hurt him so much.'

Elise cocked her head. 'I didn't know she'd retired.' For a while she'd kept up with what Georgie was doing, but it had all fizzled out. Elise's insides squirmed. She was so bad at keeping in touch. Something she couldn't let happen with Hayley and Genevieve.

Come break time, sitting at her desk with a fresh coffee, Elise made a decision. She couldn't keep hiding. If Glenbriar was to be her home again, even temporarily, she needed to talk to her friends, and soon.

With slightly trembling fingers, she composed a group text to Hayley and Genevieve.

Hi you two. It's been too long, and that's entirely my fault. I'm back in Glenbriar (long story) and would love to see you both if you're willing. Dinner this week maybe?

She almost deleted it three times before finally pressing send, then immediately put the phone face-down on her desk and tried to focus on inventory reports. Ten minutes later, when it buzzed twice in quick succession, she could hardly bring herself to look. What if they said no or told her to get stuffed?

When she finally flipped it over, her heart soared.

HAYLEY: Elise!!! OMG yes!! When and where? So much to catch up on!

GENEVIEVE: You're back! Holy shit! What's the story? How about Thursday at The Cross Keys? Around 7?

No anger. No recriminations. Not yet anyway. Elise stared at her phone, tears pricking at her eyes.

ELISE: Thursday works for me. Thank you both. Really. I'll tell you everything when I see you.

Living with her brother and his family during the week had seemed like the practical solution while she figured out her housing situation. A long commute from Glasgow each day wasn't feasible, and she couldn't afford to maintain two separate full-time residences. But after just a few nights, she was already regretting her decision.

Her sister-in-law Amanda was well-meaning and nice enough – in small doses. She ran the household with military precision and maternal warmth in equal measure. The problem was, she applied the same approach to Elise's life as she did to her children.

'I've put fresh towels in your bathroom,' she announced on Thursday the second Elise appeared home. 'And I was thinking, you really should join the tennis club now you're back. I could do with a partner for the women's doubles and David said you're rather good. I can introduce you to everyone there. Lovely people.'

'Um... Ok. That sounds... fun.' Though she hadn't played for years and wasn't sure that was how she wanted to be spending her free time.

'Great. I'll put your name down. I've done Bolognese for dinner. David's working late, so we're eating at six.'

'Actually,' Elise said, 'I'm meeting friends for dinner at seven. I thought I told you that.'

Amanda's face lit up like Elise had announced a royal visit. 'Of course! Silly me. And so lovely that you're seeing your friends again.' She pulled a pitying expression. 'Things have been rather strained, haven't they? But this is good. Who are you meeting? And where? Anywhere nice?'

'Hayley and Genevieve. At The Cross Keys.'

'Oh, great. Your besties. I love Genevieve, her cookware is amazing. And Hayley does my hair sometimes. She's an absolute gem.'

As Elise changed into a simple blue dress and touched up her makeup, she felt a mixture of dread and anticipation. There would be questions, of course. Explanations needed. But overall, she felt positive about the meeting. She sat on the end of the bed and sighed. Now, if ever, she needed her friends so badly. Because her heart ached, and she wanted to tell them something she couldn't tell anyone else in the world.

The Cross Keys stood at the edge of the river, its old stone walls softened by climbing roses and fairy lights strung along the raised deck that surrounded it. Elise arrived seven minutes early and hovered outside, debating whether to wait or go in.

'El-eee-yeeess,' came a sing-songy voice.

Elise turned to find Hayley approaching, her long dark hair hanging in elegant waves over her shoulders. She wore a black jumpsuit and nude heels as she rushed up and wrapped her arms around Elise's neck.

'Hayley.' Elise breathed in Hayley's familiar scent of salon products and floral perfume.

'God, look at you.' Hayley pulled back to examine her. 'Still as glamorous as ever.'

'Says you,' Elise said. 'Looking like a model.'

Hayley linked her arm through Elise's. 'Come on, Gen texted that she's inside already. And before you tie yourself in knots, she's not angry. None of us are. We're just curious. We didn't like to push too hard when it seemed like you needed space.'

Elise gave her a grateful smile as Hayley guided her into the restaurant, a cosy space with exposed beams and soft lighting. Genevieve sat at a corner table by the window. Her caramel-coloured hair was pulled into a loose updo, and she wore a simple dark green maxi dress.

'Hey!' Genevieve waved, but didn't stand for a hug.

'Hi.' Elise slipped into a chair opposite her. 'You look well.'

'So do you. And sounds like we have lots to catch up on… You're back for a start?'

'First week in a new job, yeah.' Elise shrugged. 'And I'm staying with David and Amanda, which is…'

'Exhausting?' Genevieve said, a hint of a smile appearing.

'Amanda's lovely, but she has the energy of a border collie on Red Bull.'

'She means well.' Hayley settled beside Genevieve. 'And her kids are so beautiful.'

'Yeah, she's blessed with bonnie babies.' Elise smiled. This was pleasant, but she couldn't shake a raw edge surrounding them. Things couldn't go back to exactly how they were… not after everything that had happened, and all Elise had missed. But she had to try.

A waiter approached. They ordered drinks – wine for Hayley and Elise, sparkling water for Genevieve – and studied the menus.

'So,' Hayley said once the waiter departed, 'tell us everything. How did you end up back in Glenbriar? What's the new job?'

'It's a long story.' Elise sighed. 'The short version is that it's the same company but I'm taking on the branch here – or I should say I was blackmailed into taking it.'

'Blackmail?' Genevieve's eyebrows rose. 'That sounds dramatic.'

'Someone filed a complaint about me being "unprofessional" on a tour.' Elise carefully avoided mentioning the specifics. 'Gill used it as leverage to get me to take this job she's been trying to fill for months.'

'That's rough,' Hayley said sympathetically. 'Though selfishly, I'm glad you're back, even if it wasn't your choice.'

'It's temporary,' Elise said quickly. 'I mean, I'm looking at it as temporary. I haven't really settled on a long-term plan yet.'

They ordered food, then Elise handed her menu back to the waiter and took a deep breath.

'Listen,' Elise said quietly, her fingers curling around the stem of her wine glass. 'I owe you both an apology. I know I hurt you, and I know I disappeared when I should've shown up. I'd like us to be close again. I miss what we had. And Gen' – she looked up, her voice catching – 'missing your wedding was... unforgivable.'

A silence fell. Genevieve's expression shifted – still cautious, but softening.

'It's ok,' she said at last. 'I understand. It was awkward for me and Finlay too.'

'It was mostly for his sake that I stayed away.' Elise dropped her gaze. 'I didn't think he'd want his evil ex ruining the day. Everything was so tangled – me and him, and then you and him. And Hayley... you being his sister, and Aidan's cousin, just made it harder. I felt like everyone must be judging me. Like I'd become a... walking mess of bad decisions.' She gave a hollow laugh. 'And instead of fixing it, I ran. Because living with the shame was easier than facing the people who'd seen the worst in me.'

'Elise.' Hayley reached out and touched her arm. 'We never thought that way. We figured you needed space.'

'I did,' she said. 'But now, I need you both. More than I realised. And I know I don't have a right to ask that of you after shutting you out.'

She blinked fast, pressing her fingers to her eyes. A warm hand closed over hers.

'Hey.' Genevieve's voice was gentle. 'We understand. And please – don't call yourself evil. You made mistakes. We all have. My mistake was not admitting my feelings for Finlay sooner.'

Tears still pricked at Elise's eyes. 'I was so awful when you started seeing him. I assumed he was doing it to get back at me... just like I'd used him to punish Aidan. I couldn't even see how I'd hurt people. I was just trying to stop everything spinning out of control.'

'We forgive you,' Genevieve said quietly.

'Of course we do.' Hayley squeezed her arm. 'You were hurting. We saw it, even if we didn't always know what to say.'

'I've been in counselling,' Elise said. 'It helped me untangle things – what was actually mine to carry, and what never should've been. I learned that I'd spent so long shaping myself into what I thought people wanted, I didn't even know who I was anymore. But I'm trying. And I don't want to be the version of me who runs away when things get real.'

Hayley let out a shaky breath. 'Well, we're still here. And we're glad you are too.'

'Life's too short for grudges,' Genevieve said, her eyes shining.

'So let's not waste any more of it,' Hayley added. 'You're not alone anymore, Elise. Not if you don't want to be.'

'Especially now.' There was something in Genevieve's voice that made Elise's brow furrow. 'What do you mean, especially now?'

A smile bloomed across Genevieve's face. 'Well, I was going to wait until dessert to tell you both, but...' She placed her free hand on her stomach. 'I'm pregnant.'

'What?' Hayley squealed, drawing looks from nearby tables. 'Oh my God! I'm going to be an aunty.' She wrapped her arms around Genevieve. 'Has Finlay told Mum? She'll be overjoyed!'

'He's telling her now, so she knows at the same time as you.'

Elise's stomach swooped. 'That's so lovely.' She squeezed Genevieve's hand, the warmth of the moment settling in. A fleeting thought crossed her mind – how, at one point, *she* had imagined having children with Finlay. But that had been before she realised their relationship had been doomed from the start. Now, knowing he and Genevieve were happy and starting a family together filled her with a deep, unexpected warmth. Neither Aidan nor Finlay had been the right fit for her. She saw that clearly now, but only because someone else had opened her eyes. Someone she didn't really know that well. Someone she'd spent a large part of her life hating, yet someone who had looked at her – and seen her – like no one else had. He'd cracked through her walls and awakened feelings she didn't know she possessed.

It may have been brief, but it had felt so real, and it lingered in her thoughts, refusing to fade.

'How far along are you?' Elise shook herself.

'Twelve weeks.' Genevieve beamed. 'We had the scan yesterday. Everything looks perfect. But morning sickness is brutal.'

'You don't look sick,' Hayley said. 'You're actually glowing.'

'Trust me, the glow comes and goes. Mostly when I'm not hanging over a toilet bowl.'

Their waiter appeared with their food. As soon as it was on the table, Hayley raised her glass. 'A toast! To Gen and Finlay and the little bun in the oven.'

'And to friends.' Genevieve raised her water. 'And new beginnings.'

'To friends.' Elise clinked her glass against theirs, a lump forming in her throat.

The conversation flowed more naturally now they'd cleared the air. Genevieve talked about her pregnancy symptoms and how her cookware line was expanding. Hayley shared gossip and stories from the salon. Elise found herself laughing more than she had in months.

'I've missed this,' she said. 'I've missed you both so much.'

'We missed you too,' Hayley said. 'We were never angry. We were just waiting until you were ready to share.'

The dessert menus arrived, and Genevieve immediately perked up. 'I'm eating for two, so I'm definitely having the chocolate fondant.'

Elise traced the rim of her wineglass. 'There's something I want to tell you both,' she said. 'But I need you to promise it stays between us.'

Hayley and Genevieve exchanged a glance, curiosity sparking in their eyes.

'Of course.' Genevieve settled back in her chair. 'Are you pregnant too?'

'Definitely not. Now, swear.'

'Hand on heart.' Genevieve did the action with a solemn look.

'Pinky swear,' Hayley added.

Elise took a deep breath. 'I told you about the complaint at work. The one Gill used to strong-arm me into taking the Glenbriar job.'

'The unprofessional behaviour thing?' Hayley leaned forward.

'Yeah, that.'

'*Did* you behave unprofessionally?'

Heat crept up Elise's neck. 'Kind of. Well, yes. I shouldn't have but... There was this guy and we—'

'You hooked up?' Hayley's eyes gleamed.

'Yes.' Elise swallowed. 'We agreed to a fling, and it was good. Really good. But it's a lot more complicated than that.'

'Why?' Genevieve frowned.

Elise stared into her coffee, unable to meet their eyes. 'Because he wasn't a stranger. I already knew this man. And I don't get on with him in the real world.'

'Who is he?' Genevieve exchanged a glance with Hayley.

'Do we know him too?' Hayley asked.

Elise nodded. 'It was Gabe Wilder.'

Silence. Complete, stunned silence. When Elise finally looked up, both women were staring at her with identical expressions of shock.

'Gabe,' Genevieve repeated flatly.

'Aidan's best friend Gabe Wilder,' Hayley added, her voice rising slightly.

'The very same.'

'Oh my god. You were guiding the tour Aidan and Lilah went on?' Hayley goggled, the penny obviously dropping. 'So you must have seen all this drama with Scarlett.'

'Yeah. That was part of the complaint. Though I couldn't exactly do anything about that crazy boyfriend of hers.'

'True.' Hayley pulled a face. 'But Gabe? Was it a bit of...' She glanced around and lowered her voice '...angry sex? Because you hate him, right?'

Elise snorted. 'You always love the gory details, don't you?'

'Sure do.'

'It maybe started off like that.'

'But?' Hayley prompted.

'It stopped feeling like just a physical thing.' Elise gave them a helpless look. 'It started to feel... significant. Which is terrifying.'

'You mean you caught feelings?'

Elise inhaled sharply. 'Something like that.'

'And have you seen him since you've been back in Glenbriar?' Genevieve asked.

'No.' Elise took a sip of wine. 'If I see him, I'm not sure what I'd say to him. "Hey, thanks for the mind-blowing sex that got me demoted"?'

'Mind-blowing, was it?' Hayley grinned wickedly.

'Shut up,' Elise groaned, feeling her cheeks burn. 'That's not the point.'

'It's a pretty important point.' Genevieve grinned. 'It's always good to get someone you enjoy getting down and dirty with, especially if you're thinking of seeing him again.'

'I'm not. We ended it. It was a fling. That's all he wanted. I have to respect that. It would have been too complicated.'

'Because of Aidan?' Hayley asked.

'Exactly. Gabe is Aidan's best friend. And well...' She looked between the two of them. 'Look at the mess we all got ourselves into when friendship mixed with romance.'

'It could get messy,' Genevieve agreed. 'Though Aidan is happily married now.'

'So what are you going to do?' Hayley pressed. 'Just walk away and forget it ever happened?'

Elise let out a long sigh. She didn't know what to do. But one thing was certain. Whatever she decided, it felt a lot better having her two friends back beside her to help her if she needed them... And something told her she would.

CHAPTER TWENTY-FOUR

Gabe

Gabe rinsed out his mug and placed it on the drying rack, glancing around his compact living space. This flat had suited him fine for years as a place to crash between adventures, podcast recordings, and environmental campaigns. But lately, it felt confining, like a too-small jumper that pinched at the armpits.

The buzzer rang. His mother – fifteen minutes earlier than expected. Well, maybe it was better to get this over and done with. His sense of duty was strong, but her visits and their interactions were never real. How could they be when she still had loyalty to her husband?

'Hello, son.' His mother swept in, trailing perfume and nervous energy. She kissed his cheek, her lips barely grazing his skin. 'It's so lovely to have you back in town. I always worry when you're far away doing all these dangerous things.'

'Dangerous? Hardly, Mum.'

'Well, all the outdoor stuff.' She frowned. 'You never know what might happen.' She pulled back to examine him.

'Is it really any worse than keeping three cats, two dogs and two donkeys?' He raised his eyebrows. 'Plus those birds that practically mug you on the way to the front door?'

His mum used the grounds at their house to keep quite a menagerie. She'd always loved animals, and Gabe was pretty sure they were an escape for her. It didn't take too much to imagine her consoling herself with doggy cuddles when her husband decided to unleash a tirade, and Gabe knew he did exactly that – frequently.

'I've brought you those chocolate biscuits you like.' She pulled a packet out from a shopping bag.

'Thanks.' He took the packet, noting it was the brand his father preferred, but saying nothing. He pretty much ate anything. 'Do you want a cup of tea?'

'No time, I'm afraid. Your father's waiting in the car. We've got to be at the airport in two hours.'

'You could have posted the keys through my letterbox.'

'Don't be silly.' She rummaged in her bag. 'I wanted to see you. And go through the instructions.'

Gabe leaned against the counter. 'You already messaged me.'

'Yes, but I've written it down in case the message gets deleted.'

Gabe didn't like to say he'd be more likely to lose the bit of paper than delete a message.

She pulled out a jangle of keys and a folded piece of paper. 'Now, the feeding schedule is on here, along with the vet's number and the emergency contacts. The peacocks keep trying to get into the house; please don't let them. They make a terrible mess. And the same goes for the guinea fowl, though they usually stay near the trees.'

He took the list from her and caught her giving him an almost sad smile. Despite everything, he loved her fierce attention to detail, her obsessive care for her animals. He'd love to be closer to her, go back to the house, help with the animals more often. But he wouldn't. Maybe it meant his father had won the silent war, but Gabe didn't care. For his own self-preservation, he couldn't bring himself to have anything to do with the man ever again.

'Don't worry, Mum. It'll all be fine. You have fun.' He meant it too – at least, he wanted to. But with his father there? It was hard to believe *anyone* could have fun around that man. Gabe had learned that lesson early: that the anticipation of a family holiday could be shattered in seconds by a raised voice or a wrong move. The wrong shoes, asking the wrong question, breathing too loud – it didn't matter. His father could find fault in anything, and did. By the time Gabe was twelve, he'd stopped getting excited about going anywhere.

Worse still, his mum had never really stopped making excuses for it, and would always add, '*At least he's faithful. He's not a cheat.*' Those words had become a mantra, and sometimes Gabe would repeat them back inside his head in a mocking voice, hating how his mum held his father's only attribute high enough to exonerate him from all his misdeeds.

'Thank you, Son. And I am pleased you're back. I hope you'll stay this time.'

He gave her a tight smile, then turned to the window. Rain spattered the glass. Outside, his father's car idled with all the simmering impatience Gabe remembered. 'I don't know if I can,' he said.

He didn't want to go. But staying felt impossible too.

'I've been offered a year-long contract,' he said. 'An environmental podcast in Cornwall. Still under the *Wilder at Heart* brand, but with a potentially bigger audience. Decent money too.'

All good things. On paper, it was a dream opportunity. The kind of thing his younger self would've jumped at. A sign that he was getting somewhere.

But he hadn't jumped.

Because something wasn't sitting right.

Elise.

He could still taste the sweetness on her skin. Still hear her laugh, the real laugh, not the fake version others saw. And the way she'd looked at him. The way he could really talk to her, the way she "got him"... And he got her.

But it was just a fling. No promises, no regrets.

So why couldn't he let it go?

Maybe because something about being with her had cracked him open in a way he hadn't expected. She'd inadvertently made him question the version of himself he'd built up for public consumption – the confident, free-spirited Gabe who always had a new adventure lined up. But what if he didn't want to keep chasing? What if, for once, he just wanted to belong somewhere? With someone.

He glanced at his mum, who was fiddling with her scarf, avoiding his gaze the way she always did when she suspected he wasn't telling her the full truth.

'I'll think about it,' he said, not just to her but to himself.

His mother clutched her pendant. 'But Cornwall is so far.'

'That's rather the point,' he muttered. The further away from Elise, the better – for himself. And he wasn't kidding. He'd even considered opportunities in New Zealand.

'What about your flat?'

'I don't know. I might sell it or let it out.' He shrugged. 'It's too small anyway.'

His mother looked around the space. 'It is a bit cramped. You could stay with us if you needed—'

'No thanks.' His tone left no room for discussion. His mum knew his feelings about his father, but she couldn't help herself. Just as she believed she could fix her husband, she believed she could bring Gabe round. But it wasn't going to happen. His parents' house was a gorgeous place, with easily enough room for him, but memories sullied it so much Gabe couldn't look at it with anything but disgust.

She sighed, touching his arm. 'Glenbriar's your home. People care about you here.'

'I know.' He softened his tone. 'I do love it here... I'm just not sure it's practical.'

His mother checked her watch. 'I should go. Your father will be getting impatient.'

'Heaven forbid we keep him waiting.' Gabe was unable to keep the bitterness from his voice.

'He's excited about the trip,' she said. 'We both are. First holiday in three years. And will you at least think about staying?' She stepped forward and hugged him. 'Feels to me like you're running away from something. I just hope it's not me.'

He stiffened. 'I'm not running away from you. I'm moving towards an opportunity.' Though he couldn't deny he was running from Elise – or the memory of her.

His mum held his gaze for a long moment, then nodded. 'The spare key to the shed is under the blue plant pot. Don't forget to water my orchids – just a thimbleful for each, no more.'

'Got it.' He waved her out, watching as she headed down the stairs, then closed the door and leaned against it. He looked down at the keys in his hand. Maybe a week at his parents' house would seal the deal. If anything made him want to run away, it was that place.

The road to Glenview House where his parents lived took Gabe past Woodend Cottage, where Aidan and Lilah lived. The September trees in the wood nearby were beginning their slow surrender to autumn, but the weather had stayed nice, and it still felt more summery than autumnal, though perhaps the air was a little chillier come evening. Gabe drummed his fingers on the steering wheel. He could nip in and say hi to Aidan. Of course, he was procrastinating, but he pulled the car up beside the house. Tucked in at the side of it was a bright yellow shed with flowers and bees painted on it: The Crafty Bee Barn, where Aidan's mum had a studio and she and Lilah sold crafts. Scarlett had worked there for a while too, but she didn't seem to stick at much for long.

As Gabe approached the fence, a beautiful grey and white husky padded up to it. 'Hey, Maya.' He leaned over and rubbed her soft fur.

'Oh, it's you.' Aidan looked around the side of his house. 'You come for some honey?'

'Um... Yeah.' He hadn't, but Aidan kept bees and had the best honey in the county, so Gabe wasn't going to turn it down.

Aidan led him into the kitchen and filled the kettle. Lilah turned around and smiled. She had a pair of garden gloves in her hand, her ginger curls escaping from a messy ponytail. 'Oh, hi.' She gave him a quick hug. 'How are you holding up after that mad coach tour?'

'Fine. It was... interesting.'

'That's one word for it.' She exchanged a look with Aidan. 'We quite enjoyed it, but Scarlett's been completely traumatised.'

'Really?'

Aidan nodded. 'Yeah. She's not doing well. She hasn't left Mum's house since we got back.'

'Won't talk to anyone about what happened,' Lilah said. 'We all thought it was about Leon, but her mum thinks it's something even worse.'

'But we're not sure what.' Aidan shrugged. 'She won't say.'

'Weird.' Gabe let out a sigh.

'And what about you? Is this you off to play zookeeper at your parents?'

'For my sins.' Gabe took a mug from Aidan. They chatted some more about the garden and the bees until Gabe couldn't prolong the inevitable anymore. After hugging them both good-bye, he got back in his truck. He sat for a moment, taking a few deep breaths, then started the engine and headed into the countryside on the hills behind Glenbriar. About a mile up, he turned off the main road and up a winding private track, trees closing in on either side. Glenview House was a sprawling Victorian building with mullioned windows and creeping ivy. Gabe parked in the sweeping drive, his stomach already knotting. This place should be somewhere he loved returning to. It had originally been his maternal grandparents' house, and his mum had inherited it... Then his father had moved in, taken over, and turned it into the doom place that it was.

The minute Gabe unlocked the front door, the smell hit him – expensive cigars, leather, furniture polish. His father's scent. He breathed through his mouth, dropping his bag in the hallway.

The cats appeared almost instantly, winding around his ankles, meowing at him.

'Alright, alright,' he muttered. 'Dinner's coming.'

He went through the routine, feeding the cats and letting the dogs out into the garden. Later he'd walk them to the donkeys and check they were ok. The peacocks screeched at him from the trees, their cries echoing across the grounds like lost souls.

Inside, he opened windows to clear the cigar smell. Objectively, the house was beautiful – antique furniture that had belonged to at least two generations on his mum's side, oil paintings, thick oriental rugs. But to Gabe, every room held memories he'd rather forget. His father's study, where he'd been lectured for hours about his 'disappointing' grades – even if they were actually perfectly acceptable. The dining room, where silent meals had stretched into eternity. The annex – which had seen better days – but had been the perfect place to hide when the shouting started.

He grabbed what he needed from the kitchen – a few bottles of water, some fruit, bread and cheese – and headed back outside. The September evening was balmy, the sky still light though the sun was low. He rolled the truck around the perimeter of the grounds, past the formal gardens his mother kept immaculate, to a small wooded area that sloped down to a stream.

Here, at least, he could breathe. This had been his childhood refuge – a place his father never bothered to visit, deeming it too wild and unkempt.

Gabe reversed the truck into a level spot beneath an old oak tree. The roof tent was his pride and joy – a canvas and aluminium affair that unfolded from the top of his vehicle into a comfortable sleeping platform. He'd spent more nights in it than in his flat over the past year, chasing stories for his environmental podcast, camping in remote glens and beside lochs.

After all the animals were sorted, he sat in a folding chair beside his makeshift camp, listening to the burble of the stream and the distant calls of the peacocks. The low sun reflected off the windows of the main house, still visible through the trees, but here he felt separate from it and from the memories that were built into its walls.

A light breeze ruffled the leaves above. For the first time since returning from Skye, Gabe felt something like peace.

Tonight, he'd sleep under the stars, with only the trees as witnesses to his thoughts – thoughts that, despite his best efforts, kept circling back to dark eyes, long chestnut hair and a smile that messed with his mind completely.

Friday morning greeted the grounds of Glenview House with the kind of sunshine that almost mocked the summer as it came too late for most people's holidays. But getting to enjoy it from the beauty spot in his parents' garden was refreshing, perhaps more so than the whole five days on Skye. Gabe nipped into the house to use the facilities. He showered, then fed and exercised the animals.

His mum had left food, but most of it seemed to be chocolate treats, and while that was kind, he needed something more substantial. Instead of packing away his tent, he decided to cycle back to Glenbriar. His dad had a brand-new e-bike and probably didn't want Gabe anywhere near it, but what he didn't know couldn't hurt.

He wheeled it out of the shed, found a helmet, and headed towards Glenbriar. The track stretched before him, lined with hedgerows heavy with brambles not quite ready to eat, but there were plenty of wild raspberries which were ripe and looked delicious. He stopped to pluck a few, then carried on.

Once he reached the town, he chained the bike in the supermarket car park. He might get a couple of things in here, but he preferred to use the independent shops. The Deli was great, and he headed down the hill towards the High Street.

He paused outside the window of the outdoor equipment store, eyeing a new pair of hiking boots. Perhaps he should invest in some gear for Cornwall, if he decided to take the job.

Cornwall. The word felt both enticing and hollow. An escape route from...

He turned away from the window, and his eyes widened. Had his thoughts conjured the woman in person? Maybe he'd somehow manifested her into being before him.

'Elise.'

She was wearing a smart blazer and pencil skirt in the Highland Horizons' colours. Was she doing another tour? Or perhaps visiting their branch here.

'Oh... Hi.' She adjusted the strap of her handbag on her shoulder.

'Hey.' He rammed his hands into his pockets. 'I didn't know you were in town.'

She gave him a brief smile. 'Well, I am... And so are you, it would seem.'

'I'm house-sitting for my parents. They're in Italy.'

'Ah yes. I remember you mentioned that.'

'I thought you were in Glasgow.'

Something flickered in her expression. 'Not anymore. I've been... reassigned.'

'To Glenbriar?' He couldn't keep the surprise from his voice. 'Since when?'

'Just a couple of weeks.'

'So, you're working here?'

'For now.' Her smile tightened. 'I'm the branch manager, on a fixed-term contract.'

'Wow. You took the job they offered you then? And... congratulations?' He studied her face, sensing there was more to this. Something wasn't quite right. Or maybe she was just feeling awkward around him. He could relate – this was kind of weird.

Elise sighed. 'It's not exactly a promotion.'

A group of tourists bustled past them, forcing them to step closer to the shop window.

'Oh? What happened then?'

She met his eyes directly. 'You did.'

He blinked. 'Me?'

'Someone on the tour complained about my "inappropriate conduct" with a passenger. Gill – my boss – got wind of it. She was ready to fire me.'

Guilt hit him like a physical blow. 'Elise, I'm so sorry. I had no idea—'

'It's not your fault.' She cut him off. 'Well, not entirely. It takes two. I wasn't exactly fighting you off.'

Their eyes met, and memories played in Gabe's mind. Why did it feel like she was reliving the same ones?

She looked away first. 'Anyway, I talked my way out of being fired. But Gill saw an opportunity. You know how she wanted me to do this job?' Elise's fingers tightened around her bag strap. 'Well, she told me if I took it the complaint would "disappear".'

'That's blackmail.' Gabe's fists tightened in his pockets.

'I know.' She shrugged. 'But I didn't want to lie. And I don't want to get fired. That wouldn't look good on my CV. So, I'm doing this for now. But I'm looking for something else.'

'What kind of thing?'

'I don't even know.' She pulled a face. 'It's not all bad. The salary's decent, and I have more autonomy than in Glasgow.'

'But you didn't want to come back to Glenbriar.'

'No.' Her voice softened. 'But I've made up with my friends and that's helped.'

His stomach twisted. Here he was considering running away to Cornwall, while Elise had been backed into a corner because of him – because of them.

'Let me make it up to you,' he said suddenly.

Her eyebrow arched. 'And how exactly would you do that?'

'I don't know. Dinner? A drink?' He hesitated, then added, 'A romantic weekend in a truck and rooftop tent?'

She snorted. 'Excuse me?'

'I'm serious.' He leaned forward. 'I'm camping at my parents' place... I told you I can't stand being in the house. I've got a beautiful spot by a stream, under the stars. Private, peaceful.'

'You're insane.' But she was smiling, a real smile that reached her eyes.

'Probably.' He grinned. 'But think about it. No tourist complaints, no judgmental colleagues. Just us, a warm sleeping bag, and more stars than you can count.'

'That's your pitch? Sleep in a glorified tent on top of your truck?'

'The tent is very comfortable, I'll have you know.' He raised his eyebrows suggestively.

She shook her head, but her smile remained. 'You're ridiculous.'

'Is that a no?'

She studied him for a long moment. 'We agreed what happened on Skye was just a holiday fling.'

'We did.' He nodded slowly. 'But that was before you got exiled to Glenbriar because of it. Seems only fair I help you make the best of your sentence.'

'And am I to assume this is a rekindling of the fling... Or what?' She held out her hands.

'If you want it to be. Or we can just hang out as friends. I'm easy both ways.' And he almost meant it, though his heart wasn't a hundred per cent onboard. Friends didn't seem like quite enough.

'Ok,' she said finally. 'I suppose I could come up for the weekend. I wasn't looking forward to going back to Glasgow just to sit alone in my flat. At least your ridiculous tent has company... And hopefully not such gruelling company as my brother's house.'

His heart leapt. 'Is that where you're staying?'

'Yup.'

'Well, come up later if you want. I'll introduce you to the menagerie.'

She raised an eyebrow.

'You'll see what I mean when you get there.'

'When should I come?' she asked.

'Whenever you like. Let me give you their address.' He pulled out his phone.

'Should I bring anything?'

'Just yourself.' He smiled. 'And something to sleep in, maybe a change of clothes.'

'Ok, I'll see you later then.'

'I'll be the one with the ridiculous tent.'

She watched him for a moment and her eyes dropped subtly to his lips, but she wouldn't kiss him out here – he knew it. Too many people here knew too many other people. And the news would be all around the town before Gabe got even halfway back to his parents' house.

'Later.' He took her hand and gave it a little squeeze. Yes, later.

He watched her as she headed back to work. After the doom and gloom of the last couple of weeks, a ray of sunshine had returned to his heart.

As he headed to the deli, he tried not to overanalyse what that meant exactly and where this left him in the grand scheme of his life.

CHAPTER TWENTY-FIVE

The tent perched on the roof of Gabe's truck brought a smile to Elise's face, though she wasn't sure if it was a happy smile or a what-the-hell-have-I-let-myself-in-for-please-help-me smile. Despite always having worked in travel and tourism, she'd never camped in her life before. And camping on top of a truck seemed completely insane, especially when there was a perfectly good house just across the garden. A totally stunning house in fact.

'Well?' Gabe gestured towards his setup. 'What do you think of Château Wilder?'

'It's wild alright.' Elise raised her eyebrows. 'I can see why you didn't want to stay in the house. I mean, this is so much better.'

Gabe laughed and shook his head. 'You'll love it. Just wait and see.'

The late afternoon sun bathed the secluded corner of his parents' garden in golden light. The spot he'd chosen was sheltered by a cluster of mature silver birches, their leaves rustling gently in the breeze. Elise wasn't a massive fan of nature – not that she didn't appreciate natural beauty – and being out in it at close quarters wasn't something she craved, but she could understand why it appealed to some people. And actually the idea of being out in the open like this had a certain pull, though she wouldn't be doing it without Gabe.

She watched as he climbed the first few rungs.

'Come on up. I'll give you the grand tour.'

She approached the ladder cautiously, conscious of the slim-fitting jeans she'd chosen that morning – practical enough for the countryside but still flattering. 'If I fall and break something, you're explaining to Gill why her new Glenbriar manager is out of commission.'

'You'll be fine.'

When she reached the top, Gabe's hand closed around hers and pulled her onto the platform. The contact sent a jolt through her.

'Welcome to my humble abode.'

Elise ducked inside, surprised by what she found. The interior was bizarrely cosy, with a sleeping area covering most of the floor space, dressed with proper bedding – not the sleeping bags she'd expected. Small battery-powered lanterns hung from the ceiling poles, and there was even a tiny shelf with a Bluetooth speaker.

'This is actually quite nice.'

'Don't sound so shocked. I have standards, you know.'

The tent wasn't tall enough to stand in, but sitting, there was plenty of headroom. Through the mesh windows on either side, she spotted glimpses of trees and sky. It felt intimate without being claustrophobic.

'And you prefer this to your parents' perfectly good house?'

Gabe's expression clouded briefly. 'The house reeks of my father's cigars. I can't sleep there without feeling like I'm breathing him in. It brings back so many bad memories.'

Elise patted his arm. 'Yeah. That's not good. Your mum must be grateful that you're doing this though.'

'She is. She very rarely goes anywhere as she's so worried about leaving the animals.'

'It's a really nice place for a house. It's beautiful.' She looked across the wide lawn. A stream ran through the middle of it. 'And so peaceful.'

'Wait until the peacocks start their morning screaming. Not so peaceful then,' Gabe chuckled. 'But at night, it's magic. You can see every star.'

'Sounds lovely.'

He shifted closer. 'Much better than the coach, huh? No schedule, no complaining passengers, no one to report us for fraternising.'

Elise rolled her eyes. 'Don't remind me. I still can't believe someone complained. We weren't exactly hurting anyone. But people sure love minding everyone else's business.'

'Don't they just,' Gabe murmured, his eyes briefly dropping to her lips before meeting her gaze again. 'Even though I do feel really guilty about it.'

'Well, it's done now.' She gave a little shrug. 'I'm actually enjoying being back more than I thought I would. Hayley and Genevieve have been amazing. It's so nice to be close to them again. And Kate, who I work with, is lovely.' Things were oddly falling into place in a way she hadn't expected. Of course, she couldn't stay with David and Amanda indefinitely – for many reasons – so she'd need to sort out somewhere once the lease on her Glasgow flat came to an end. But it felt like a happy homecoming. A new start. Everything was going well... Almost. She kept her eyes on Gabe and her insides flickered.

What if...?

The question fluttered around her chest and for the first time she properly allowed herself to wonder if somewhere along the line they might have a future together. This felt more like a date – albeit a weird one – than a continuation of their fling. And if he was back, and she was back... But of course, there was Aidan. And there would always be Aidan. Even if Aidan didn't publicly object to his friend dating his ex, the levels of awkward would never not be there.

Gabe let out a sigh. 'I'm pleased you're finding your way back. I know it's been a tough few years... probably not helped by me.'

She smiled. 'I forgive you.'

He took her hand and squeezed it. 'Thanks.'

'What about you? What's next for *Wilder at Heart*?'

'Well...' He glanced down at their joined hands, then back to her face. 'I've just been offered a year's worth of podcast work in Cornwall.'

'Cornwall?' The word felt heavy in her mouth. 'That's... far.'

So much for her thinking he was sticking around. Apparently not.

'The money's good, and it would mean working with some big names in conservation.'

'Sounds like a great opportunity.' A cold weight settled in her stomach as she spoke. Of course he was planning to leave. Gabe Wilder never stayed in one place for long. Tying him down would be like trying to cage a wild animal. It wasn't fair. Just as she thought she'd found home and someone she could care for, he was about to up and leave again.

She steeled her heart. Whatever she felt for Gabe, she didn't want it to hold him back or impede him. She'd been selfish in relationships before – used people. She wasn't ever going to do that again. Being with Gabe made her happy, but she wouldn't attempt to make him stay just for that. His happiness mattered as much as her own.

'Do you want to come with me to feed the animals?' he asked.

'Sure.'

The path to the donkey paddock wound through a section of garden that had been left deliberately wild. Elise picked her way carefully over the uneven ground. Gabe's mother's dogs bounded ahead – a shaggy brown terrier mix called Sting and a black labrador called Nero – occasionally circling back to check on their temporary human caretakers with expressions of barely contained excitement.

'Careful there.' Gabe caught Elise's elbow as she stumbled over a hidden root. 'Mum believes in letting nature do its thing in this part of the property. Dad hates it, of course. I'm surprised he's let her keep it like this. He's such a bully.'

'Oh dear.' She sighed 'Parents.'

'Do you get on with yours?'

'Mostly, but they spend a lot of time travelling. They've always loved it and now they're both retired they're away more than they're here, so I don't see them that often.'

'Is that where you got the idea to work in the travel industry?'

'Probably, though I don't think I ever looked at it like that, but yeah. Makes sense. It was something we always did as children – they took us everywhere.'

'Sounds like great experiences. I was the opposite. We hardly ever went anywhere – only wherever my father wanted us to go, which was usually Largs. The place *he* went for his holidays every year as a child.'

Elise smiled. 'You've made up for it now.'

'I guess.'

The evening air carried the sweet scent of late summer – grass, wildflowers, and a leafy, earthy kind of smell. As they crested a small rise, Elise saw the donkey paddock ahead, a spacious enclosure bordered by wooden fencing. Two grey donkeys with short bristly manes stood watching their approach with pricked ears.

'That's Mabel and Dolly.' Gabe pointed to the donkeys. 'Mabel's the bigger one with the white nose. She's the boss.'

'They're bigger than I expected.' Elise eyed the animals with a mixture of interest and wariness.

Gabe laughed. 'Yeah, donkeys can get quite big. A lot of people think they're smaller than they actually are. And these ladies are absolute sweethearts.' Gabe approached a small feed shed beside the paddock. 'Though they might nibble your fingers if you're not careful.'

'That's reassuring,' Elise muttered, hanging back as Gabe unlocked the shed and emerged with two buckets of feed pellets.

The dogs circled around them, the terrier yapping excitedly while the labrador sat patiently by the gate, tail sweeping the ground in steady thumps.

Gabe unlatched the gate and stepped into the paddock, the dogs staying obediently outside. Mabel and Dolly approached immediately, their large heads bobbing as they walked. Gabe greeted them, stroking their necks and murmuring to them.

After Gabe had checked their water trough and their shed, they collected the now empty buckets and returned them to the store.

'Have you heard anything from Scarlett?' Gabe shut the door and bolted it.

Elise shook her head. 'I'm not really in touch with her. Why?'

'Aidan's worried about her. Says she's not left her room at their mum's house for weeks.'

'Sounds like she's in a bad way.'

'Yeah. That breakup on the coach was pretty hideous. I don't know how she lasted the week, especially when those busybodies started having a go at her.'

'Do you think there was any truth in the rumours about her and Lloyd?'

Gabe glanced at her and pulled a face. 'Na, surely not. That was just his mother being paranoid.'

'But why would she be? Did he look like someone who has holiday flings with women around fifteen years younger than him?'

Gabe gave a little shrug. 'Not really.'

'Exactly. So why would his mother think that?'

'Maybe she thought Scarlett was looking at him in a funny way...' He screwed up his forehead like he was trying to imagine something or recall something. 'You know... I just remembered. That day we went canoeing, Scarlett got in a canoe with him. I thought it was a bit odd at the time, but what if... Maybe...'

'Yeah, exactly. This is what I'm thinking. What if it's true?'

They reached the edge of the lawn where several peacocks strutted around regally, their magnificent tails dragging behind them like royal trains. On a small courtyard next to the lawn some speckled guinea fowl darted about near a large silver bin, making strange chattering noises.

Gabe lifted the lid on the bin and filled a scoop with grain. 'I don't see Scarlett going for someone like him though. And even if she did have a fling with him... Well, a fling's a fling, right?' He tossed the scoop of grain in a wide arc, and the birds converged from all directions.

Yup. That was so true. A fling was a fling.

'I just hope she's ok,' Elise said.

The sun was beginning to sink lower in the sky. Ahead, the house loomed, its windows reflecting the golden light. They ambled towards it, the dogs bounding on, chasing invisible scents.

'When I was dating Aidan, Scarlett used to latch onto me sometimes.'

Gabe nodded and rubbed his hands. 'I can imagine. She probably thought you were very cool... Which you are, of course.' He winked.

'Ha. You've changed your tune.' Elise side-eyed him. 'But Scarlett would turn up when Aidan wasn't there or call me to go shopping. At the time, I found it annoying.' She winced at the memory.

'Scarlett can be a lot,' Gabe said.

Elise wrapped her arms around herself. Without comment, Gabe shrugged off his fleece jacket and draped it over her shoulders. The lining retained his warmth and scent.

'Thanks,' she murmured.

'Can't have you freezing before we make it back to the tent,' he replied with a wink. 'So, Scarlett adopted you?'

Elise nodded, slipping her arms through the too-large sleeves of his jacket. 'Looking back, I wonder if she just didn't have many friends of her own. She was always talking about people who'd let her down or betrayed her. At the time, I thought she just thrived on the drama.'

'I can see that,' Gabe agreed.

'But now I'm not so sure,' Elise went on. 'I don't remember her with a consistent group of friends. You said she was friends with Lilah now, but I guess that's fairly recent.' Elise stopped beside him and looked up at him.

Gabe nodded. 'Yeah, it is.'

'Scarlett used to be so angry with her,' Elise said with a rueful smile. 'Because she accidentally knocked out one of Scarlett's front teeth during a hockey game when they were teenagers. Scarlett had to get a crown, and according to her, it was a deliberate attack.'

Gabe groaned. 'Oh god, yes.'

'Scarlett held onto that grudge for years. When Aidan started seeing Lilah, she would call me constantly with updates about how ridiculous it was that Aidan was so nice to Lilah. I think for a while she even wanted me to get back together with Aidan to push Lilah out.'

'And did you want that?'

Elise shrugged. 'Maybe at the time. But definitely not now.'

'Good.' Gabe turned to face her and stroked a strand of hair behind her ear. 'Because that would be far too weird.'

'You're not wrong.'

'Let's get these two inside.' Gabe nodded to the dogs, who immediately perked up at his movement. 'And then I'll show you the luxury bathroom facilities that come with Château Wilder.'

Elise laughed, allowing him to lead her towards the house. 'You mean we don't have to use the bushes? Thank god.'

She was up for many things, but that wasn't one of them.

Chapter Twenty-Six

Elise

As Elise and Gabe approached the back door of Gabe's parents' house, a pang of guilt grew in her chest; her earlier judgments of Scarlett had been based on a superficial opinion, which didn't seem fair now. Perhaps they were more alike than she'd realised – both hiding behind public facades, both making questionable relationship choices, both sometimes feeling like outsiders even among friends.

The house enveloped them in warmth as they stepped inside, but Elise immediately understood what Gabe had meant about the cigar smell. It lingered in the air like an unwelcome ghost, clinging to the drapes and furniture no matter how clean everything looked. Gabe flicked on the lights as they moved through the dim hallway.

'Welcome to the mausoleum,' he said wryly, watching her take in the tired, formal décor. 'Best bathroom's upstairs, second door on the left. Kitchen's here if you need anything. I'd offer a tour, but...' He gestured vaguely.

'But you'd rather sleep in a tent than spend time in here,' Elise said. And she could almost see why. The house was all stiff, old-fashioned grandeur – furniture that had once been expensive, heavy curtains, faded wallpaper – like someone had stopped caring halfway through keeping up appearances. The place wasn't neglected exactly, just... emotionally hollow. As if no real joy had ever lived here. If Gabe hadn't been happy growing up, no wonder it still made his skin crawl.

Pity, really because beneath the scent of furniture polish and sickly air fresheners that barely masked the stale cigar smoke, the house had the bones of something beautiful.

The dogs trotted ahead of them, clearly familiar with their evening routine. The black Lab paused at a large wicker basket in the corner of the kitchen, looking expectantly at Gabe.

'Yes, your majesty, dinner's coming,' he told the dog. To Elise, he added, 'Make yourself at home. Bathroom's got everything you need – towels, toiletries.'

'I'll just grab my overnight bag from the car,' Elise said.

Outside, it felt colder now. The wind had picked up and Elise felt a smidge of rain.

'Is the tent waterproof?' she asked when she returned to the kitchen.

'Completely,' Gabe assured her, moving to a cupboard and pulling out a bag of dog food. 'That tent's been through storms, gales, and a blizzard. A bit of rain won't bother it.'

Elise wasn't entirely convinced but nodded anyway. 'If you say so.'

'Trust me,' Gabe said with a wink, measuring out food into two bowls. 'The cats usually appear once they hear the food bags.' He reached into another cupboard for cat food. 'They're probably lurking somewhere.'

As if on cue, a sleek grey cat slunk into the kitchen.

'That's Minerva.'

'She's beautiful.' Elise crouched down to offer her hand to the cat. Minerva sniffed her fingers before turning her attention back to Gabe and the food.

'You've made a friend there.' Gabe set down a dish. 'She's a sucker for anyone who might pet her.'

'She's very sweet.' Elise straightened up. 'Are we getting dressed for bed here, then walking back to the tent in pyjamas?'

'That's the camping way.' He smiled broadly.

Elise headed upstairs. The bathroom was as tired as the rest of the house, but the shower was hot. She dried herself off and changed into the sleep clothes she'd packed – soft cotton shorts and a loose t-shirt. She brushed her teeth and washed her face, studying her reflection in the oversized mirror. Her dark hair fell loose around her shoulders. It was a weird kind of vulnerable, standing here like this – way off-brand from her usual self, about to sleep in a roof tent of all things. She didn't know exactly what this thing was between her and Gabe yet, but for once, she wasn't spiralling about it or planning her escape route. She just wanted to be here.

With him.

When she returned downstairs, Gabe had changed as well, into sweatpants and a tight black t-shirt that hugged his shoulders in a way that made her mouth go slightly dry.

He glanced up, his eyes taking in her bare legs before meeting her gaze with a heat that made her skin tingle. 'Well, that's all the animals fed, so let's get going.'

The wind gusted more forcefully now and rain lashed against the windows. Elise accepted a pair of waterproof trousers to wear over her PJs and she put Gabe's fleece back on.

'We'll dash for it.' Gabe grabbed a large golf umbrella from a stand by the door and led her out the front. The moment they stepped outside, the wind whipped around them, tugging at their clothes and hair. Gabe pushed up the umbrella and pulled Elise close against his side.

They ran across the garden. The umbrella provided minimal protection as the wind kept changing direction, but Gabe's arm around her was solid and warm. By the time they reached the truck, they were both damp and breathless.

'Up you go.' Gabe urged, holding the umbrella over the ladder as best he could while Elise scrambled up. At the door, she took off her shoes, the waterproof trousers and the fleece and left them in the little porch so they wouldn't get the bedding wet. She shivered.

Gabe climbed in after her, taking off his boots and outerwear too, then zipping up the tent. 'Not so bad, right?'

'I'm freezing.'

'Let's get cosy then.' Gabe arranged the pillows against the rear of the tent and patted the bed. 'Very romantic, floating off into the sunset.'

'It's nighttime.' Elise smiled despite herself.

'Details.' He waved dismissively.

She got under the covers, and it did feel a little warmer. She pulled out her phone and checked the time. 'You know what? I'm going to message Scarlett. I feel bad for her. It must be really hard for her, no matter what she's going through.' And god knew there had been times in the not-so-distant past when Elise had wished someone had messaged her with random words of kindness. 'I think I still have her number.'

She opened a new message. The last one was dated over a year ago, but that wasn't going to stop her.

ELISE: Hi Scarlett. I know it's been ages, but I heard you're going through a rough time. Just wanted to say I'm back living in Glenbriar now, and if you ever want to talk or grab a coffee, I'm around. No pressure at all. Hope you're doing ok.

She hesitated, then added: *I know how it feels when everything seems to be falling apart. Sometimes it helps to talk to someone.*

Her finger hovered over the send button. Was this overstepping? They'd never been close, and their last interactions had been awkward at best, but Scarlett had tried. She'd always tried, even when Elise hadn't appreciated it. She pressed send before she could overthink it further.

Gabe settled under the blanket next to her. 'Thanks for doing that.'

Elise shrugged. 'After our conversation earlier, I just feel like it's wrong not to do something – or at least try.'

'You're full of surprises, Elise Reid.' Gabe smiled at her.

'She probably won't respond.' Elise set her phone aside. 'But at least she knows someone's thinking about her.'

The tent swayed again as a stronger gust of wind hit it, and Elise instinctively grabbed Gabe's arm.

He chuckled, covering her hand with his. 'Don't worry. This tent's not going anywhere. I was going to bring my guitar up and sing us a song, proper camping style, but it's in the truck and I really don't want to go outside again.'

'Sing to me anyway. Amanda keeps telling me how wonderful you are.'

He smirked. 'Yeah, she had me sing at that church concert, and she was such a groupie.'

'I know. She never shuts up about you.'

He turned to look at her, and the proximity of his body sent a wave of warmth through her. And she really needed to leach some of that heat, so she shifted closer.

Softly, he started humming a tune, then turned it into a song. His voice was a little rough, but still tuneful and very real. A smiled grew on her face as the sound vibrated through the small space. *'I'd keep you safe.'* The words were part of the song, but they seemed to be a promise too and she believed them.

Their eyes met in the lantern light as Gabe's song finished. He reached up and turned off the light.

'You are a very good singer. Maybe you should do music videos instead of environmental ones.'

'I sometimes sing on the podcasts.'

Elise smirked, thankful he couldn't see her in the dark. 'You know I've never watched them.'

'What?' he said in mock outrage.

'Well... You annoyed me too much. I couldn't bring myself to give you the credit for doing anything that good.' Though now she wished she'd watched them all... And perhaps if she had, it would have nudged her brain into the place that it was now. Maybe she'd always secretly had a thing for Gabe, but the timing had never been right.

'You're naughty,' Gabe murmured.

'I'm also cold,' she said.

He moved closer. 'Shall I warm you up? I know a really good way.'

'I'm counting on it.'

His thumb traced the line of her jaw. She leaned into him and their lips found each other, tentative at first, then with growing certainty.

Gabe's mouth was warm and gentle, his stubble creating a delicious friction against her skin. Elise melted into him as he wrapped her in his arms.

The kiss deepened, his tongue teasing along the seam of her lips. She opened for him. He tasted faintly of toothpaste.

'I've missed this,' he murmured against her mouth. 'Missed you.'

'Same.' Two weeks had felt like an eternity after the intensity of their fling.

His mouth left hers to trail along her jaw, down the sensitive column of her throat. Elise tilted her head back, giving him better access as his teeth grazed her pulse point. Her hands slid beneath his t-shirt, exploring the warm, taut skin of his back, feeling the muscles shift as he moved.

'I love... this,' Gabe muttered against her collarbone, his hands finding the hem of her shirt.

Elise raised her arms, allowing him to tug the garment over her head, her heart hammering. She'd been sure for one second he'd been about to say something else... Something that terrified her. Goosebumps raised on her exposed skin, quickly chased away by the heat of his palm as it travelled over her bare breasts.

'You're beautiful,' he said.

Before she could respond, his tongue was circling a nipple that had already peaked in anticipation. Elise gasped, her hands clutching at his shoulders. The sensation sent sparks of pleasure straight to her core, her body arching instinctively into his touch.

Gabe took his time until Elise was writhing beneath him.

He pulled back just long enough to take off his t-shirt. Elise ran her hands over him greedily, exploring the contrasts – the softness of chest hair against firm muscle, the smooth skin and rough calluses. There was something so undeniably masculine about him, so rugged.

She leaned forward to press her lips to his chest, just over his heart. It pounded beneath her mouth, its rapid pace betraying his outward composure. Was it wrong to feel love? Could this be love? Or just a burst of happy hormones tricking her?

The tent swayed more dramatically as a strong gust of wind hit it, the canvas snapping taut before relaxing again. The sound of rain intensified, but neither of them paused in their exploration. If anything, the wildness outside made their shelter feel even more intimate, their connection more vital.

Gabe's hands found the waistband of her shorts, his fingers dipping just beneath the elastic, teasing the sensitive skin of her lower abdomen. 'Can I?' His voice was rough with desire.

'Yes,' Elise breathed, lifting her hips to help as he slid the shorts down her legs, taking her underwear with them.

The cool air on her heated skin made her shiver, but then Gabe was there, his hands warming her thighs as he positioned himself between her legs.

Elise felt herself flush, not from embarrassment but from sheer want. This was his signature move, and he did it so well.

'Please,' she whispered, her hands fisting in the bedding beneath her.

The first touch of his mouth made her gasp. Elise closed her eyes, giving herself over to sensation. The skilled movement of his tongue against her most sensitive spots, the slight scrape of stubble against her inner thighs, the occasional hum of appreciation that vibrated through her core – it was overwhelming in the best possible way.

Outside, the wind howled, rattling the tent poles and creating an eerily beautiful soundtrack. The occasional lash of rain against the canvas punctuated the rhythm of Gabe's attentions.

Elise's breathing grew ragged. A particularly violent gust of wind made the entire tent structure shudder, and Elise cried out, her back arching, fingers grabbing Gabe's hair as waves of pleasure crashed through her. He stayed with her through it all, gentling his touch but not stopping, drawing out her climax until she was trembling.

Only then did he pull away.

'Beautiful,' he murmured, making his way back to her. 'Absolutely beautiful.'

Elise was still catching her breath, her body liquid with satisfaction. The tent continued to flap and move. She wrapped her arms around him, loving his heat, her hands tracing the solid planes of his chest, his abdomen, feeling the hard evidence of his desire against her thigh.

Gabe supported his weight on strong arms that bracketed her shoulders. Even in the dark, his eyes held hers with an intensity that made her breath catch. Elise reached up to trace the line of his jaw, feeling the rough stubble beneath her fingertips.

Gabe shimmied out of his pyjama bottoms and reached under the pillow, retrieving a foil packet. 'Always prepared,' he said.

'Boy Scout?'

'A very naughty one.' He tore the packet open.

Elise watched as he rolled the condom on. There was something incredibly intimate about witnessing this moment.

Gabe settled between her thighs, his weight a delicious pressure. He braced himself on one elbow, his other hand gently brushing hair from her face.

'You ok?' His eyes searched hers.

'Very,' she whispered.

He kissed her deep and positioned himself at her entrance. The first push inside her was exquisitely slow, a careful claiming that had Elise gasping against his mouth. She was still sensitive, every nerve ending heightened and receptive.

'God, Elise,' Gabe breathed when he was fully within her. He rested his forehead against hers, his breathing ragged. 'You are amazing.'

She wrapped her legs around his waist, adjusting to the fullness, loving the weight of him on her. Outside, the wind lashed against the tent, making the structure shudder.

'The tent,' she gasped as Gabe began to move, drawing out slowly before pushing back in with deliberate control. 'Can it take it?'

'Is fine,' he said, his voice a low rumble against her ear. 'Focus on us.'

It was easy to obey. Each thrust sent sparks of pleasure through her, building on the afterglow she still felt. Gabe set a measured pace, unhurried but thorough, each movement deliberate and deep. Elise's hands roamed his back, feeling the shifting muscles, the slight dampness of sweat beginning to form.

The limited space of the tent meant they were pressed close, chest to chest, every point of contact between them electric. The intimacy of it – here in this small, swaying space, with rain pattering above them and wind howling around them – was intense.

Gabe shifted slightly, changing the angle, and Elise gasped as he hit a spot deep inside that sent a jolt of extreme pleasure through her. He noticed her reaction, repeating the movement.

'There?' he murmured, watching her face with heated concentration.

'Yes,' she breathed, her fingers digging into his shoulders. 'Right there.'

He maintained the angle, his thrusts becoming more forceful but no less controlled. One hand slipped between them, finding her sensitive bundle of nerves, circling them with just the right pressure. The dual stimulation had Elise trembling beneath him, pleasure building rapidly once more.

The storm battered the tent, wind howling and canvas snapping, but it only seemed to feed the fire inside her. Wild matched wild. She was done holding back.

'Kiss me,' she demanded suddenly, needing more. 'I need—'

She couldn't finish. But Gabe obviously understood. His mouth found hers, deep and consuming, his kiss echoing the rhythm of his body. Elise clung to him, lost in the rising tide, her mind clear of everything but the way he felt – strong, present, hers.

She arched her back, a cry tearing from her throat. Her eyes rolled out of focus and pleasure crashed through her in relentless waves. The sensation seemed to go on forever, so intense and powerful, leaving her breathless and trembling.

Gabe continued to move, drawing out her pleasure until she was boneless beneath him. Only then did his control finally slip. His rhythm faltered, becoming more erratic, more desperate. Elise, still floating in her own afterglow, wrapped her arms tightly around him, encouraging him wordlessly.

He groaned, his face buried in her neck, body tensing above her. The moment he found his release, his hips pressed flush against hers, a shudder running through his powerful frame.

For several long moments, they lay entwined, both catching their breath, hearts pounding against each other. The storm continued unabated outside, rain lashing the canvas, wind buffeting the structure, but inside their cocoon, a different kind of peace had settled.

Eventually, Gabe lifted his head and brushed a gentle kiss against her lips before carefully withdrawing and disposing of the condom in a small waste bag.

When he returned to her side, Elise turned into him instinctively, her body seeking his warmth. He pulled the blankets over them both, creating a cocoon of comfort against the storm's chill. His arm wrapped around her, drawing her close, their bodies fitting together so perfectly it almost hurt.

'Warmer now?' he murmured against her cheek.

'Very.' She curled into him, breathing in the scent of him, letting herself be held.

'Told you the tent would hold,' he said, a smile in his voice.

Elise laughed softly. 'I never doubted it.'

What she *did* doubt was her ability to hold herself together when he left for Cornwall. These stolen moments felt like a balm to her soul, a rare safe space where she could simply be herself. Being with Gabe had allowed her to accept parts of herself she'd long hidden. But how long would she stay whole if it all came crashing down again?

It looked like that was going to be tested.

CHAPTER TWENTY-SEVEN

Gabe

Rain thrashed against the canvas of the roof tent, making it bow and flex like a living thing. Gabe pulled Elise closer. Outside, the storm raged, but inside their small shelter, wrapped in blankets and each other, a strange sense of peace washed over him.

Her breathing had steadied into the gentle rhythm of someone on the edge of sleep, her head resting in that perfect spot between his shoulder and chest. Her hair tickled his chin, and he smoothed it down. It was odd enough being here, camping out in his parents' garden, but being here with Elise made it even stranger. Since Gabe had left home, he'd never had much desire to come back. His mother had financially supported his purchase of his Glenbriar flat years ago before he had the money. And he knew why. She wanted to keep him here. She thought if he had a flat here, he'd want to stay, but it hadn't worked like that. During the lockdowns, when he'd made a name for himself, it had become his studio, but as soon as he could travel again, he did.

So why was he now lying here thinking about how wonderful it would be to settle in Glenbriar with Elise? Would she want that? He was thirty-five, maybe time had caught up with him and he needed something more stable. Did she want that too? She was happier with her friends now and enjoying being back.

A perfect opportunity, right?

Except for his job.

Except for Aidan.

The thought of his best friend sent a fresh wave of guilt through Gabe. Here he was, holding Aidan's ex-girlfriend in his arms, contemplating big feelings... relationships, the future. What the hell would Aidan make of this? After all the pain he'd gone through with Elise, he didn't need her back in his life on the arm of his best friend. And Gabe didn't want to lose Aidan. He'd been like a brother to him; stood by him, always been there for him. Gabe doing something like this to him would do nothing but aggravate him. Even if Aidan didn't say as much, it would always be there. The past cut so deep.

The storm seemed to intensify, as if responding to the tension in Gabe's head. Rain hammered against the canvas, and the wind whipped around them.

Elise stirred slightly, but Gabe was certain she was asleep, or almost there. He kept her tight in his arms, where he wanted her to be for a very long time. If he just stayed like this and didn't move, maybe he could prolong this moment. Closing his eyes, he drifted to the sounds of wind and rain.

When he woke, pale light was filtering through the tent and the comfortable weight of Elise's head was on his chest. The storm had blown out sometime in the night, with only a light breeze remaining. For a moment, Gabe simply breathed, cataloguing sensations: Elise's hair tickling his chin, the steady rhythm of her heartbeat against his ribs, the distant calls of his mother's peacocks demanding their breakfast.

Reality intruded with those indignant squawks. The animals needed feeding, and judging by the light, he was already later than they were used to. Still, he couldn't bring himself to move just yet. If he did, he'd break the spell.

He allowed himself another minute, watching the gentle rise and fall of her back beneath the blankets. Last night felt simultaneously like a vivid dream and the most real thing he'd experienced in ages.

One of the peacocks let out a particularly demanding cry, and Elise stirred against him.

'What in god's name is that noise?' she mumbled, her voice rough with sleep.

Gabe chuckled. 'The peacocks.'

Elise lifted her head, blinking owlishly at him. Her hair was a magnificent mess, her eyes still heavy with sleep, and a crease from the pillow marked her cheek. She looked absolutely beautiful.

'They don't sound too delighted.'

'I better feed them soon or they won't shut up.' He lifted his phone from under the pillow to check the time. As he flipped up the opening screen, he saw a message from Aidan. A fresh wave of guilt hit him. *Shit*. Did Aidan know – or guess – what was going on with Elise? And was this a message to admonish Gabe?

Gabe opened the message and frowned, taking a moment to process the contents.

'What is it?' Elise asked. 'Has something bad happened?'

'Um...' Gabe blinked. 'Aidan says they've just had a call from their mum saying Scarlett's disappeared overnight and they're seriously worried about her. He's wondering if I can help them look for her.'

'Oh god.' Elise clutched her face. 'You have to help them.'

'Yeah, I will. I better get these animals fed first.'

Elise sat up fully. The blanket slipped, revealing the smooth expanse of her bare shoulder, and Gabe felt a renewed surge of desire that he reluctantly tamped down. Responsibilities first.

'I should help too.' She rolled over and lifted her phone. 'No messages. I hope she's ok.'

Gabe unzipped the tent, and they emerged into the reasonably bright morning. The storm had left its mark – puddles dotted the ground, and the grass squelched underfoot as they made their way back to the house.

The dogs and cats greeted them, and Gabe opened the doors, letting them into the garden while he headed to get the food ready.

'I'll grab my clothes,' Elise said. She pulled her phone from her back pocket. Gabe watched as she tapped at her screen, a frown growing.

'Everything alright?' He took a step closer.

Elise looked up, her face pale. 'It's Scarlett. She's just messaged me.'

'What does it say?'

Elise held out the phone, and Gabe took it.

SCARLETT: Thanks for reaching out. You're one of the only people who has. I'm really tired of trying. Nothing ever gets better. I think everyone would be happier if I wasn't around anymore. Sorry for the drama. Just wanted someone to know I appreciated them before I go.

Gabe felt a cold weight settle in his stomach. 'Christ. And this just came in now?'

'Yep.' Elise looked up at him. 'Let me call her and see if she picks up.'

Gabe ran a hand through his hair as she called.

'Voicemail. Should we call the police? Or do you have Aidan's mum's number?'

'I don't have it, but I can call Aidan and tell him. They might already have called the police. I'll check,'

Elise nodded. 'Probably best.'

'Can I tell Aidan about that message?' He eyed her phone. 'If I do, I'll have to explain why you were here.'

Elise sucked on her lip. 'Yeah... You have to tell him. He needs to know.'

'Ok.' He let out a sigh. This was it. Once Aidan knew, there was no going back. And confessing to a fling felt a whole lot easier than trying to make sense of feelings he couldn't fully comprehend himself.

'Listen, Gabe...' Elise didn't quite meet his eyes. 'About last night.'

'Yeah?'

'It was wonderful. Really, truly wonderful. In fact, everything we shared has been so good.'

Something in her tone made his heart sink. 'I sense a "but" coming.'

She smiled sadly. 'No buts... Just thank you.' She closed the distance between them, pushed up, and kissed him on the cheek. 'I'll get dressed and drive down to David's. I know it's not that likely, but she might have gone there looking for me. If I hear anything, I'll message you. And can you do the same?'

'Yeah, sure.'

'Great. I'll, um, well... I'll go as soon as I'm dressed. You better call Aidan.' Elise gave him a little wave and left. Just like that. Gabe watched her, listening as she headed up to get her clothes. He sensed she didn't want a long, drawn-out goodbye. He didn't either. In fact, he wasn't ready for their story to be over, but it couldn't continue until everything going on around Scarlett was resolved.

Even as he hit call, he wasn't sure how he was going to explain it.

'Hi,' Aidan said, before Gabe was suitably prepared.

'Hey. Any joy finding Scarlett?'

'No. Nothing. I've no clue where she is. Mum thinks she might really do something awful this time. She's been on the verge of this kind of thing before, but it seems to have come to a head.'

'Have you called the police?'

'Yes, they're aware.'

'And does anybody have any idea where she is?'

'Nope. We've been everywhere we could think of.'

Gabe swallowed and took a deep breath. 'Look, this is possibly not going to help – in fact it might make it worse. But I have to tell you.'

'Tell me what? Are you having a relationship with her or something?'

'No.' Gabe ran his fingers through his hair. In some ways that might have been simpler. But he'd never looked at Scarlett like that. 'She messaged this morning to say she was feeling at rock bottom. But she didn't give away any details about where she was.'

'Ok... But why was she messaging you? I didn't think the two of you were that close.'

'It wasn't me she messaged. It was Elise.'

'Elise? What's she got to do with this? And how do you know about it?'

'All good questions.' He huffed, almost grunting. 'Elise and I have been having a bit of a fling since the coach trip... I'm sorry. She was here with me, and we were talking about Scarlett. Elise reached out to her yesterday, and this morning Scarlett messaged her back.'

Silence.

Not good.

Gabe hadn't expected any less, but surely this was better than lying to his best friend?

'Aidan?'

'I'm speechless. You and Elise?'

'Yup.'

'How long?'

'Just since the tour.'

'Are you sure?' Aidan sounded less than convinced.

'Well, yeah.' Though he wasn't in all honesty. But it felt even worse saying he'd always fancied her. That was something he'd never allowed himself to fully acknowledge – coveting your best friend's girlfriend was definitely a sin, possibly even a crime. And he'd made damn sure he never looked at her or spoke to her in a way that might be misconstrued – the absolute opposite in fact. He'd made himself hate her. But that wasn't how he'd felt at all.

'Listen, Aidan, this isn't a good time to talk about it. I know that. I feel bad about it, but I don't want us to fall out. It was a fling—'

'One you're still having.'

'Until I leave for Cornwall.' And now, more than ever, he felt the need to get away and leave this mess behind, though an equally powerful force was begging him to stay. 'Let me come and help look for Scarlett. We can talk about it another time.'

'Ok. See you in a bit.'

With a sigh, Gabe ended the call.

Gabe didn't want to choose between Elise and his best friend, but he wasn't sure he could meet them on common ground either.

Chapter Twenty-Eight

Glenbriar church was a place Elise hadn't set foot in for a long time. If she'd had the guts to come back for Genevieve's wedding, she'd have been here last year, but the last time she was here was probably at one of David and Amanda's children's christenings. She wasn't likely to go to a church for herself. She wasn't exactly a believer, but she was hoping for nothing short of a minor miracle now.

She went around to the backdoor and scanned the ground to the side. As she'd left the driveway at Glenview, her phone had buzzed again, and she'd pulled in at the side of the road to see another message from Scarlett. This one said where she was – hiding in the church. And how to get in – using a key that Scarlett remembered from primary school as being hidden under a slate. Elise didn't like to comment on how lax church security was, not when Scarlett had willingly given up her location, though she'd also asked Elise to come alone and not tell anyone.

As soon as she saw Scarlett was ok, she'd message Gabe and tell him to pass on a message to Aidan. And she was praying everything *would* be ok.

The vestry door looked weathered, its green paint peeling at the corners. She bent down, lifting the slate where the ground was damp and sure enough, found a key. She unlocked the door, put the key back, and went inside. The door closed, the snib lock securing it. Elise headed straight through the back passage and into the main part of the church.

'Scarlett?' Her voice echoed in the empty space that smelled of furniture polish and aged hymn books. 'It's me. I'm here... Are you...'

Weak morning light filtered through stained glass, and for a moment, Elise saw and heard nothing. Her heart hammered as she imagined a hundred and one gruesome scenarios.

Then a muffled response from above: 'Up here.'

Elise looked up towards the gallery. She couldn't see anyone, but she headed out a side door and up the cold stone stairs.

'Scarlett?' As soon as she was up, she peered around.

Scarlett sat on the floor against the far side wall, knees drawn up to her chest, her bright red hair falling across her face. Her mascara had run, leaving dark tracks down her cheeks.

'Hey.' Elise lowered herself to sit beside her. 'What's going on?'

Scarlett looked up, her eyes red-rimmed. She wore an oversized black jumper over leggings. 'You actually came.'

'Of course I came. You asked me to.'

'I wasn't sure if you would.' Scarlett wiped her nose with her sleeve. 'People usually don't care.'

Elise reached out, hesitated, then gently tucked a strand of hair behind Scarlett's ear. She recognised that feeling, the sense that no one cared, even though she knew it wasn't true. Lots of people cared for Scarlett. But Elise had been there herself, too lost in her own darkness to see the love that was still there for her from her friends and family. 'I'm here now. Talk to me.'

Scarlett's laugh was hollow. 'You're going to think I'm stupid. Everyone does. I know people talk about me all the time. They call me dramatic... And look at me. What am I doing? Being dramatic.'

'I'm hardly in a position to judge, am I?' Elise sighed. 'I've been pretty dramatic sometimes myself. I know a cry for help when I see one, and I also know how it feels when no one answers. It's easy to shut yourself away and think no one cares. Only recently, I decided to reconnect with my friends – but it meant a good hard look in the mirror.'

'Yeah... I've done that. And I don't like what I see there. No wonder everyone hates me.'

Elise rubbed her shoulder. 'That's not true. It's how you feel, but you have friends... And family. Aidan, Lilah, your mum... Me.'

Scarlett scoffed. 'You didn't used to want to be my friend. I think I annoyed you.'

'I was in a bad place. Lots of things annoyed me, and I'm sorry for it. Truly.' She pulled out her phone. 'Let me just message someone and tell them you're ok. Everyone's worried.' She sent a brief message to Gabe saying she was with Scarlett, and they could stop searching.

'Everyone thinks I'm an idiot for going out with Leon. Before that, there was Zeb Buchanan. I've had so many toxic boyfriends.'

Elise nodded. 'Is that what's upsetting you? That business with Leon on the coach was really horrible.'

'Yeah... And what did I do?'

Elise raised an eyebrow. 'You kept going.'

'No.' Scarlett shook her head. 'I slept with Lloyd... Jumped into bed with the first available man.'

Elise's mind scrambled in ten different directions. What the hell? The rumours were true.

'Well... Did he hurt you or something?' He didn't look the type, but wouldn't it be just the thing for him to be a Jekyll and Hyde. Poor Scarlett.

Scarlett sniffed. 'No. He was really nice. Like so nice. Kind and gentle.' She let out a little laugh. 'He thought I was insane coming on to him. He backed off at first, but I didn't give up – I probably should have – but well, apparently his wife died last year, and he was feeling sad, lonely. I was a distraction, I guess. And I was so pissed about Leon ruining everything. I wanted a distraction myself. That's why I got annoyed when I thought he was with you… And his mum was annoyed with me for starting rumours, then she guessed what was going on. It was so horrible for him. I shouldn't have pestered him.'

'Look, that's not on you. It takes two.'

'That's what he said. He was so sweet about it all.'

Questions buzzed in Elise's head like trapped wasps. 'And is that why you're upset now?'

'Yes.' Scarlett swallowed hard. 'I wish I hadn't done it.'

'Why? Are you pregnant or something?'

'No.' Scarlett hid her face. 'But it was so good… It felt like…' She sobbed into her hands. 'Like love. Like he really loved me. But I know it's not true. I'm just so used to rough guys who don't care. Now, I feel so lost. Like I've tasted something so good, but I know I'll never find it again.'

Elise nodded, understanding her despair. Much as she wanted to help, she wasn't going to offer useless platitudes. She remembered people doing that to her when Aidan had left for Canada. Scarlett may have plenty of time to meet other nice guys, but it wasn't guaranteed.

Scarlett peered up at Elise, her eyes wide and vulnerable. 'What should I do?'

'I don't know what to tell you,' she said. 'But I'm here to listen.'

Scarlett leaned her head against Elise's shoulder, her hair tickling Elise's cheek. 'That's more than most people offer. They just think I'm an idiot.'

'Do you think you might see him again?'

'No.' Scarlett shook her head. 'I can't. He lives somewhere else, and he has three kids. His life is too different from mine.'

'Yeah. I know how that feels.'

Scarlett lifted her head from Elise's shoulder. 'Really? Are you seeing someone too?'

'I had a holiday fling too,' she said. 'With Gabe.'

Scarlett's mouth fell open. 'Gabe? Gabe Wilder?'

'The very one.'

'But he hates you!' Scarlett blurted, then immediately looked apologetic. 'Sorry. That came out wrong. But he's always been so... I mean, whenever your name came up, he'd get this look on his face like he'd swallowed something sour.'

'I know.' Elise couldn't help but smile at the accuracy of the description. 'The feeling was mutual, believe me. Until it wasn't.'

'And what are you doing about it?' Scarlett had shifted to face Elise fully now, her earlier distress ebbing away.

'Nothing.' Elise tucked her hair behind her ear. 'He's going to Cornwall and I'm staying here. So, yeah, I get it. Different lives, different things.'

'Bloody hell.' Scarlett let out a low whistle. 'Does Aidan know?'

'Possibly. Gabe might have to tell him.'

'But you like him.' It wasn't a question.

Elise sighed. 'It's complicated.'

'It's always complicated, isn't it?'

'Yeah.' Elise managed a small smile. 'Please don't tell Aidan. If he hears about it, it should be from Gabe... or me.'

'I promise,' Scarlett said.

But even as she said it, Elise felt a flicker of doubt. Scarlett was known for many things, but keeping secrets wasn't one of them. Her emotions ran hot and fast, often bypassing any filter between her brain and her mouth.

Confessing this to Aidan's half-sister of all people was possibly not a smart move. Elise had spent years trying to minimise the damage she'd caused her reputation in Glenbriar, and now she might have just created another issue.

'Really, Scarlett. Not a word.'

'I get it. Secret. Like me and Lloyd.'

'Yes. And I won't tell anyone about that.'

From below came the sound of the church door opening, followed by footsteps on stone. Elise and Scarlett froze, exchanging alarmed glances.

'It's Sunday,' Elise whispered. 'People will be coming in here.'

Scarlett's eyes widened in panic. 'Shit.'

'We need to get out of here.'

'How? We can't just waltz down the stairs in the middle of everyone arriving.'

Elise peered over, then crouched down again. 'It's the minister. I'll go down and explain. Surely a minister will be understanding.'

She nipped down the stairs and crept through the door into the main part of the church. The minister was a very young, good-looking man, and Elise suddenly realised he was the one Amanda talked constantly about. He blinked when he saw Elise, like he was covering up his shock.

'I'm so sorry,' she began. 'I can explain.'

'Are you alright?' he asked.

'Yeah, there was a bit of a problem with a friend of mine.' Elise explained about Scarlett, and the minister nodded.

'Would she like to move into the backroom? I can get her a cup of tea or something.'

'I'm not sure,' she said. 'Maybe if I just take her home.'

A woman dressed entirely in black – ripped jeans, a faded band t-shirt, and Doc Martens – came through the backdoor. Multiple piercings lined her ears and a small silver ring adorned her left nostril.

'Hey.' She smiled at Elise.

'This is Kristi,' Grant said. 'My partner.'

Elise smiled back at her, remembering Amanda's stories about the minister's scandalous partner... Well, only because she didn't look the part, though apparently, she was very nice.

The church door swung open, and more people came in. Elise winced. One of them was Amanda.

'Elise! What are you doing here? I thought you were back in Glasgow for the weekend.'

'Amanda's my sister-in-law,' she told Grant.

'I see.'

'I'll explain later,' Elise told Amanda. 'It's really complicated.'

'Is everything ok?'

'Yeah, it's nothing to worry about.'

Grant whispered something to Kristi, who nodded.

'How about we go up and get your friend?' Kristi said to Elise. 'I can let you both out a side door.'

Elise agreed and saw Grant distracting Amanda.

Back upstairs, Elise beckoned Scarlett, who came forward. She sucked on her lip when she saw Kristi.

'This is Kristi. She's going to open the side door. I'll take you back to your mum's house.'

'You're Zeb's sister, aren't you?' Scarlett said.

Kristi raised an eyebrow. 'Yeah... for my sins. You used to go out with him, didn't you?'

Scarlett nodded. 'We split ages ago... He was into, well...'

'You don't have to sugarcoat it for me,' Kristi said. 'I know what a piece of work he is.' She led the way down the stairs and threw open a side door. Elise thanked her and she and Scarlett left the building.

Elise pulled out her keys. 'I'll drive you home.'

Scarlett nodded, following Elise to her car. They drove in silence for a few minutes, windscreen wipers creating a hypnotic rhythm against the light rain.

'The minister and Kristi are a rather unexpected couple.'

A small smile tugged at Scarlett's mouth. 'Yeah. She's nice, even though she's related to Zeb the twat.'

Elise snorted a laugh. 'Don't you think that could happen with you and Lloyd if you tried?'

Scarlett sighed. 'No. It was just a fling.'

'Relatable.' Elise watched the road for a minute, and she turned onto the street where Aidan's mum lived. 'Scarlett... It's not for me to say, but would you consider going to counselling? I saw someone in Glasgow when I first arrived there. We only had a few sessions, but I learned a lot about myself. I think it would really help you make sense of things. She told me it's ok to choose yourself. I did... And I have. If I really wanted I could go to Cornwall and follow Gabe in the hope of something happening. But I don't want to live in Cornwall, so I'm choosing what I want, which is to stay here.' Her insides squirmed a little. She knew that meant giving up someone she'd grown to care deeply for, but she wasn't going to try to pin him down here. She'd ruined enough men's lives for her own selfishness. Not this time.

'I might do that.' Scarlett smiled at her. 'And thank you for caring enough to help me.'

'You're welcome. Text me sometime and we'll go for a coffee or a walk. Just let me know.'

With a last smile, Scarlett was out of the car, jogging through the drizzle to her front door. Elise watched until she was safely inside, then put the car in gear and pulled away.

She could go back to Gabe, but that probably wasn't the sensible option. She needed space and time to think.

Monday morning hit like a gentle but persistent hangover, not painful, exactly, but lingering niggles and aches plagued her head. Yesterday afternoon, she'd returned to David and Amanda's house and faced Amanda's inquisition about why she'd been at the church, who Scarlett was, and so on... Work was actually a relief. But she really needed to get somewhere to stay.

She sat at her desk in Highland Horizon Travel's back office, scrolling through customer feedback forms.

'Cuppa?' Kate peeked in from the main room.

'Yeah, thanks. That would be great.'

Kate returned moments later with two mugs. 'It's quiet out there, so I'll hover and natter. You had any luck finding a house yet?'

'I've got a property viewing booked tomorrow and it really can't come soon enough. Honestly, living with Amanda is...' She shook her head. 'She's so helpful, but sometimes she'd just too much.'

Kate laughed and sipped her coffee. 'We all need our own space. Kerr, my youngest son, lived with us when he came back to teach at the high school, but he soon got fed up with that. He moved in with a friend for a while.' Her smile widened. 'Eddie, who's about my age, but they're best buddies. It's very sweet. He's got his own place now on Kirk Lane. It's not exactly his ideal home, but Glenbriar is not an easy town to find a house in. It's either too expensive or there's nothing available.'

'As I'm discovering.'

'You could always try a flat share.'

'I might end up doing that.' Though she really wanted her own space. If she had to share with anyone, there was only one person who fit the bill, and he was going to Cornwall.

The day passed reasonably fast. Elise left early, as she had an appointment at Cutting Edge where Hayley worked. The walk from the office took less than five minutes. Elise smiled, loving how she was back so close to people who mattered to her.

'Perfect timing.' Hayley dusted her hands together as she emerged from the backroom. 'How are you doing?'

'Apart from the weekend drama...' Elise dropped into the salon chair that Hayley patted the back of invitingly.

'Do tell.' Hayley draped a cape around Elise's shoulders.

Elise chatted, confessing to what had happened with Gabe and how other issues had made Elise hit the brakes on her fling. It was time to be sensible. To choose herself and not blindly chase a fragile hope.

'Is it that fragile?'

'Yes,' Elise said quickly. 'It was just temporary.'

'You said it had started to feel significant.'

Curse Hayley and her good memory.

'Maybe... But we're very different people heading in very different directions.'

'I think you're scared,' Hayley said.

'I'm not scared,' Elise protested. 'I'm realistic. We'd never work long-term.'

'How do you know? You're scared of messing things up again – for yourself and for him.'

Elise sucked on her lip and dropped her eyes to her hands. 'I can't afford to do that. I've been there too many times.'

Hayley moved around to trim the front of Elise's hair, her expression thoughtful. 'But maybe this time it's worth the risk.'

'You think?'

'Look at me and Oliver.' Hayley raised an eyebrow. 'He moved to London, and I thought we were done, but he came back. He risked it for us, and it's all worked out.'

Elise frowned at her reflection in the mirror.

'Give love a chance,' Hayley said. 'You've spent so long punishing yourself for what happened with Aidan and Finlay. Maybe it's time to forgive yourself and see if there's a way to make this work for both of you.'

Elise pulled in a deep breath. 'I'll think about it.'

Maybe it was a terrible idea. Maybe it would end in disaster. But she really should try. Gabe was leaving whether she did or not, so laying her cards on the table might change nothing... Or perhaps it could change everything.

Chapter Twenty-Nine

Gabe plastered on his professional smile as the Cornwall Coastal Conservation Initiative team beamed back at him through his screen, oblivious to the chaos churning in his gut.

'I can make some catchy straplines to go with that.' Simon – the man in the centre of the screen – adjusted his webcam. 'We can figure out the best platforms once we start airing and hone the campaign to that audience.'

'Right… Yeah.' Gabe shifted in his chair. Every moment spent discussing his impending move to Cornwall felt like a betrayal of something. It made his chest ache and his head spin, but a grey fog surrounded his mind, obscuring his vision, so he couldn't see any other path.

'*Wilder at Heart* is such a great name, and it instantly gives that image of you, Gabe, full of energy and excitement.'

'Thanks.' Gabe unleashed a smile, but it felt fake. The energy and excitement he'd had for the podcasts had dwindled. His whole life felt flat.

His gaze slid to the clock in the corner of his screen. Twenty minutes until the viewer was due. Once that was done, he could pack up and go back to the tent and the animals. He was enjoying being with them. Maybe he should do something wacky like buy a field and raise alpacas. That honestly appealed more to him than going to Cornwall.

'Listen, folks,' Gabe said. 'I need to shut down in a moment. I've got a viewer coming round to see the flat.'

'Perfect,' Simon beamed. 'I'll email you the schedules. Cornwall is bloody excited to have you joining us.'

'Likewise,' Gabe said, his smile tight. 'Looking forward to it.'

The call ended, and Gabe's smile dropped immediately. He exhaled slowly, leaning back in his chair and staring at the ceiling.

What the hell was he doing? The Cornwall gig should be right up his alley. Yet he couldn't muster any excitement for it at all. He scrubbed his hands over his face. The Zoom call had left a sour taste in his mouth, like he'd been lying to everyone: the Cornwall team, himself, the invisible viewer who would soon be wandering through his flat. He needed coffee, or something stronger, but before he could decide which, his phone chimed. One new message. From Elise.

Aidan's less than zero degrees reaction to Gabe's news about the fling had been exactly as Gabe had thought. How could he pursue a relationship with Elise if it was going to harm his friendship with Aidan?

He opened the message.

ELISE: Hey, how are you? That was wild with Scarlett on Sunday. Hope things are going well with the animals.

Gabe stared at the screen. How was he? Confused. Conflicted. Caught between the future he'd thought he'd mapped out and the unexpected detour that was Elise Reid.

'Fine' would be the standard response. Easy. Noncommittal. But was he fine?

He typed and deleted three different variations of the same lie before settling on something equally meaningless.

GABE: Yes, fine thanks. What's up? How are you?

His thumb hovered over the send button. Too casual? Too abrupt? Was there a hidden code to text messages that he'd never bothered to learn because he'd never cared this much before?

'Christ almighty,' he groaned, pressing send before he could overthink it further. 'It's a text message, not a marriage proposal.'

He set the phone down on the coffee table and deliberately walked the few steps to the kitchen. He wouldn't wait around for her response like some lovesick teenager. He was a grown man with a flat viewing to prepare for. A potential tenant who might help facilitate his move to Cornwall, his exciting new life that definitely wasn't giving him heart palpitations every time he thought about it.

The kitchen was spotless, but he wiped down the already clean counter anyway, just for something to do with his hands. His gaze kept drifting back to his phone, still silent on the coffee table.

Why did his stomach feel like it was trying to climb up his throat at the thought of being so far from her?

The phone chimed. Gabe nearly vaulted over the kitchen island in his haste to get to it.

ELISE: I'm alright. Been thinking. I want to talk to you. About... Well, everything. Can we meet soon?

Gabe sat heavily on the edge of the sofa. *Everything.* A dangerous word. And if they were to discuss everything, it meant Aidan. Cornwall. Feelings. A future... Or no future.

His thumbs hovered over the keypad.

What did he want to say?

He wasn't good at this kind of thing. Nothing too deep. But she'd rocked feelings in him he hadn't experienced before. If he wanted them to exist beyond this moment, he had to act.

GABE: Sure, we can meet up and chat. When were you thinking?

ELISE: Today, if you're free? I know it's short notice.

Today.

Well, when better? It wasn't like he had a lot of time.

The doorbell rang, startling him so he nearly dropped his phone. The viewer wasn't due for another few minutes but they were obviously being extra punctual.

GABE: Sounds good. Where?

He'd be done here shortly and he'd rather not have her visit here – he was pretty sure she didn't know where he lived and he didn't need that to change. This place didn't feel like his anymore. He wanted space. Room to move – for him, and a partner. A family. Pets.

Was this him growing up?

Who'd have thought it?

He shoved his phone in his pocket and took a deep breath. Focus on the viewing now, deal with Elise later. One issue at a time.

Gabe swung open the door with a smile, only for it to freeze on his face like badly applied plaster. Elise stood there, her hand halfway raised as if caught between knocking and fleeing, looking just as stunned as he felt.

'Elise, you're here.' So, she did know where he lived.

She wore her purple blazer over a simple white blouse, her work clothes, hair pulled back in a neat ponytail.

'Gabe,' she replied, eyes wide. 'I... What are you doing here?'

'I live here – obviously.' He frowned. 'And I'm waiting for a viewer.'

A smile crept over Elise's face. 'That would be me.' She raised her hand.

'What?'

'I didn't know it was your flat. The estate agents don't give out personal details.'

'Right.' His brain struggled to process this new information. 'Of course... Ok... Well, come in.'

She tucked a loose strand of hair behind her ear. 'How bizarre... Though I should have worked it out. I knew you were planning on renting this place and there aren't that many properties available in Glenbriar. I just didn't quite grasp how far down the line you were.'

'Yeah... I'm in pretty deep.' And wasn't that the truth? And now Elise wanted to rent his flat while he was away.

He shook his head. Well, there was an almost twisted poetry to that scenario, though it had a somewhat tragic air about it.

CHAPTER THIRTY

Elise

E lise stood frozen in the hallway, her rehearsed flat-viewing questions evaporating like morning dew. This wasn't just some random flat. This was Gabe's flat.

Her heels clicked on the wooden floor like a timer counting down. 'I, um, was just going to message you about where we could meet,' she said.

'Yeah.' He scraped his hand through his hair. 'Looks like the universe had other ideas.'

'Apparently so.' She glanced around at the small living area with its dormer windows framing the rolling hills beyond Glenbriar. 'It's a lovely place.'

'It's not bad. It's just not me.'

'I can see that. I'm not sure it's me either to tell the truth, but I can't stay with David and Amanda indefinitely.' She met Gabe's eyes and, for a moment, they just stared at each other. Elise's mind raced. She had two choices: pretend this was a normal flat viewing and leave their personal issues aside or speak now while she had the chance.

She watched him for any signs of which he would prefer. If she left it, was she simply delaying the inevitable?

'Gabe, I—' she started, then stopped. Old habits tugged at her, tempting her to retreat, to brush it off or change the subject.

But not this time. Not anymore.

He watched her closely, those blue eyes never straying from her face. 'What did you want to speak to me about?'

She took a steadying breath that came from somewhere deeper than her lungs – from her gut, her heart. The part that was done hiding.

'About us.'

Gabe went still. 'What about us exactly?'

'Well, you're going to Cornwall and I'm... staying here. And we had a fling, which was... nice.' The room seemed to close in, the air thick with everything unsaid. Elise's breath caught, but she held her ground. This wasn't easy – but she'd had enough of easy choices that had left her hollow.

She glanced at him. His expression gave nothing away, and her heart pounded harder for it.

'Nice?' Something flickered in his eyes. 'That's one word for it.'

'Well, yes. And now I'm...' She exhaled shakily. 'I'm not sure what I'm doing, except trying not to run away from something real. I've spent so long defining myself by what I got wrong. The girl who hurt Aidan. Who said yes to the wrong man for all the wrong reasons. Who ran from every consequence before it could catch up with her.' Her voice caught, but she didn't falter. 'I don't want to do that anymore. I don't want to make another mistake by walking away.'

Gabe stepped closer. 'Walking away from what? Glenbriar?'

She shook her head slowly. 'No. I want to stay. I've never been more certain of that. But the idea of letting you go... it hurts. And I need you to know – I have feelings for you. Not convenient ones, not easy ones. The kind that terrify me because they matter. Because you matter.'

He took another step, almost close enough to touch. 'Are you saying you want us to be together? Like, properly together?'

She met his gaze fully this time, and her nod was firm.

'Yes,' she said, the word barely above a whisper. Then louder, clearer, steadier: 'Yes. That's exactly what I'm saying.' Her heart thundered in her chest, but she didn't back down.

'I want us to be together too,' Gabe said softly. 'But... I thought you were happy keeping it casual. It was easier to believe that. Because, honestly, I'm scared too.'

'Scared I'd mess it up?' she asked, though there was no accusation in her voice – just curiosity.

'No,' he said immediately. 'Not of you. Of having to choose between you and my best friend. I don't know how to face that. Cornwall feels like an escape. If I go, I don't have to choose.'

'Gabe, I'd never ask you to choose.' Her voice was quiet, but certain. 'I know Aidan's your best friend. Yes, it might be awkward. But I respect that bond. I'm not here to come between it.'

'I know that. I do. But it's not just about now – it's about everything I've been trying to avoid for years. When I told him we'd had a fling, he didn't take it well. And if he ever finds out that…' He ran a hand through his hair, frustration etched in every movement. 'He'll have every reason to be angry.'

'Finds out what?'

He looked up, meeting her gaze. 'That it's always been you. Even back then. Even when I convinced myself I couldn't stand you. The first time I saw you, I fancied you. But you were with Aidan. And he's like a brother to me. I wanted him to be happy – but it didn't stop how I felt. So I buried it. Covered it up with anger. Told myself you were off-limits. Safer to hate you than admit I wanted you.'

Elise blinked, stunned. 'Wow. I honestly had no idea.'

'Now you do.'

She nodded slowly, letting it settle. 'So… what do we do with that?'

He exhaled. 'I think we both need to stop hiding. I've been pretending for a long time – about how I feel, about what I want from life. Not just with you, but… everything. The podcasts, Glenbriar. It felt like wanting something different made me a failure. But maybe it just means I'm finally being honest with myself.'

Her heart softened at that. She reached for his hand. 'It's not failure, Gabe. It's growth. And it's brave.'

He smiled, but there was pain in it. 'I'm not proud of how I treated you. I used your history with Aidan as a shield. Pushed you away when you were already trying to carry so much on your own.'

'Then let's stop doing that. No more shields. No more pretending. We've both made mistakes – but we're not those people anymore.'

He stepped closer, his thumb brushing hers. 'You really believe that?'

'I do. We got over this first hurdle. Together. That says a lot.' Her voice softened. 'If we can face that, I think we can face the rest – whatever it looks like.'

His smile grew, more real now. 'Then let's do it.'

'Aidan's a good man. I think he'll come around. Maybe not right away. But he will – if he sees this isn't some reckless mistake.'

'It's not.' Gabe locked eyes with her. 'It's the first thing that's made real sense in a long time.'

They stood smiling at each other, the tension between them transforming into something warmer, more hopeful.

'But what about Cornwall?' she asked quietly.

'Cornwall was a job opportunity, I realise that now,' he said. 'A good one, but just that – a job. There are other paths, and they're not failures, just choices. I applied because I thought there was nothing keeping me here. But now—' He reached for her hand, threading his fingers through hers. 'Now there's every reason to stay.'

The warmth of his touch spiralled up her arm, anchoring something inside her that had felt loose for years.

'You mean that?' She needed to hear it again.

'I do. You've changed everything for me, Elise. Being with you... it made me realise I don't have to chase the next big thing to feel fulfilled. I want to build something lasting. Here. With you.'

His thumb traced soft circles on her palm, and Elise felt her breath catch.

'I'd like for us to date properly,' he said. 'We can go places with the tent, and you can take me on one of your fancy holidays – though maybe not a coach tour.'

She laughed, the knot in her chest easing. 'No coaches. Promise.'

Gabe looked down at their hands, then back at her. 'Can I seal the deal with a kiss?'

'Of course.'

He leaned in, his calloused palm cupping her cheek, lips brushing hers in a kiss that was gentle, grounding, and real.

'I have another idea,' he murmured as he pulled back.

'Which is?'

'It might be too soon – feel free to shoot it down – but... what if, instead of you taking this flat, we looked for a place together?'

Elise blinked, heart lifting like a balloon. 'Together? You mean... properly live together?'

'Or not, if it's too fast,' he said quickly. 'We could find places nearby, or you could take this one and I'll just—'

'Gabe.' She cut off his ramble. 'I'd like that. Let's see if we can last a week without murdering each other.'

His grin was boyish and full of hope as he slipped an arm around her waist. 'At least let me choose the weapon.'

'Dare I ask?'

'Better not.'

She shook her head, laughing. 'Well, if we pool our incomes, we can afford somewhere bigger than this.'

'With a garden,' he added.

'Sure, but a house with actual walls and plumbing. I'm not moving into your tent full-time.'

'No? Even after that glowing review you promised me?'

'It did have certain... perks.' She poked his chest. 'You know what you're doing in a sleeping bag.'

'Why don't you come over this weekend?' he said. 'We'll look at listings. I'll talk to Aidan, and let the Cornwall team know where I stand.'

'Ok.' She smiled, still slightly dazed. 'This is wild. Half an hour ago I came here to view a flat, and now I'm planning to house-hunt with you.'

'Life's weird like that.' He pulled her close again. 'Or maybe it just makes sense when you find the right person.'

Elise leaned into him, her forehead resting against his. 'We're possibly going to drive each other mad.'

'Definitely. But we'll have snuggles and kisses to get through it.'

She closed her eyes, letting herself picture it: a shared home, sun on tangled sheets, late-night arguments and laughter in the kitchen, quiet mornings and everything messy and magical in between. And for the first time in a long time, it didn't feel like a dream. It felt like hers.

'Do you play tennis by the way?' she asked.

'That is the most random thing you've ever said to me.' He grinned and shook his head. 'I have played in the past, yeah. I wouldn't say I'm much good though. Why?'

'Amanda wants me to join her club. I'd feel a lot happier about it if you were with me. She loves you, after all.'

'Fine. Let's do it. It can be one of our first couples' bonding experiences.'

'Thank you,' she whispered. 'I want to give this a real chance. *Us* a real chance.'

'Me too. No more hiding. No more pretending.' He sealed the promise with another kiss.

As his lips moved against hers, gentle and sure, Elise finally understood what it meant to stop running. What it meant to stand still and let herself be seen – not just for how she looked or what she offered, but for who she truly was. To choose someone, and to be chosen not despite her flaws, but with them. To stop guarding every inch of herself and trust that she didn't have to earn love through control or perfection.

It wasn't the flat viewing she'd expected. She still didn't have a home that was hers, but this moment, this choice, *was*. And it put her exactly where she wanted to be.

CHAPTER THIRTY-ONE

Gabe

Woodend Cottage had never looked so intimidating. Gabe had been coming here since childhood, but now he hesitated on the threshold, unsure if he had the courage to walk through the door. He'd stood his ground with angry farmers, environmental sceptics, even his own father's scorn, but the thought of this conversation with his oldest friend tied his stomach into a sailor's knot.

The door swung open, and Aidan smiled out. Maya, the husky, bounded up and nosed Gabe's leg. 'Gabe? Is everything ok?' Aidan's smile was genuine, but Gabe caught a sharper look beneath it.

'Is this a bad time?' He should have texted first, but he was on a tight schedule today. He was meeting Elise at the tennis club, and stranger even than that, his mother had decided to come along too. Not to play – she had the dogs with her – but to observe and to chat more with Elise. They'd only met once briefly so far, but his mum had taken a shine to her and was keen to see her again.

Anything that got her out of the house and away from his father was a good thing, as far as Gabe was concerned.

'For you? Never.' Aidan stepped back, gesturing for Gabe to come inside. 'You want a coffee?'

'Na. I better not. I'm playing tennis shortly.'

Aidan raised an eyebrow. 'Tennis?'

'Yeah.' He ran his hand through his hair. 'But first, I want to clear the air between us.'

'Ok... But what do you mean?' Aidan gave a little shrug.

'About Elise. I told you we had a fling, and I know you weren't thrilled about it. Thing is, it's gone further than that. We're going to try and make things work between us. We want to find somewhere to live – together. But I don't want to lose you in the process.'

'But Gabe—'

'No, let me finish.' His fingers tightened around the back of a wooden kitchen chair. 'I didn't plan this. It just happened, and now it's real. And I don't want to have to choose between my best mate and the woman I've fallen in love with.'

Aidan was quiet for a moment, frowning. Then he sighed. 'Is that what you think? That I'd make you choose?'

'You seemed pretty angry.'

'I wasn't angry about you and Elise.' Aidan clapped Gabe's upper arm. 'I was so worried about Scarlett. The whole Elise thing just caught me off guard.'

Gabe blinked. 'So... you're not angry?'

Aidan shook his head. 'Not really. I suppose there might be some awkward moments, but we'll cope. Because I'm married to the love of my life now. Elise and I were never right for each other – we both know that.'

The tension in Gabe's shoulders began to loosen. 'You're sure?'

'Yeah. I mean, I would never have predicted you'd end up with Elise Reid. Considering you always seemed to hate each other.' Aidan huffed a laugh. 'But I'm not going to stop you. It's your life.'

Gabe rubbed at the back of his neck. 'She's changed. And so have I. We understand each other.'

Aidan smiled. 'Then that's all that matters. You're still my best friend. And if you're happy, I'm happy.'

'I am,' Gabe said. 'Happy, I mean. With her.'

Aidan's smile widened. 'Then good.'

'Thanks,' he said. 'For understanding.'

'Nothing to understand. You deserve to be happy. And if Elise makes you happy, then I'm all for it.'

'Thank you.' Gabe let out a breath. 'Is Scarlett ok now? Elise seems to think she is. I think they've made a bit of a friendship too.'

'Yeah, Scarlett mentioned that. Elise talked her into going for counselling, which I think is a good start.'

'I'm glad to hear that.' Gabe checked the time. 'I better get moving.'

'Yup. We don't want you to be late for your date.' Aidan walked him to the door. 'And Gabe? I mean it. I'm happy for you. Both of you.'

'Thanks, mate. You're the best.'

As Gabe drove towards the tennis club, the sun broke through the clouds. He wasn't typically one for omens, but that felt like a good sign if ever there was one.

He'd walked past the club a thousand times. It looked like it had been plucked from a 1950s postcard: whitewashed walls and hunter-green trim, perched on the hill overlooking the town like a duchess surveying a fancy tea party. It was just off a well-trodden route up a local hill that eventually led to Ben Vrack, Glenbriar's "mountain". But he'd never actually set foot inside. It always looked too posh a place for him.

He didn't have a racquet of his own, so he'd take whatever spares Elise and Amanda had. Apparently there was no dress code, which was just as well. These combat shorts and his white t-shirt were as 'tennisy' as he got.

As he approached the entrance, he spotted Elise outside the fenced off court area. She wore black lycra shorts that showed off her long, tanned legs, and a red polo vest, that looked amazing with her long dark hair, which was pulled back in a high ponytail.

For a moment, he just looked at her. She was so beautiful. He could hardly believe his luck.

'Hey.' He approached her and Elise looked up from her phone.

'Hi.' She rose on tiptoes, pressing a kiss to his lips. 'Glad you're here. That was your mum messaging me. She's on her way.'

'You've got yourself a fan. I've never known her this into anyone. She loves you more than me.'

Elise narrowed her eyes slightly and Gabe's chest flickered. He knew his words were ambiguous. They could mean his mum loved Elise more than she loved her son… Or they could mean that she loved Elise more than he did. Only he'd never actually said the words. Yet.

'Well, I'll take her and you can have Amanda. She's wetting her pants at the thought of playing tennis with you. I think she's jealous that you're not dating *her*.'

He smirked. 'She's funny. When I sang at that church show, she treated me like I was a celebrity.'

'You are, remember? I mean, look at all those groupies on the tour.'

He ran a hand through his hair. 'Like a g-list celebrity, maybe.'

'She's in there.' Elise pointed to the courts that were screened with huge banners around the wire fencing. 'Let's go and meet the people she wants to introduce us to.'

He followed her through the door onto the court, where several heads turned as they entered.

'Elise!' Amanda almost ran over. 'And Gabriel.' Amanda beamed up at him, extending a hand adorned with a tennis bracelet. 'I'm so glad you came and that you're with Elise. Honestly, it's just the best news.'

Gabe shook her hand. 'Thanks, that's—'

'I'm actually delighted you're back to stay Glenbriar. I'm on so many committees and we really need someone who'll make a stand for the environment. I'll be picking your brains constantly.'

'Great.'

'And I must say.' She lowered her voice to a stage whisper, 'I'm so excited about this.' She gestured between him and Elise with a knowing smile. 'When Elise told me you two were an item, I nearly fell off my chair. It's so romantic!'

Elise cleared her throat. 'So what's the plan?'

'I need to find Eddie. He's my partner for our doubles game. You'll adore him. He's an absolute duck. He's in his late fifties, but so dapper and charming. I just love him.'

Elise craned her neck, her attention caught by something – or someone.

Gabe looked around, expecting to see his mother, but Elise appeared to be looking at a young man standing by the far court, talking to an older man. The young man was tall, handsome and laughing loudly at something the other man had said.

'That looks like Jake Halley.' Elise narrowed her eyes slightly.

'Who?' A possessive, rather green streak fired through Gabe.

'Someone I was at school with. Kate, the woman I work with, is his mum.'

Amanda turned to look at the man and smiled. 'No, that's *Kerr* Halley.'

'Ah, yes, Jake's brother.' Elise nodded. 'They look so alike.'

'Kerr is Eddie's friend. They work together at the high school. Apparently, Eddie used to be his teacher and now they're best buddies. Such a funny story.'

'Oh, my god. *That's* Eddie?' Elise was gaping at the older man. 'You mean Mr Caldwell? He was my teacher too. I had him for history.'

'I remember him vaguely,' Gabe said.

'He's been teaching at the high school forever,' Amanda said. 'He doesn't look old enough, does he? He's so dapper, and an absolute darling.'

'He was a good teacher.'

'I don't think I ever had him,' Gabe said. 'I didn't take history.'

As if sensing eyes on them, Eddie and Kerr looked over. Eddie waved to Amanda and signalled that he would just be a minute.

'I'll just nip to the bathroom before we're up,' Elise said. She headed into the clubhouse, and Gabe was left with Amanda, who grinned at him.

'I'm still so thrilled you were able to sing for the church celebration.' Amanda patted his arm. 'It really made the whole thing extra special having our local celeb.'

'I'm not really a celeb. You had Tavrach singing. I think they're more famous around here than me.' The local band had quite a following in the town.

'They were wonderful too. The frontman has a house just along the street from me... Which reminds me of something I want to talk to you about.'

'Oh?'

'Houses!' She clasped her hands together. 'I know you and Elise are still in the early stages, but the market in Glenbriar is frighteningly competitive.'

'Houses?' Gabe opened his mouth, then closed it again.

'I've already got a few properties in mind,' Amanda continued. 'There's a lovely cottage on Birch Lane, needs some work, but it has character, and it has literally just come onto the market. Or if you prefer something more modern, there's a new development on the edge of town with excellent eco-credentials. I checked specifically because I know how important that is to you. Elise's friend Hayley already lives there, though I'm not sure if any of them are actually for sale at the moment.'

'Um... Thanks.' He glanced around, hoping to see Elise. And soon. Lots of people got annoyed with Amanda's meddling, even though she meant well and seemed happiest when she was organising everyone else's business. Gabe wasn't sure he wanted this conversation with her though.

'Psst, Gabe.'

He looked around and saw his mother waving from outside the court through a gap in the banners,

'Hi, Mum.' He smiled at Amanda. 'Excuse me. I should go and speak to her.'

'Of course!' Amanda clapped her hands together. 'I'd love to meet her too – later if it's convenient.'

'Absolutely.'

Elise came out of the clubhouse, and Gabe caught her. 'I'm just going to say hi to mum.'

'I'll come with you.'

They made their way around the fence.

'She looks really well,' he said. 'I think it's your influence.'

'Hardly.' Elise laughed. 'I barely know her.'

His mum held the two dogs back as she hugged Elise, then Gabe. 'Lovely place this, and so nice to see you both together.' She smiled at them, then looked away, wringing her hands on the dog leads. 'I have something to say... It's not easy, but I want to tell you both. It's highly unpleasant, but, well...'

Gabe frowned, horrible visions running through his head. Was she ill? Or had his father sent her to say something belittling to him and Elise?

'I discovered your father has been having a secret affair for many years.' She didn't look at Gabe as she spoke. 'He didn't want me to find out obviously.'

What? Gabe's brain struggled to compute the information. So much for "at least he's not a cheat".

'The thing is... I've cut him a lot of slack. An awful lot,' she went on.

That was an understatement.

'All our lives.' She glanced away, watery eyed. 'But I can't do it anymore. Cheating is something I can never forgive. The house belongs to me. It was my parents' house before me. It makes me so sad that you won't visit me there.' She blinked up at Gabe.

'Because one day I'd like you to have it.' She held up her hand before he could speak. 'I know you hate it.'

'I hate it because he's there.'

Elise's hand slipped into his, and she applied gentle, reassuring pressure.

'That's what I'm trying to say. He won't be there anymore. I've told him to leave. I've checked all the title deeds and with my solicitors. It's definitely mine.'

'You've thrown him out?' Gabe's eyes almost popped. Elise squeezed his hand.

'Yes. Because I want the house to be somewhere my son can visit. Somewhere you can bring this lovely lady.' She patted Elise's shoulder, tears shining in her eyes. 'And maybe one day, even grandchildren.'

Gabe and Elise exchanged a glance.

'I know I might be jumping the gun, but I need to do it... Just in case. I'll have it all cleaned. No more cigars. And if you want, I'm happy for you to live in it, until you find somewhere of your own. There's plenty of room. Too much for me on my own. Even with all the pets. I could have the annex done up and that would be fine for me. But only if you want to... I don't want to put you under pressure.'

Elise reached out and hugged her. 'You're so brave. And thank you.'

Gabe's mum patted her on the back. Gabe wrapped his arms around them both, sealing their hug. 'I'm glad, Mum. Shocked, but I'm sure you've made the right choice. It won't be easy, but we'll be here for you.'

'I know, son. I'm counting on it.'

They stood for a long moment in a group hug, not talking, just absorbing the information and letting it settle.

His mum pulled back first, took a tissue from her pocket and dabbed at her eyes. 'It's all a bit strange for me, but do you know what?'

Gabe shook his head.

'I don't feel sad. It's like I think that I should, but I don't. If anything, I'm excited. No doubt there will be bad days, but I'm so hopeful.' She rubbed Gabe's arm. 'I know you tried to tell me so many times and you thought I wasn't listening. But I was. Always. It just seemed easier to stay, but now I see how much I've missed by putting up with a life that wasn't my own.'

'Such a brave thing to do.' Elise gave her another hug.

'Thank you, dear. And I am very serious in hoping the two of you might want to live in the house one day. But only if that's what you want.'

The dogs were watching rather uncertainly. She bent over and gave them both a gentle rub. 'I should take these two for their walk and go clear my head. I'll come back after and watch you playing. Maybe we could go for some food later, if you don't have other plans.'

'Um...' Gabe glanced at Elise.

'Sure, I'm up for it, if you are.'

'Yeah.'

His mum smiled. 'Lovely. Right, I'll be about an hour.' She headed off with a little wave.

Gabe spent a moment just hugging Elise, not even able to take in what it all meant, but a huge weight had lifted from his shoulders. Without his dad lurking at the house, the idea of going back was much more appealing. So much land – the animals. Maybe that alpaca dream wasn't so far off after all.

'Do you still want to play?' Elise said. 'Or leave the tennis for today?'

He pulled back and smiled. 'No, let's play. I'm just in shock. This'll help bring me back down to earth with a crash.'

Amanda and Eddie were chatting near the gate. Eddie bounded up to them, smiling. 'Hello, hello. I hear you're our first opponents.'

'Yes,' Elise said. 'You used to be my history teacher.'

'Did I?'

'Yes.'

'My mind's like a sieve these days and once the students have grown up, I hardly ever recognise them. But it's very nice to see you again.'

'I feel like you're about to whip us into shape.' Elise smiled at him.

'I'll do my very best.' Eddie twirled his racquet. 'Or if I don't, Amanda will.'

As they took their positions, Gabe looked over at Elise and winked. This was bound to be chaos, but he didn't mind. His head was so light, he was almost floating.

Eddie bounced a ball on his racquet effortlessly. 'Right then, let's begin. I'll serve first, shall I? Go easy on you youngsters.'

'Going easy' for Eddie apparently meant serving a ball that whizzed past Gabe's ear before he'd even registered it was coming.

'Fifteen-love,' Eddie announced cheerfully.

'Looks like we're about to get our butts thoroughly kicked,' Gabe muttered to Elise.

By the time Eddie had won his service game without dropping a point, Gabe had already accepted they were going to be thrashed. When it was his turn to serve, he managed to hit the net twice, his own foot once, and, on his final attempt, achieved what Eddie generously called 'a proper serve', which Amanda promptly returned with such force that neither Gabe nor Elise had a chance of reaching it.

But it was fun and once they warmed up, they got in a few rallies, though predictably, Eddie and Amanda won fairly easily.

Amanda smiled at Eddie. 'Who's up next?'

'Kerr is about to be annihilated.'

'Looking for their next victims already,' Gabe muttered.

'Come with me a second,' Elise said.

'Where are we going?'

'For a breather. We need it. That was a lot to take in with your mum.'

'It'll take a while to sink in, that's for sure.'

Elise took his hand and led him up the path, which wound through a small copse of trees before emerging onto a grassy hillock at the top of the park grounds. From there, the whole of Glenbriar spread out below them, the River Briar cutting through the centre of town, a patchwork of fields and the rolling hills beyond.

'Such a beautiful view.' Gabe took a deep breath, then side-eyed her. 'I hope my mum didn't scare you with talk of grandchildren.'

Elise shook her head. 'Not at all. It was quite touching. And really, Gabe, I'm not against the idea, if that's where the road leads.' She took his hand, and he pulled her close and wrapped his arms around her.

'I love you,' he said. 'I've wanted to say that to you for quite a while now, and I want to keep saying it every day for the rest of our lives.'

She let out a breathy little laugh. 'I love you too.' She looped her arms around his neck. 'It took us a long time to get here, but I feel like we've arrived somewhere really special.'

'We took the scenic route.'

She leaned her head on his shoulder. 'We certainly did.'

'And I'm not letting you go.' He pressed a kiss to the top of her head. 'Tomorrow, we keep going. Together. Figuring it out as we go.'

'Sounds perfect,' she murmured.

Gabe had to agree. Maybe it was a messy perfect, but it was real, and it was theirs, and that was enough. He let out a soft sigh. A couple of months ago, he'd have been more likely to fight with Elise Reid than anything else. But now, all he wanted was to keep her close for the rest of his days.

The End

More Books by Margaret Amatt

Scottish Island Escapes

1. A Winter Haven

2. A Spring Retreat

3. A Summer Sanctuary

4. An Autumn Hideaway

5. A Christmas Bluff

6. A Flight of Fancy

7. A Hidden Gem

8. A Striking Result

9. A Perfect Discovery

10. A Festive Surprise

The Glenbriar Series

1. Stolen Kisses at the Loch View Hotel

2. Just Friends at Thistle Lodge

3. Pitching up at Heather Glen

4. Two's Company at the Forest Light Show

5. Highland Fling on the Whisky Trail

6. Snowdown at the Old Schoolhouse

7. Starting Over at the Crafty Bee Barn

8. A Surprise Proposal in the Rose Garden

9. Cutting it Neat for the Wedding

10. A Classy Affair in the Country

11. Mix Up under the Mistletoe

12. A Fresh Start on the Bridle Path

13. Last First Kiss at the Village Church

14. Fight or Flirt on the Scenic Route

15. Love Match on the Road Home

Love on the Edge – Barra Series

ACKNOWLEDGMENTS

Huge thanks go to my wonderful husband for always supporting my dreams (and for patiently enduring all the writing chat that never stops!). And to my son, whose curiosity and enthusiasm for storytelling always makes me smile – watching him create his own worlds is one of my greatest joys.

I'm also incredibly grateful to the editors who helped shape this book, and to the fellow authors and friends who continue to cheer me on behind the scenes – your support means the world.

But most of all, thank you to the readers. Whether you've just picked up one of my books or have been with me from the start, I appreciate you more than words can say. Your messages, reviews, and recommendations keep me going and remind me why I love doing this so much. I hope these stories bring you as much joy as I had writing them.

And an extra thank you to Sarah Steel who had the bright idea of putting Elise together with Gabe! At first, I wasn't sure about the idea, but the more I thought about it, the more I realised how great it was! Thank you for that Sarah.

Big love. Margaret XX

About the Author
Margaret Amatt

Margaret has told and written stories for as long as she can remember. During her formative years, she spent time on long walks inventing characters and stories to pass the time.

Writing books is Margaret's passion and when she's not doing that, she's often found eating chocolate, walking and taking photographs in the hills around Highland Perthshire. Those long walks still frequently bring inspiration!

It's Margaret's pleasure to bring you the **Scottish Island Escapes** series, **The Glenbriar Series** and the **Love on the Edge – Barra** series. Each series features interconnected stories for those who enjoy inhabiting Margaret's world but each and every book can be read as a standalone if you'd rather dip in and out.

You can find more information about Margaret on her website or by signing up for her newsletter

www.margaretamatt.com